On My Way Home

By
Allie Walker

Cathy! Thank you for the support

Allie Walker

ISBN: 1499391994
ISBN 13: 9781499391992
Library of Congress Control Number: 2014908667
CreateSpace Independent Publishing Platform
North Charleston, South Carolina

For Doug and Tammy
without you this book would not be possible.

Prologue

Clare LaFrace stared into the endless road on her way home Saturday night. It twisted and turned with the promise of life's greatest answers around the next bend. The moon had finally become victorious in the battle against the sun, which had decided it would be best to retreat until morning. Clare was exhausted, and the synthetic energy of coffee and various flavored sodas was beginning to give way. Clare had had a busy few days, but most of her days were busy—after all, she was a single mother of three young girls. She rested her head on one hand, leaving the other on the steering wheel and letting the day's events soak into her mind for total understanding.

Clare made an extra-long drive every Saturday to various local towns in search of fresh new talent. That was her job; she was a talent scout. This particular Saturday, Clare was making the tedious three-hour drive back from Valley Mines, Ohio, to her home of Laking, Ohio. She was only an hour or so away from home, and she started to daydream about her feather bed and firm pillows awaiting her arrival. She had completely forgotten about the singer she had heard so much about, who was supposedly the next Whitney Houston, because Clare never made it inside for the showcase. He had been there waiting for her outside of the venue, as he said he would be, and of course she had not believed him. That was something she had learned from her own history, which included many broken promises from that man.

Clare's career as a successful talent scout had been long and rewarding. She always had an ear for what could be the next big thing, and she had discovered a few big names along the way who had made her a respectable amount of money. With that she had established herself well enough to be mostly a referral service, but Clare still scouted once a week for any untapped talent that resided within a reasonable driving distance of home. She would go to local plays, karaoke bars, small venues, and even the occasional high school football game. People out in the small, sporadic towns were always on the lookout for that special quality or skill that could skyrocket them to the big city. Clare often thought people took small towns for granted, and they didn't appreciate the homey feeling they provided—the feeling that no matter how much trouble you were in, you always had a home to come back to. Take Laking, Ohio, for example. Laking was a traditional old town with the town square in the center, and it was still functional in the present day, filled with all of the important government buildings along with some scattered shops and cafes on the adjacent streets. The streets were still named Main, First, Second, Third, and so on and so on. They were covered in untouched cobblestone, which made it difficult to walk around in high heels. There were monuments to honor the various fallen heroes—some from the Civil War, some from World Wars I and II—and there was a bronze statue of Stewart Laking, the founder of the town, the most revered man in town. Stewart Laking's remaining descendants, the Knopes, were still quite a prestigious presence in the town.

Despite Clare's love for small towns, she too had big dreams once upon time. She had dreamed of being an actress, famous, sitting on a talk show's couch and explaining how she had overcome such a painful childhood in the foster system. She wanted to give other foster children hope and provide evidence that it really does get better if you put in the work—the ones who weren't considered good enough for adoption, the ones who fell through the system, and the ones who got bounced around as soon the checks stopped coming. Clare had bought her ticket to Los Angeles when she was only sixteen years old, and she had every intention of going, convinced that her life would be vastly better than it was in Laking, but she never got to use it. It now sat in a box full of distant memories from a past life, hidden beneath her bed. Clare did not regret her decision to stay; however, she wished sometimes she could have changed the timing, but even that made her feel guilty. She thought about how different her life could have been if she had not gotten pregnant at sixteen and how different her relationship would be with Austin Knope if they had not been forced to be teenage parents.

Clare LaFrace promised herself that she would never let her children go through what she did. She would always love them fiercely, and she would do anything to make them feel that love and to feel wanted—and most of all, to be appreciated. Clare was a single mom of single moms. Though she didn't know it, others looked at her in awe, wondering how she made it look so simple. Some would say that she gave up everything for her children, but Clare thought that her children gave her everything that she had never had, including hope and purpose. She lived her life with no regrets, and she loved her children more than her own life. Every decision in her life was in the best interest of her girls. She retired her youth at sixteen when she saw the second pink line appear. She did not resent that pink line. In fact, she felt that she had made the conscious choice to have sex unprotected, and she had gotten pregnant, so she had to take whatever came with that. For her and Austin, that was a baby at sixteen. Clare had never married, yet she had only loved one man her entire life. Sure, there had been other crushes, but nothing compared to Austin James Knope, the father of all three of her children.

Clare LaFrace and Austin Knope had a fantastic, written-for-the-movies love story going for them. People of the small, close-knit community of Laking always gushed about how adorable they were together, how in love they were with each other, and how inspired they were by the way they looked at each other. Austin was from a wealthy family, descendants of the very founder of the town, and Clare had no family—not even a trace. They were from opposite sides of the tracks, polarized moons, and perhaps even different planets, but they saw no validity in any of that. They just knew that their love was the real thing, and they were destined to be together. Clare and Austin met in sixth grade, when Clare first moved to Laking to stay with what would be her final foster family, and Austin told her three days after their first meeting that he was going to marry her someday. From that moment on, they were inseparable, like peanut butter and jelly—sure, you can have one without the other sometimes, but put them together, and it was pure magic. Clare knew that Austin would be the man she would marry, and it was not so secret that she still believed it to this day. Their life together was going hand in hand—all the right dances, a shoo-in for prom king and queen when the time came—but everything was put on hold when that faint pink line appeared and Clare was pregnant at sixteen.

Austin was the son of the wealthiest man in town, and his father had already planned his life for him. Two things that did not include were Clare LaFrace or any teenage pregnancies. Austin was forbidden to see Clare, or he would run the risk of losing his family's support. At sixteen, he couldn't bear that thought, nor could he bear the thought of losing Clare. After many endless nights of fighting and screaming, which Austin some years later had explained to Clare, he came to her with his mother and asked Clare to get an abortion. After that, Clare did not question the fact that she was on her own, and the fairytale was over without the happy, valiant Prince Charming on a white horse to save the day—he must have taken a wrong turn. But despite everything, her love for Austin was never scathed. Austin kept his distance during Clare's pregnancy except for the secret rendezvous under the bleachers and the awkward encounters in the school hallways. And though he was present at Gabriella's birth and promised Clare that even though he couldn't be there, he would take care of them, of course his parents had demanded a DNA test to prove that Austin wasn't the father. The secret and awkward encounters ceased, and amazingly in the small town that they lived in, they managed to avoid each other for three years without any contact or sight.

Three years later, Gabriella was growing like a beanstalk fueled by magic beans. She was an ostentatious toddler with a curiosity for life and sense of adventure. Clare took her to the park almost everyday after she finished her shift at the Sunrise Diner, before her night classes. Clare often would daydream about Austin when she saw the other fathers playing with their children on the monkey bars, the slides, and the swings. She longed for him more than she would have liked to, but one fateful day at the playground, there was Austin strolling through, looking around with a cup of coffee in one hand and a backpack slung over his shoulder.

Austin stopped in his tracks at the sight of Gabriella. He saw in an instant what Clare had seen her entire life: the spitting image of the man she loved wrapped in her daughter's eyes. Austin could not peel his eyes away from Gabriella. He was mesmerized; he had fallen in love as quickly as he had with Clare all those years ago, and that afternoon, they were the family that Clare had imagined since Gabriella's birth.

Austin and Clare picked up right where they had left off. He explained his actions to Clare, and it was nothing that she had not suspected in the first place. He told her it was the only way that he could be a good father—by keeping his distance in exchange for his parents' help in covering Gabriella's expenses. Clare knew that he was telling the truth, and she knew in her heart that Austin would never hurt her unless he was forced to do so.

Austin and Clare's reconciliation did not last long, but it was long enough for Clare to conceive another child. Once again, Austin's parents stepped in to protect their son—but most importantly, their family's reputation. Austin allowed history to repeat itself, and he was not present in the life of Gemma, their second daughter. Clare was devastated once more, and though she still loved Austin for reasons that she could not put into words, her disappointment grew with each day that he was absent from their family's life. But she refused to play the victim of a broken heart, so she raised her two daughters to the best of her abilities and worked extremely hard to make a life for them that she never had.

Clare and Austin went eight years with barely any communication. He went away to school, and Clare was almost positive it was orchestrated by his mother and father, Parker and Penelope Knope. When Austin returned to Laking, Gabriella was seven and Gemma was four, but Austin didn't make an effort to see them. One day Clare read in the *Laking Herald* that Austin had married a woman named Alice, and they were expecting twins. He was making his first run for public office to follow in his father's footsteps.

Austin and Alice Knope were part of a high society that Clare really never understood. They had their twin boys and a girl shortly after that, and Austin devoted himself to them. Clare's jealousy would encircle her body every time she saw them out in public, looking like a walking Christmas card no matter the season. If she tried to avoid him, she only saw him more. They would exchange longing looks, but neither would act on them. It was as if they were separated by an invisible locked door and they both had lost their key.

Clare had tried so many times to forget him. She had tried dating. She had tried throwing herself into work and any hobby, but every day, his image was burned into her mind. She could see him looking out through their children's eyes. She could see their special moments as if they were yesterday every time she dropped the girls off at school, and sometimes when she closed her eyes, she saw him there extending his hand to her once more. No matter what she did or whatever he did, she could not bring herself to stop loving Austin Knope.

Clare jerked back into the present, the tires on her compact SUV squealing to avoid hitting a deer that had ventured into the road. Gaining control and allowing only a few tears to trickle down her face, she turned her thoughts back to Austin. She knew that Austin had done what he thought he had to do, but there were times, many times, when she had tried to hate the man she loved so deeply for the pain that he had caused her and their kids. Gabriella, Clare's oldest daughter, didn't have to try hard to hate Austin. Gabriella could not remember the small amount of time that they had been two peas in a pod while Clare was pregnant with Gemma. Clare had given it a real effort to get her to warm up to him somewhat in recent years because he had made a substantial effort with their third daughter, but Gabriella wouldn't let go of the past. Clare understood Gabriella's hurt, abandonment, and feeling of being unwanted, and the only way Gabby could express her feelings was anger toward him. Clare let out a deep sigh, worried that Gabriella would never be able to forgive Austin for leaving her.

Night had set in, and the moon was the only source of light except for a few lampposts on the lightly traveled highway. The sight in front of her was so majestic and alluring, it made her think of the small miracles people witness every day without realization. Like the sun rising, the stars shimmering, helping someone less fortunate, a baby being born— small actions indeed, but to those involved, miracles undoubtedly. She thought about her own miracles that had taken place in her life, and how Austin had been apart of almost all of them. And with those happy thoughts, she took a ride down memory lane to a night that changed her life forever.

Clare gazed at herself in the mirror. Her tight pink dress was long enough not to be too revealing, but it hugged her in all the right places. She wore a sapphire diamond pendant necklace with the silver still shining despite its ten-year age. Her heels were high enough not to make her giant, but they defined her calves. She had spent a prodigious amount of time meticulously working on her makeup and fixing her brunette locks, which curled without trying. That night she defined the words *sex appeal,* and she needed to look her best for her ten-year high school reunion. Clare had never had a problem with confidence about her appearance; she took it as the one thing in her life that she didn't have to struggle with. Her defined features made her stand out in such a small town. She had beautiful light-blue eyes—they were not as deep blue as the ocean, but blue like the sky on a clear day. And she was slender and tall, with curves in the right places, which made men glance over their shoulders while holding their wives' purses. Clare had always been the wife every eligible bachelor wanted, but for some reason, she could never get over the boy who had stolen her heart in the sixth grade.

Clare walked into the cheaply decorated gymnasium on that warm September night seven years ago, and in an instant, Austin and Clare couldn't take their eyes off of each other. No one else in the room mattered, not even Austin's wife, Alice. Alice and Austin argued through gritted teeth all night until Alice got so angry that she left without her husband in tow.

It seemed that it was exactly what Austin wanted. He made his way over to Clare. It was something out of a movie or a romance novel. He was moving in slow motion toward her, his deep green eyes with glimmers of amber shining through. She was frozen waiting, longing for him to embrace her, her heart beating so fast that she thought it might pop out of her chest to surrender. Austin was mysterious, charming, and ruggedly handsome, and he was coming toward her. He didn't blink. He was walking, with her as his prey, and she was paralyzed with love and agony.

He put his hand on the small of her back, pulled her in close to him, and gently kissed her cheek. Clare knew that if she pulled away, that would be the end of it, and they would not be together that night. But she could not help that she was in love with a married man. Austin had a spell over her, and she could never find the antidote to save herself from his charm.

They spent the night getting lost in each other. They reveled in the past, they did not care who saw them, they did not care that they were being gossiped about, and Austin did not care that he was about to cheat on his wife. The magnetic pull between them was too intense to resist. Clare loved Austin with all of her heart, and even though they were not married, there was not a doubt in her mind that they were soul mates. The night of their ten-year high school reunion was the best night of Clare's life.

Austin and Clare's night of passion resulted in another daughter. Austin did not leave his wife for Clare, but he did not deny that Giuliana was his daughter. From the moment Giuliana was born, Austin started making efforts to become part of his daughters' lives. Gemma liked the idea of having a full-time dad, but she never let her guard down completely. She still wore the fear of her father's leaving on her sleeve. Gabriella, on the other hand, did not care that Austin was making an effort. It seemed to make her resent him more than before. The harder he would try, the more she would hate him. Despite Austin's pleas with Clare to help him with Gabby, she didn't want to push her daughter into a relationship she wasn't ready for. Clare put herself in Gabriella's shoes, and if her parents had just reappeared in her life, she would not be impressed. She would not fling herself into their arms. She would make them earn her love and respect. Clare had grown up in the foster care system, so the feeling of being unwanted by a parent or anyone was all too familiar to her. Clare had never felt sorry for herself because she reasoned that she would not be the strong, independent woman she was now if she had not gone through all of the struggles in her life. She decided to let Gabby forgive in her own time if that was what she wanted to do. Clare had come to terms with her life, and she was grateful for everything she had.

Clare was suddenly brought back to reality by an oncoming blinding light. Before she knew what was happening, there was a loud crashing sound. The sounds of splintering metal and cracking glass filled her ears and ignited a deep fear. Gravity lost its hold for a second that felt like hours. She looked around to try to grasp what was happening. The headlights that had blinded her now illuminated the specks and shards of glass that were floating in the air around her. She knew she would not be walking away from this. Panic, deep and consuming, settled in, and all Clare could do was close her eyes to the horror and hold on for her daughters. All her strength was not enough to keep gravity at bay. The car landed violently, leaving Clare unconscious and bleeding.

Distant, indistinct shouts made something in her mind click. She opened her eyes to a blurred vision of flashing lights and darkness. She tried to rise, but her legs were pinned underneath the steering wheel, and one arm appeared to be broken. She felt a warm sensation in her stomach but smiled ever so slightly.

"I'm alive," she whispered only loud enough for herself to hear. She tried to crane her neck to see what had happened and where she was. The flashing lights were too much for her to see anything that would give away her location. She tried to remember how far away from home she had been, but she could not remember the last mile marker she had seen. A man in a yellow suit was beating on the outside of her door with some sort of hammer. Even though the man was only inches away, it sounded as if she were underwater, and all she could hear was a faint echo of his voice.

"We'll get you out of there!" the man shouted.

Clare thought she managed to nod at the man, but she wasn't sure. She tried to take a deep breath in, but it wasn't an easy task. It was something she did every second of every day, but now it seemed alien to her, and it felt as if she had never done anything as difficult before. She began to feel weaker, and she realized that she might be more severely injured than she had previously thought. Flames danced in Clare's eyes as the tractor-trailer exploded. She heard the distant sounds of struggles and panic. As she watched the flames engulf the road and everything in their path, she knew that she would not be going home tonight. She felt tears begin to slide down her face and fear settle in her stomach. An image of her three beautiful daughters came into her mind. She didn't want to miss out on their lives; she wanted to be there for everything, as she had always promised. Clare thought that this might be her punishment for being in love with a married man, and perhaps she should have tried harder to stay away from Austin.

Clare felt the anger and resentment building up inside of her. She was weak, but she felt she might be able to do some damage with the hammer the man in the yellow suit was using against the car. She closed her eyes and let her thoughts and prayers consume her completely.

How can God do this to me? Everything is falling into place. I have three wonderful children who are about to achieve and embark on such a great journey. I guess being mad at you isn't going to get me anywhere. Please, God, I am responsible for three young, fragile lives. I have a six-year-old daughter who needs me to teach her things that you can only learn from your mother. I need to be there for her. She is almost ready to take the training wheels off of her bike. I need to be there to read her favorite stories and introduce her into the magic of books. I need to help her with homework, I need to kiss her boo-boos. I need to love her the way every little girl deserves to be loved. Giuliana needs her mother. I cannot leave her.

Gemma—she is at the age where you need your mother more than ever. She is fourteen, and she is about to become a young woman. I want to be there for her first date, her first love, her first heartbreak. I need to be there when she needs someone to talk to just because, or when she needs advice on something that she only feels comfortable talking to me about. I need to be there for all of the successes that she is going to have. I need to be there so she can get mad at me. She needs me. I need to be there when she realizes how great she really is.

Gabriella. Gabriella. I have grown up with her, and I know that she will do great in her life. I could not have raised her any better if I had tried. She learned as I learned. She respected me, and I respected her. She has always been able to do anything and everything she has ever set her mind to. I want to be there when she realizes that she is in love, and I want to see her get married, and I want to see her be the best at whatever she does. I know she won't settle for anything but the best. I want to see her one last time. Please, God, let me see my children again. I am not ready to go yet.

The tears were gushing now, and her thoughts lingered with Gabby for a moment. It suddenly became clear to her. She saw her daughters smiling at her, reaching for her hand, but they were just out of reach. Clare saw Austin's face one last time. She felt at peace knowing that she had loved him unconditionally with all of her heart. She knew that he loved her the same. She didn't have the luxury of being mad or disappointed, but if she had a little more time, she would make sure that she and Austin were together as they were meant to be.

Clare felt the warm sensation in her stomach again and realized it was her blood. She felt her breath become scarce. She knew that she would not be seeing her daughters again, but she took pride in knowing that she had hugged and kissed them good-bye this morning. She had told them that she loved them. Her last tears filled her eyes and trickled down her face.

The man in the yellow suit was still too far away to reach her. She closed her eyes and smiled faintly. She pictured Gabby, Gemma, Giuliana, and Austin all smiling at her. She knew that somehow they would be fine. They would miss her and want her back, but they would understand why she could not be there. They would become stronger people because of it. It was too late for her. Her fight was over. She knew that her children would know how she loved them, and they would remember what had happened on her way home.

1

Gabriella Knope, a normal teenager with so-called normal teenage problems, had been accepted at the ripe age of eighteen to Brown University, and she was still counting down the minutes as her time to leave drew nearer. Gabriella was practically drooling at the thought of escaping what she considered to be a prison, but the map called it Laking. Everyone knew everyone's business, everyone knew the ins and outs of your daily routine, that nosy neighbor was always peering over the slightly overgrown hedges for a tidbit of gossip, there was no question about whom you were romantically involved with, and scandal and rumors ran rampant across the town. There was a clan of older women who all went to the same beauty parlor, and they were always in cahoots, devising new tactics to get any new information. And when they got it, you could be sure that it would be at the bingo hall that night, in the high schools by morning, and in the business district by late afternoon. Last week, Gabby and Jason, her best friend, were having lunch in the park, and by the time her actual boyfriend, Alex Hickins, had heard about the innocent lunch, it was proven without a trial that Gabby and Jason were basically having sex for everyone to see. Gabriella then had to spend three hours of her Friday night fighting with Alex, trying to convince him for the thousandth time that she and Jason were only friends and nothing more.

Gabriella often thought that Laking had stopped progressing around 1930, that the rest of the world had moved on and modernized, but here was a little blip on the map, Laking, just as it had been in the "good ole days." There wasn't anything particular that she was sad about leaving except for her friends and family, but she thought she could use a break from everyone in general. Gabriella craved to know what the world was like past Interstate 4. She could not wait to go somewhere where no one knew her name or somewhere where people didn't gossip about you when you got a new haircut that took a few tries to get the styling down. Most importantly, she wanted to live somewhere where people didn't know her father. She wanted to live somewhere where people didn't look at her as if she were the daughter of a whore whose life ambition was to destroy the reputation of the Knopes. Gabriella wanted to experience real life, she wanted to see what other people were like, she wanted to be free.

Gabriella's life ambition was to be a novelist, but she had not found her story yet, or it had not found her—either way, it was her dream. She knew that the moment it happened, it would be something so great, such a wonderful idea, that she would not be able to stop writing until it was finished. She had started numerous stories, but had never finished any more than thirty or so pages. She always had a deep-rooted feeling that her work was not good enough for anyone to see; all she could think about was the possible judgment and criticism that would come from it, but that was all about to change. Brown University had one of the best writing programs in the country. She would be able to perfect her skills and set out to prove what everyone had always doubted, and the fact that it was in Rhode Island only made it that much more appealing for Gabby.

Gabriella was lucky in that she was good at almost anything with minimal effort. She never had to study very hard, she could run a mile in about nine minutes, she wasn't shy, and she had secured a group of friends she was sure she would take with her throughout her life. Gabriella had been blessed with her mother's effortless beauty—not the height, but she made do with step stools and tiptoes. Gabriella had an athletic build from her four years as a semisuccessful volleyball player. Her chestnut-brown hair was even with her shoulders; she never managed much more than a ponytail. Her eyes were her father's, a stunning rare green with glimmers of amber. Gabby never bothered with makeup; she was attractive enough without it. She received enough attention from boys to feel confident, but on the rare occasion when she put on makeup, she noticed heads turning to take a second glance. The insecure part of her wondered if she didn't know how to apply the makeup properly, but she never paid much attention due to her overly jealous longtime boyfriend, Alex.

It was Saturday night, and she was at Alex's house. He had been in the bathroom for a while. She assumed he had eaten too much at the Mexican restaurant where they had had dinner. Gabriella was lying half on the bed staring up at the ceiling, and she could still see the outlines of the glow-in-the-dark stars that had eased his mind about the dark in his younger years. Alex's phone went off again. She had ignored it the previous three times, but finally, annoyed with the constant beeping, she picked up the phone casually to silence it. The name Danielle D flashed across the screen. Gabriella never cared that Alex hung out with other girls, regardless of his feelings about her talking to another guy in her chem lab. It just never bothered her. She wasn't in the relationship for marriage and a baby, and she assumed that it would end within the next few weeks, as she was leaving for school. She was trusting enough, but Danielle was someone that Gabriella did not like. Gabby didn't even pretend to like her, and Danielle made it quite plain that she couldn't stand Gabby. They had been enemies since the first grade. Danielle and Gabriella had been best friends for a year and half, which in first-grade time is an eternity. But after Christmas break, Danielle came back with a new backpack and new barrettes for her hair, and she had decided that Gabriella was the enemy. Danielle would blame everything on Gabriella and more than once cost her recess, and she had even gotten her into trouble with her mother, Clare. What sealed the unspoken eternal enmity was the incident with Gabriella's favorite snow globe, which she had brought for show-and-tell. It was the first gift she had received from Jason Throne for her birthday. It was beautiful, the pink ballerina standing on one pointed foot, her arms gracefully reaching for the falling snow. She turned to the song "Somewhere over the Rainbow," the outside porcelain roses intertwining around the base with red bows tying them together. Danielle Dickert had purposely knocked it off of Gabriella's desk just as she finished her own presentation of some goofy-looking bell. From that moment on, Danielle became the inspiration for all of Gabriella's villains in her stories.

So without much hesitation, Gabriella opened the phone and read the text:

She gone yet? Did you tell her? I miss you!! Xoxoxo

"Wow!" she said aloud to herself. Her face got hot, she wanted to scream, she wanted to hit something—maybe someone—but then a brilliant idea came into her mind. She smiled spitefully and sent a text back from Alex's phone:

Yes, can you come over?

Gabriella's mind had calmed slightly, but she was still furious. She felt slightly stupid for not seeing the signs, but they had been dating off and on since sophomore year. They were more on than they had been off. They had had their petty fights and their petty breaks, and she didn't think that he had ever cheated on her. Even though she felt that the relationship had run its course, it did not excuse Alex's behavior. Alex knew how Gabby felt about Danielle, and she was truly hurt that he would cheat on her with that girl.

Gabriella tried to quickly play out the scenarios that could take place. She felt a small amount of relief circling around her. She had been dreading having "the talk" with Alex, and now Danielle had given her legitimate reason instead of the so cliché "it's not you, it's me" speech. Gabriella laughed aloud to herself and wondered for a moment if her mortal enemy Danielle Dickert had unknowingly done her the biggest favor. The phone beeped again, and Gabby picked it up—without any hesitation this time. She wasn't surprised when she saw Danielle's name appear across the screen. She clicked her name to open the text message: *"Yes! I can't wait to see you sugar bear!! Muah!"*

Gabriella replied from Alex's phone: *"Ditto"*

Gabriella wasn't sure how everything was going to play out, but she was certain that it would make for a good story for Jason.

Alex came out of the bathroom with a satisfied grin on his face, as if he had done the porcelain gods proud. Alex was a tall, handsome boy with deep green eyes, wavy hair that was darker than brown but not quite black, and muscles that were just enough to be comfortable for Gabriella to snuggle up inside. He had always been considered a rare gem among the girls of Laking, but he had a soft spot for Gabriella. He saw her as a challenge, as she did not throw herself at him, and she would barely give him the time of day before they started dating two years ago. Alex was captain of the very popular high school football team, but even with college offers rolling in, he had opted to go to the state college. He saw no need to leave a life where he was already respected and looked up to. As long as he was the biggest fish, the size of the pond didn't matter. He made no effort to pick up his feet, and he scooted across the floor toward her. He stopped short of her, noticing his phone was in her hands.

Gabriella, slightly nervous, hurried to come up with a believable explanation. "Oh," she said, waving the phone and smiling warmly, "I can't get any service here, so I just used yours to let my mom know I was not going to be home tonight." She tossed the phone back to him and smiled seductively at him.

He looked at her with a questionable expression, not sure whether he had heard her correctly. He looked around the room, waiting for hidden cameras to jump out and reveal that he had almost fallen for the practical joke. Alex scratched his head, making himself look dumber than normal. "Gabby, we need to talk."

"How about we talk in the morning?" she replied, trying to imitate a seductive pose she had seen in a magazine once. Gabriella could not help but smile at Alex's expression. He was dumfounded, and he probably thought that he might have dozed off in the bathroom and was dreaming because Gabriella had made her feelings about sex very clear to him. She wanted to wait until she was ready, and if he ever tried to pressure her, she would be out the door. And surprisingly, Alex respected that and never pushed her, not even on prom night.

"Don't you have to leave?" he asked. He was searching her face for any signs of truth to what she was suggesting.

"No." She reached out and lightly grazed his arm with the tips of her fingers. "I want to stay here tonight." She nestled herself in his arms and

looked up to him. Gabriella was quite entertained by Alex's bewilder-
ment and excitement. "Alex," she whispered, "I love you. And I know
we have our problems, but we can work on those, and we can be happy
again." She smiled up at him. "Let's start fresh."

Alex started to pull away, but Gabriella closed her arms tightly
around him. She pressed her lips against his and pushed her tongue
deep into his mouth, making the kiss as passionate as she possibly
could. She began to shudder with soft moans of pleasure as Alex ran his
hands up and down her back, being very aware of his hand placement.

Gabriella was doing everything she could to make the kiss last as
long as possible. It was indeed their good-bye kiss, and she wanted
Danielle to walk in on them. She wanted to see the horror on Alex's
face and the embarrassment on Danielle's. Alex began to make timid
moves that were forbidden in their relationship. She wasn't going to
give anything up to him, but she decided to let him think that that was
her intention. She pulled back so she could look into his deep-green,
cheating eyes. He smiled slyly up at her, slid his hand up her blouse, and
began to caress her breast. He made small circles with his finger around
her nipple. Gabriella started to become aroused and let small whimpers
of desire. She had to quickly remind herself of what her plan was, and
she had to immediately put her emotions on lockdown.

He smiled that charming, hypnotizing smile that had so many other
girls under his spell. "Are you OK?" He sounded as if he genuinely cared.

Gabby smiled weakly back at him.

She heard a car pull up in the driveway and let out a louder whimper to distract Alex. She had to make the scene worthwhile. Gabriella
pushed Alex onto the bed and straddled him. She began to kiss Alex up
and down to drown out any sounds coming from downstairs. Gabriella
heard Alex's brother telling Danielle exactly where she could find her
boyfriend. Gabriella's heart began to race with anticipation as she
heard Danielle walking toward the room. Gabriella turned to Alex and
jammed her tongue in his mouth. He responded by rubbing his hands
down her backside and up again, trying to unhook her bra. Gabby heard
Danielle right outside the door. She rose to let him breathe and watch
the show he thought that he was going to get. His eyes were wild. She

began to lift her shirt. A smile of anticipation, wild curiosity, and exhilaration spread across Alex's face like fire upon a dry stack of brush. The door swung open. Gabriella acted startled and quickly put her shirt back down. She jumped off of Alex as if they had been caught by his parents.

Gabriella had to fight the urge to smile as the taste of sweet victory was in the air. Danielle's face was better than she could have imagined. She was confused, angry, and horrified at the sight she had walked in on.

Gabriella, excited to play the part, didn't have to try too hard to be angry at Danielle. "What the hell are you doing here?" Gabby screamed.

Danielle Dickert stood, frozen, in a tight green dress hugging every curve with an absurd white jacket that some magazine had probably labeled as high fashion. Danielle glared at Gabby, too angry to speak. She looked at Alex to explain, and Gabriella was certain that death rays would escape from her eyes.

"OK." Alex put his hands up as if he were calling a timeout. He had never been fast on his feet to come up with an explanation; it was his downfall as a player. Alex was searching his room for some unknown exit to mysteriously appear. He looked between Danielle and Gabriella, back and forth, back and forth, and finally buried his face in his hands and looked to be almost pulling out his own hair.

"Alex," Danielle began in a soft, soothing, understanding tone, "what is she doing here?" She got angry and snapped, "Why would you invite me over here when you are making out with that dirty slut?"

"Excuse me," Gabriella chimed in without meaning to, but she was not going to let anyone talk about her that way. "I do think that Alex is my boyfriend, so please inform me how that makes me a slut when I have never slept with anyone, and you have probably done the entire football team, and from the way it looks, including my boyfriend as well." Gabriella gave Danielle a moment to process what she had just said. "So if I am a dirty slut, what does that make you? A twenty-four-hour convenience store with no intention of closing anytime soon."

Alex unintentionally laughed and then immediately clapped his hands over his mouth and tried to sink farther into the corner as the girls argued.

Danielle's anger was protruding from her face. It was obvious that she was offended and slightly caught off her game. Gabriella's insults were never anything compared to Danielle's. She was silent for at least two minutes before she spoke again. "Trust me, I do not sleep around."

Gabriella rolled her eyes immediately and let out a chortle of disbelief.

"I only sleep with the ones whose girlfriends aren't satisfying them. They come to me begging. Alex came to me begging, saying you were as dried up as a rotted-out apple core." Danielle folded her arms across her chest and stood to one side with her hip pointed out, as if she were posing for a picture.

Gabriella kept her cool while an image of strangling Danielle danced across her mind. "Aw, sweetheart, you forgot your vocab lesson."

Danielle looked confused. As she was about to laugh at Gabriella's lame attempt to insult her, she was silenced.

"Begging is asking for freebies over and over again. Now, I did dumb that down for you a little bit so you could understand." Gabriella moved within striking distance of Danielle. "And freebies are what you give every guy in town, because, honey, we're eighteen, not in our twenties. So there are a lot of boys not being 'satisfied' by their girlfriends."

Danielle clinched her fists at her sides. It was as if Gabriella were daring her to hit her. The anger was boiling off of her face. Danielle seemed too rattled to continue in what would be an endless rain of insults directed toward each other.

She turned away from Gabriella to focus her anger on Alex. "What is going on here?" she demanded.

Alex only cowered into the corner farther, trying to avoid eye contact with either of them. He was likely praying for invisibility so he could slip out unnoticed. An awkward silence fell upon the room. There were just glares and imaginary daggers being thrown in every direction. Gabriella smiled to herself, knowing that she was about to be vindicated for all the torture Danielle Dickert had ever bestowed upon her.

"Alex," Gabriella said, breaking the silence with a soft, tearful voice, "can you talk to me, please?" Her eyes were wide with sadness, making the amber in her eyes sparkle.

Alex looked up at her and reached out for her hand. Gabriella walked toward him but stopped short and turned her head down as if she were inconsolable. "Gabby." His voice cracked as he choked back his own tears. "I am so sorry."

"What are you sorry for?" She wanted to hear the words leave his mouth. She wanted to make sure Danielle heard every word he had to say.

Alex moved closer to Gabriella, not quite close enough to touch her. He opened his mouth to speak, but he had lost his words. He looked into Gabriella's eyes, trying to make her see the regret in his deep emerald-green eyes, but she turned away so as not to fall victim to what had lured her in so many times before.

"Gabby," he began, "you know we have had our problems, and I thought that you would be breaking up with me because you are going to Brown in a few weeks." His explanation was honest, but Gabriella found it to be pathetic, only infuriating her more.

Gabriella's fake sobs left without hesitation as she listened to what Alex had just told her. "So let me get this straight." She moved closer to Alex and poked him on the shoulder with force. "Because I got accepted to a good school that isn't in this crap town, you felt that it was OK to cheat on me with her, with that slut?" She glared at Danielle.

"Listen here," Danielle started, but Alex cut her off at once.

"Stop!" He put his hand up to make her shut up. "Danielle, I do not know why you even showed up here." Alex's tone was ruthless.

Danielle looked understandably confused. "You texted me to come over because you said that you broke up with her."

"Gabby, that's not true," Alex said at once. "Danielle, I have not sent you any text messages today." Alex seemed sure that he hadn't texted her, but then his face read like a child trying to decide whether the tooth fairy really did exist. He looked back and forth between Gabriella and Danielle. "Danielle, you need to leave right now." He was firm, and he ushered her to the door.

Gabriella thought the look of utter humiliation on Danielle's face was enough to find a new villain for her stories, because that villain had finally lost. Danielle was so furious that she did not say a word. She grabbed her purse and slammed Alex's door. Gabriella was almost sure that the door would fly off the hinges and that Danielle was bound to go through one of the steps, she was stomping so hard. There were two more doors that Danielle tried to break, and the sound of her tires squealing in the driveway was the only communication left. Gabriella tried not to smile, only letting her small dimples show.

Gabriella looked at Alex, waiting for him to say something. The silence was uncomfortable. She was becoming impatient and let out an annoyed sigh.

"Gabby, I am so sorry." Alex held out his arms as if she were supposed to jump into them.

"Alex, save it." Gabriella put her hand to motion him to stop at once. "I cannot believe that you would cheat on me with her. Not that you were off base that I was going to break up with you, because I was—I mean I am going to break up with, but you know how I feel about her." Gabriella was talking a mile a minute and trying to gather everything so there would be no need to ever see Alex Hickins again. "Oh, by the way"—she stopped to smile at him—"I sent the text to Danielle, and I am the reason she came over."

Alex's mouth was wide open in disbelief. He regained his composure. "Come on, don't you think we can work this out? I realized tonight that I really do love you, and I don't want to lose you." He was starting to sound desperate. "You are smart, funny, beautiful—what more could a guy want?"

"A twenty-four-hour convenience store," Gabriella replied.

"Gabby, I do love you." He sounded sad and defeated.

"Why all of a sudden are you sure of your love for me? Because I made you think we were going to have sex?" Gabriella knew that she was right.

Alex shook his head. "No, that's not it. I realized how it would be without you."

Gabriella put up her hand to silence him. "Save it, Alex, and do me a favor. Delete my phone number from your memory. Don't bother trying to call me or waste your 'I'm sorry' on me, because you will be stuck in this little town forever with the town whore as your wife, remembering the good old days when you had someone with class." Gabriella picked up her things, grabbed her keys, and headed for the door.

"Gabriella, wait!" Alex said in desperation. "I am sorry. If you could just give me one more chance, I promise you won't regret it."

She turned to face him. "The only thing I would have regretted is if I had given up my virginity to you, so I'm good." She walked out of the door. She knew that she was leaving her childhood behind as she closed the door to her car. There were no holes for it to creep back into. She was now an adult and about to start the greatest adventure of her life—college.

Gabriella rummaged in her purse for her cell phone. She pulled it out and lit the screen up. She glanced and quickly had to glance back to make sure she had seen the number correctly. She had missed twenty-three phone calls. Gabriella was eager with curiosity to see why she had suddenly become so popular. She flipped the phone open and skimmed the list: five were from Jason; six from a number she did not know but assumed it was Danielle's friends trying to mess with her; eleven were from Cindy Throne, Jason's mother, which led her to believe something must have happened; and one was from her own mother. A small amount of panic came into her mind, and not knowing what had taken place, her imagination went wild. She quickly called home, but there was no answer. She tried her mother next, but it went straight to voice mail. Mystified by not being able to reach anyone, she looked at the phone again and noticed that she had a voice mail from her mom. Her mind eased a bit. She assumed her mother had left her a message explaining whatever was wrong and telling her not to worry. She hit the button to listen, but at the same moment, her phone began to vibrate with Jason's name flashing across the screen.

"Jason?" She was hopeful.

"Gabby, where are you?" He sounded rushed and worried.

"I am on my way home." Panic came back into her mind. She had known Jason since the first grade, and she had never heard him sound so worried before. "What's going on?"

"Gab, don't go home. Come to my house. I need to see you right away," Jason said.

Gabriella could tell by Jason's tone that he wasn't asking. He was telling her. Gabriella did not want to question him, but something inside was not settling right. "Jason"—she was unsure of where her thoughts were going—"is everything OK?" She was terrified of the answer, fearing the worst.

"Gabby, just come to my house, and I will explain everything. Please. Be safe." Jason hung up the phone without giving her a chance to respond.

She looked at her phone, expecting it to tell her what had just happened. Perhaps the phone would review the conversation in play-by-play action.

Gabriella did what Jason asked and headed toward the Thrones' home, and she tried to focus on the events of the night because they seemed to be less disheartening. She tried to distract herself by thinking of things she could get for her dorm room in college and what clever Facebook status she could put up to really rub Danielle's face in her recent victory, but she had a feeling in the pit of her stomach that something was horribly wrong.

She pulled into the Thrones' driveway behind a slew of cars. The Thrones' home always exuded picture-perfect family happiness—red brick, two stories, blue shutters, wraparound porch with various hanging flowers, and small ornamental statues holding whimsical gardening tools or pulling a stationary wagon behind them. Gabriella laughed out loud to herself, realizing the obvious, and everything made sense now. The Thrones were hosting her going-away party. Even though Gabriella had insisted on no party, she knew that her mother would not listen, and she would throw Gabriella a party with everyone she had ever met in her entire life. Gabriella did not want to ruin the surprise that her mother had orchestrated so well, so she took a couple of minutes to compose herself. She straightened up her hair, trying to smooth away the flyaways, added a little bit more lip gloss, and decided it was the best she was going to be able to do.

The Thrones' pathway was perfectly decorated with the right amount of light to illuminate the perfectly tended flowers and the perfectly tended shrubberies that lined the front of the wraparound porch of their classic colonial home. Gabriella was walking at a dredging pace to give the Thrones and party guests enough time to prepare for her arrival. She was going to knock, which she never did at the Thrones' because they were like a second family to her. But still, she wanted to make sure they knew she had arrived. The door swung open before she had a chance to go up the four wooden stairs, and Gabby jumped back a few steps, almost losing her balance.

"I am so sorry, honey. I did not mean to startle you," Austin Knope said. He stood in brown slacks with a green polo shirt; he had sandy-blond hair neatly piled on his head, and his eyes were a brilliant shade of green with small glints of amber that made his face light up.

Gabriella was already annoyed, and she hadn't even gone in yet to talk to anyone. She looked at him as if she had never seen anyone as disgusting as he was, and she wanted to know immediately what he was doing at her party. She shot him a dirty look, demanding an answer.

Austin caught her familiar gaze and nodded. "If you come in, I will explain everything."

"I don't know if you know that I do not like you, and I would appreciate it if you would leave my going-away party. You know, that thing you do every time you knock up my mother." Her tone was cool and straight to the point.

"Gabby, I am not here to fight with you." He shook his head, trying to motion her inside.

She jumped back on the attack. "I don't care for your explanation." She stopped and looked him straight in the eye. "Just wait until the other two are old enough to realize what kind of person you are."

"Gabby," he pleaded.

"Gabriella." Her voice was emotionless. "Friends and family call me Gabby, but you are neither, so please—Gabriella, Mr. Knope." She didn't give him a chance to respond. Why on earth would her mother invite him? she thought. He had had plenty of chances to acknowledge her existence and do father-daughter things, but he had chosen not to.

"Gabby." Jason Throne interrupted her thoughts. He pulled her into a tight hug, as if it had been decades since they had last seen each other.

"Jason, can you please tell me what is going on?" she asked coyly. "Why is Austin at my party?"

"Party?" Jason repeated, unsure of what she was talking about.

"Yes, I know it was supposed to be a surprise, but I—" she started to explain how she had figured everything out when she arrived at the Thrones' home.

"Gabby, no, sweetheart, no. You better come in and sit down," he said. He put his arm around her to provide support, as if she were losing the use of her legs.

"Jason," she began again.

He gave her a look she had never seen on his face before. She took a closer look. He had been crying. His face was red and splotchy, and his expression was of sorrow and heartbreak. She stopped in her footsteps, barricading her feet to the ground. There were so many thoughts flying through her mind. She didn't know what was going on, but she wanted to know, and she did not want to wait another second. Gabriella naively wondered if her mother was making another attempt to force her to have a heart-to-heart with Austin, and maybe this was some sort of intervention to get her to love her father. But why would she choose the Thrones' home?

Jason forced her to move forward to the sitting room, where there were a lot of familiar faces. She saw her sisters—Giuliana sitting on Mr. Robert Throne's lap and Gemma sobbing quietly in Mrs. Cindy Throne's arms. Gabriella looked from one to the other and then back at Jason. Then it became clear. She had been wrong again about the party. Something terrible had happened, and that was why no one would tell her over the phone, why there were so many missed calls, and it was the reason Jason was treating her as if she could break at any moment. She searched the room for her mother, hoping her instincts were wrong. Gabriella felt guilty because she had just been angry at her mother for allowing Austin Knope to be in her presence.

"Where is my mother?" Gabriella asked, fearing she already knew the answer.

"Gabby, honey, sit down," Mrs. Throne said softly.

"No!" she yelled, louder than she expected to. As if sitting down would make this news any easier to take. "Where is my mom?" she asked again.

"Gabby..." Austin Knope tried to approach her.

"No!" Gabriella screamed at the top of her lungs. "I do not want to hear anything from you, not you!" She felt the tears coming. "Not you." Her voice was less audible through the sobs, her stomach knotted up, and she felt she would be sick. She was losing control. She looked to Jason, her very best friend in the entire world. He was the one who was there for her no matter what. He never asked for anything in return except for her friendship. "Jason, please tell me what is going on." She was crying now. There was no stopping it. Something was about to be revealed, and she had to hear it. She had to hear what she felt in her heart to be true.

Jason tightened her grip on her. "Gabby, there was an accident," he began softly.

"What?" she said. "No. Where is my mom?" she demanded again.

"Gabby, babe, I'm so sorry, but the accident—it was a head-on collision, and the doctors weren't..." Jason could barely bring himself to say it, knowing the pain it would cause.

"Jason, stop!" she screamed through the sobs. "You are not going to tell me that my mother is dead. You are going to take me to that hospital, and they are just going to have to bring her back." She was frantic. She rushed to the door. She knew as soon as the words and actions left her mouth she sounded crazy, but if she didn't accept the fact that her mother was gone, maybe she would wake up from this horrible nightmare.

Jason shook his head at her and followed her to the door. "Gabby, I am so sorry, but it's too late. She's gone." He cupped her face and kissed her forehead.

"No, no, no," Gabby pleaded. "Please don't take her from me." She wasn't speaking to Jason any longer. She began to convulse. She had forgotten how to breathe. She felt Jason help her to the floor. She was holding onto the door handle. He held her tight and whispered something in her ear, but it was inaudible.

Her mother's smiling face came to her mind. She thought of the time her mom had taken the training wheels off her bike. Gabriella had just fallen off on her first attempt, and she was ready to give up, but her mother insisted that she give it one more try. Gabby could see her mother's long chestnut-brown hair blowing in the wind, and she brushed it off her face ever so slightly. She saw her mother's warm, encouraging smile telling her she had the strength inside of her to do whatever she put her mind to.

And then Gabriella came back to reality, and through her tears, she saw her two helpless sisters sobbing in the arms of the Cindy and Robert Throne in the sitting room. She looked from Giuliana to Gemma and knew what she must do. She got up as she had many years ago with the encouragement of her mother, as if she had fallen off the bike again, dusted her knees off, and moved over to the sofa. She took Gemma in one arm and Giuliana in the other. They were all that she had left, and she was going to do everything she could to protect them. Gabriella, Gemma, and Giuliana sobbed together until they fell into an uncomfortable sleep.

2

Sunlight peeked in rays through the curtains into the Thrones' family room. The sounds of sizzling grease, pans clinking together, and senseless chatter escaped the kitchen. Gabriella Knope tried opening her eyes, but the attempt was lousy. She did not want to face the day, fearing that last night's dream was no dream at all. She had no desire to ever wake up again. She had decided that it would be too hard, and perhaps if she slept long enough, everything would fade way. Her face felt sticky and hot from the residue that all of the fallen tears had left behind. The sunlight was doing its best to break through her tightly eyelids, which were trying to avoid the day at all costs. Gabriella prayed silently to herself: "If you let my mother be alive, I promise I will never take her for granted again. I'll spend every day telling her what she means to me, and I won't go away to school, I promise. Just please let her be alive."

She opened her eyes, her prayers were unanswered, and there she was in the Thrones' family room, with Gemma and Giuliana lying on either side of her. They had the same tear-stained face she did. They too were motherless. With that thought, a heavy feeling in her stomach took over and made her feel as if she was going to be sick. She assumed this would be the way she would feel every day—the sickening feeling that her mother was no longer in the same world with her. She could no longer hear her voice, she could no longer see her face. Her mother, Clare LaFrace, was gone. Gabriella got up in fear that she would need to make haste for the bathroom with the heartbreak swirling around inside trying to make its way out of her body.

She walked over to the lavender curtains with old-fashioned tassels that pulled them open and close, and she examined the outside to see how the world had reacted to losing such a great woman. The sun was shining, birds were singing, cars were bustling down the street to get to a meaningless day of work—meaningless routines, everything was the same, except her mom was gone. It was a perfect day. She thought that maybe it would be rainy and dreary to match her own mood, but no, the world was still turning, and she and her sisters were all alone. She craned her neck with silly hope that this was some kind of sick joke; maybe her mother would be hiding behind a bush, or maybe she would be pulling up in the family SUV at any moment with a tale of a wild mix-up.

Gabriella could not bring herself to say the undeniable fact out loud for all to hear. If she let the words escape her lips, there would be no taking it back. She would have to face the reality, and she was not ready to let go. Tears swelled in her eyes like an army ready to stand and fight the greatest battle of their lives, but within moments, they had already suffered a casualty. She tried to breathe and wipe away the sadness. She summoned the strength from within to make the tears stop to avoid another breakdown.

She thought it was silly that something so small made her feel so good. Gabriella thought maybe that was how she was supposed to approach things: with tiny steps. Possibly with tiny steps, one after the other, she could get through the awful day that awaited her. She turned around to face a house that had provided so much comfort and so much love in the past and now looked like a stranger's home. The pictures scattered on the walls, which Gabriella had spent so many hours pointing at and making jokes with Jason about, now seemed to be faceless and foreign. Some people found Cindy Throne's décor choices slightly tacky; Gabriella usually found it comforting and refreshingly original, but today nothing was familiar. She scanned the room for something that she could possibly hold, something that might jolt back her lost feelings. She felt so numb, as if she might be invisible or in a coma and maybe it wasn't really happening.

Gabriella walked around quietly so as not to disturb her sleeping sisters. The living room was littered with one eccentric hobby after the next. There were scrapbooks piled high on a bookshelf, one dedicated to her son for each year since his birth, one for every trip that they had ever taken as a family, every holiday. There was even one for Gabriella and Jason. Next to the scrapbooks was a collection of sand art in a curio cabinet, a hoard of homemade stuffed animals lined the fireplace mantel, and pictures that contained her memories frozen in time, even with all of Cindy Throne's good-intentioned memory keeping, marching to the beat of her own drum. Nothing seemed familiar or cracked a glimmer of a smile on Gabriella's face.

"Gabby," Jason whispered as he tiptoed into the living room, "are you OK?"

She nodded toward him. "Sure."

The empathy was pouring from his voice. "How are you feeling?" Jason seemed nervous to be speaking with her.

Gabriella tried to smile. She wasn't sure whether she managed to or not. "As well as can be expected."

Jason and Gabby had been best friends since first grade. One week in school, their own friends were out for a whole week with the chicken pox at the same time, so naturally Jason and Gabby began playing at recess with each other. Jason soon decided that Gabriella did not have cooties, and Gabriella decided that Jason was not icky. And he was not icky in the slightest. He had really come into his own--he was handsome, almost in the six-foot range but not quite there, dark-brown hair, broad shoulders and biceps that were starting to form, defined cheekbones, a smile with dimples attached, and brown, sometimes hazel, eyes. Gabriella knew that Jason would always be there for her, and she would do the same for him.

Jason was fiddling with his hands, looking slightly uncomfortable, probably trying to decide whether to say anything or just sit in the awkward silence that they had created. He decided to end the silence. "Do you need anything? Are you hungry?" His intentions were sincere, but he was still very cautious with his words.

Gabriella sighed at the thought of how many times she was going to hear the question, are you hungry? And she did not want to hear it from him. "Jason, I know that you mean well. I do, but I am not glass that is going to shatter at the slightest touch." Gabriella moved a few steps closer to him. "We both know that people will be shoving food down my throat for the next two weeks at least, so please don't join in the fun with them." She almost laughed at herself. She was surprised at how easy it was to talk to Jason when only moments ago she had been afraid that if she opened her mouth or eyes, she would burst into tears. She had found the familiarity that she had been searching the room for.

He laughed quietly. "You know," he said, moving a few steps closer to her, "you are doing much better than I thought you would. I am not saying..." He broke off.

She smiled for the first time that day. "I know." She took in a deep breath and exhaled. "I'm not OK, but who would be? I just need some normalcy right now. At least as much as I can get."

He smiled, showing off his dimples, and playfully slugged her in her shoulder. "You look really bad in the morning, and you kind of smell funny."

Her mouth opened as if she were offended, and she jokingly shoved him back and let out a laugh. But she clapped her hands over her mouth, feeling guilty about what she had just done.

"It is OK to laugh, Gabby." Jason put his hand on her shoulder gently to bring her to him.

Gabriella shook her head fiercely. The guilt was overwhelming. She shouldn't be laughing. She should be grieving the loss of her.... She could not even bring herself to say it in her own mind. If she said it, it would make it true, and that would change everything. She tried to change the subject to something not so dire, "What time is it?"

Jason, caught off guard by her casual tone, turned in every direction, not able to remember where the clocks were in his own house. "Um...It's seven forty-five in the morning." He slipped his arm around her waist and pulled her in close. "Do you want to go get some breakfast? Go for a drive just to get out of the house?"

A new beacon of hope, however outlandish, had just been lit inside of her, and Gabriella wanted to jump up and down with excitement. Why hadn't she thought of this? If she were actually to leave the house, then just maybe she could realize that it was a dream after all. Perhaps her mom would be at the Waffle Hut.

Jason seemed to read her mind without trying. "Gabby, I am so sorry. If I could take your pain away, I would. She's gone."

The tears that Gabriella had ordered to stand the front lines no matter what started to fall one by one until there wasn't a front line to speak of. Jason helped Gabriella to the floor once more, and he held her in his arms, stroking her hair, trying his best to keep it out of her face, rubbing her arms up and down, and rocking her back and forth, trying his best to soothe her. Gabriella had not known that this side of Jason existed, but she had never been more appreciative of her best friend—or anyone, for that matter. If it weren't for him, she would have to set off on a quest to find her mother. She would have convinced herself of some outlandish conspiracy in which her mother was being held somewhere against her will, but still alive.

Gabriella pulled away slightly from Jason to look into his eyes. "My mom...she is gone." The words were so final that they made her sick to her stomach as they left her lips. But she knew she had to say it out loud to make it real, or she would have fallen into a downward spiral trying to convince herself that this awful nightmare was just that—a nightmare and not the harsh reality of the way the world works.

Jason held her tightly and nodded. He kissed her softly on the forehead. They sat up against the lavender curtains until Gabriella's sisters awoke.

When Giuliana and Gemma began to stir, Jason excused himself to give them some privacy, and Gabriella smiled and hugged him tightly, appreciating the kindness he had shown her in the last twelve hours.

"Hey, Giuliana." Gabriella wrapped up her six-year-old sister in a tight squeeze, more aware of the fact that life is too short to take for granted.

Giuliana stretched her arms toward the ceiling and let out a fake sleepy yawn. "Good morning, sissy." With her upbeat attitude, it was clear that Giuliana had not grasped the severity of the situation.

Gemma reluctantly sat up and just stared off into space. She made eye contact with Gabriella but said nothing. She didn't need to. Gabriella knew exactly what she was thinking because they were both thinking the same thing: Is this really happening? Gabriella moved over to Gemma and wrapped her into a tight hug, hoping it would offer some comfort. They sat leaned up against the floral-decorated couch in the Thrones' living room, not really knowing what to do or say. Giuliana was playing with her hair, trying to brush the tangles out with her fingers. Gemma had her head looking up as if that were the only way to keep the tears way. And Gabriella felt responsible, as she was the oldest, and now she had to keep what was left of her family together. She had to be the strong one; she had to be the one to put the pieces back together.

"If you guys want to talk, I am here for you. We are still going to be a family, and nothing is going to change that." Gabriella, realizing how cliché she sounded, rolled her eyes before Gemma had a chance to.

Giuliana, the youngest, tugged on Gabriella's sleeve. "Gabby?" She looked as if she was thinking very hard about what she had to say. "When do we get to see mommy?"

Gabriella and Gemma's eyes filled with tears almost instantaneously. Gabriella tried to fight them off. She hadn't even thought about how hard it would be for a six-year-old to understand the concept of death. They usually learn with a hamster, and then a grandparent. They don't have to start out with their mother, but now all Giuliana had was two older sisters to take care of her.

"Giuliana, Mommy isn't going to be back." Gabriella barely managed to get the sentence out without bursting back into uncontrollable sobs.

Giuliana looked confused. She tucked her tangled sandy-blond hair behind her ear. The tiny flecks of amber glistened in her light blue eyes with small droplets of water forming in the corners. "But I saw mommy in my dream last night."

Gemma let out a gasp followed by a noisy sob. Gabriella had dreamed about their mother as well—probably not the same kind of dream as Giuliana's—and with Gemma's reaction, Gabriella was sure that she had had similar dreams. They missed their mother, and it had only been a day. How would the loss get better with time? Wouldn't it be worse?

Gabriella shook her head and put her own thoughts on the back burner to focus on Giuliana. "Mommy will always be in our dreams, and she will be there like a guardian angel when we need her." Gabriella was trying to come up with the easiest explanation for a six-year-old to understand. "Mom loved us all very much, and sometimes people don't have enough time on earth because God needs them for his kingdom." Gabriella took in a deep breath. Her voice was beginning to crack. "Sometimes we have to do things we don't want to, and we don't get to say good-bye when we want. So we have to use our dreams and imaginations to tell that person how much we miss and love them."

"Gabby." Gemma put her arm across Gabriella's shoulders. "You aren't alone." Gemma could read Gabriella's expressions and the feelings she was hiding.

Gabriella gave Gemma a nod of appreciation, and they all huddled together, crying off and on.

Jason and his mother, Cindy Throne, entered the living room attempting to be as considerate as possible. Cindy Throne sat down on the floral-decorated couch, cleared her throat, and waited for some sort of signal from the girls that is was OK for her to speak.

"Girls, I want you to know that if you need anything, Robert, Jason, and I are here for you. We want you to feel open and stay as long as you like. We will help you with the arrangements and whatever you need," Cindy told them. "Now, who is hungry?" she said in an upbeat tone. "I have got anything you want. You name it, you can have it!"

Gabriella was quite sure that she meant it. Even if Giuliana requested ice cream, she would undoubtedly receive ice cream for breakfast.

Giuliana broke the silence. "Mrs. Throne, can I have toast with jelly piled in the middle and cut into triangles? That is the way my mommy did it, and I would like to have breakfast with her in my dreams this morning."

Gabriella saw a small tear fall from Cindy's eye. Cindy quickly wiped it away. She nodded toward Giuliana and ushered her to the kitchen. Jason followed them, sensing that Gabriella and Gemma needed to be alone.

Gemma Knope, the sensible one of the three, asked, "What are we going to do?"

"I don't know," Gabriella replied honestly.

"There is so much we have to figure out," Gemma continued. "I mean, Giuliana is only six years old. We don't have grandparents that we know. Mom was a foster kid, so no brothers and sisters. We don't really know our dad that well, but I guess we don't have a choice. It looks like we—"

"No, are you crazy," Gabriella whispered loudly, cutting Gemma off at the mention of their father. "No, Gemma, not going to happen. I will take care of everything. Don't worry." Gabriella could see Gemma looking at her as if she were the insane one. "We will not live with that man. I will stay home from school and take care of you guys. I have a good job at the paper. Maybe they will promote me, or I can get another job. You will be sixteen soon, and you can get a job and help out." Gabriella was figuring things out as she spoke, getting together a plan, trying to sound as if she had all of her ducks in row.

"Gabby," Gemma said in disbelief with a little understanding, "I know you feel you have some responsibility, but how do you think you can afford a mortgage payment as someone who gets coffee for a living?"

Gemma did have a point, Gabriella admitted to herself, but it didn't matter. She had always been a firm believer that if you want something badly enough, you can make it happen. It was something that she had learned from her mother.

Gabriella tried to sound confident. "Gemma, I am not going to let this family fall apart." She took in a deep breath to keep her calm, as she was about to talk about the man who infuriated her the most in the world. "And I am not going to let that man sink his fangs into this family like he has some sort of right! No! I am eighteen; I will do whatever I need to do to make sure that you, me, and Giuliana stay together. I will make it work. It's settled." Gabriella didn't want to think about it anymore. "Now, let's focus on getting through the next few days. I don't want you to worry at all. I will handle everything." Gabriella got up and knocked her knee into an end table, causing a ruckus, and it was just the distraction she needed for Gemma to drop the subject for the time being.

"Everything OK in there?" Cindy Throne called from the kitchen.

Gemma shook her head at Gabriella with a disapproving look, but they both decided it was not the time or the place. They walked into the kitchen to get some breakfast. Gabriella let out a shrill gasp at the sight of Austin and Alice Knope. Gabriella started to open her mouth to express her disapproval of their existence, but Cindy Throne quickly interjected.

"So, what can I get you two for breakfast?" she asked, trying to diffuse the tension.

Gabriella was not interested in breakfast. "Cindy, what are they doing here?"

Cindy Throne grimaced, pursing her lips and searching for the right words to handle such a delicate subject. "Austin, your father, wanted to be here this morning. He wants to talk with you."

Gabriella rolled her eyes and turned her attention to the first and only man to ever break her heart. "So, what do you want?"

Austin, with his sandy-blond hair, a blue polo shirt, and Levi jeans, got up and started to move toward her, but instead, he stopped halfway. "Gabriella, I know that you are angry with me, but I really just want to help and be here for you and your sisters."

Gabriella laughed mockingly. She caught the dirty glare Alice Knope shot her from across the room. Jason looked at her, imploring her to not start the same old argument.

She placed her hands on her hips. "And what do you think you can do to help?"

He took a deep breath, knowing this might be his only chance to talk to her in a civil manner. "Gabriella," he began cautiously, "I am not going to pretend I know what you are going through, losing a parent at such a young age."

Gabriella's eyes filled with the all-too-familiar tears. But it dawned on her she had lost both of her parents at a young age—first her father when he abandoned them, not once but three times, and now her mother was gone.

Austin mistook Gabriella's silence as an indication that she liked what he was saying, so he continued. "But I want to do right by your mother. I want to help. I want you and your sisters to come and live with us."

Gabriella felt her blood boil to the surface. Her sadness had been channeled into rage, and the cap on her emotions was about to explode like the bombs bursting in air from that famous anthem. How could Austin be serious? Who did the hell did he think he was? One day—not even a whole day—her mother had been gone, and he was asking such an outrageous question, and she was supposed to just run and jump and say, "Please love me like you should have all along." Not only did Austin Knope break her mother's heart on three separate occasions, he did not want anything to do with her when she was a baby. And then, when he had gotten her mother pregnant again, he left for his own unexplainable, selfish reasons. He had a "real" family, and it had always meant that he could not be bothered with Gabriella and her sisters. He had strung her mother along for her entire life, and Gabriella refused to let that happen to her and her sisters.

"How dare you!" Her voice was almost a whisper, but everyone could hear her. They could probably hear the world's tiniest mouse, it was so quiet in that room. "How dare you come in here and act like you care. You act like you care about me and my sisters when we both know that you do not. How dare you talk about my mother like she was some friend that you were on speaking terms with. You never even acknowledged me until you had enough time to get my mother pregnant again, and then you left because that is what you are best at. You left and ran right into the arms of that woman, and you left my mother like three-day-old trash!" Gabriella's jaw was clinched, her fists were balled, and she was ready to unleash everything she had kept to herself all of those years

Alice stood up, possibly to defend her husband, but Austin motioned her to sit down. "Gabriella Marie Knope, you are my daughter whether you like it or not."

Gabriella laughed in derision. "You are really going to try to use my full name. Wow." She was appalled by his misdirected confidence as her father.

"Gemma and Giuliana are my daughters too, and there is nothing you can do about that." Tears swelled in his eyes. "I am so sorry for all of the mistakes that I made with you and your sisters." He put his face in his hands, looked up, and appeared genuinely sorry. "And God knows I am so sorry for the mistakes I made with your mother, but you have to know that I love her very much. Shit." Austin was not as put together as Gabriella was used to. "I don't want another moment to pass where you guys are not in my life. Please let me make up for all of the mistakes now." Austin got within arm's reach of Gabriella. "I know that is what your mother would have wanted."

Jason, Cindy, and Robert Throne all shook their heads in unison, knowing that he had most definitely said the wrong thing again.

Tears were flowing freely down Gabriella's face; her voice was muffled in between sobs. "This is what my mother would have wanted," she screamed, and her hand connected with Austin's face. The shock in the room could be heard in audible gasps and murmurs being tossed around. "How dare you! How would you know what my mother wanted? You, Austin, only stayed around long enough to get her pregnant, and then you left every time!"

"Gabriella—"

"No!" She stopped him before he could say another word. "You listen to me, Austin. You had your chance to be our father. You don't get to pick and choose; that's not how it works. You walked out on each of us. You can't swoop in and act like everything is going to be different. I am eighteen years old. Gemma and Giuliana are my responsibility, not yours, and we are going to stick together. I am going to raise them on my own without interference from you. That is what my mother would have wanted." Gabriella started to gain her composure, to assert her confidence. "And if you don't like it, I'll see you in court." Gabriella left the room without saying a word to anyone.

Gabriella waited until she got up the stairs to let go once more. She was irate, she could feel the steam rolling off the top of her head, her face was hot from the nonstop crying, and her head hurt, but she hadn't realized how much until she was alone in Jason's room. Gabriella was truly alone for the first time since she had heard the unbearable news. Her angry thoughts quickly turned back to sorrowful thoughts about the best mother—her mother, who was gone and who was not coming back. Although she could have dreams about her, she knew in her heart it would not be the same. Why had her mother left her? Didn't she know that she still needed her mom to be there and tell her what to do? How could Gabriella keep the promises she had just made? She would have to give up everything she had worked so hard for until Giuliana was old enough to be on her own. She would have to forget about going to Brown University.

She paused her thoughts for a moment, staring at her reflection in the dusty mirror. She had not thought about not going to Brown University. It had been her dream her whole life, and now it was going to be taken away from her. She had gotten a full scholarship; she had worked extra hard to make sure she did not have to put the financial burden on her mother. "Wow," she thought. "This is what it is like to be an adult. This is what its like to be responsible. Well then, let's get serious."

A soft tap on the door startled her, causing her to almost trip over some dirty clothes on the floor. She was relieved that it was Jason and not Austin trying to try her patience again. She hated the fact that she had the same last name as he did. She wondered if marriage was the only way to change it, and her thoughts of Austin must have come across as an unpleasant expression on her face because Jason started backing out of his own room.

"Jason, wait. Don't go. I am sorry; my thoughts were somewhere else." Gabriella felt the need to be around someone, and she decided that she was not quite ready to be alone yet.

Jason nodded and sat down on his unmade bed. He looked at her with a satisfied smile. "I cannot believe that you slapped him." He laughed. "How long have you wanted to do that?"

She plopped down next to him and lay back with her hands folded across her stomach. "I would say about fourteen years." She laughed and didn't feel as guilty about it this time.

"Gabby, do you think..." Jason propped himself up on one arm. "I mean, don't you think that they are just trying to help?" He ducked back in case Gabriella decided to slap him as well. "Let's be honest. How do you think you are going to raise two adolescent girls? One who is barely out of kindergarten, and the other who is just starting high school? Gabby, I know that you're awesome, but come on, let's be realistic."

She looked at him, deciding whether or not she should make him her next victim, but he did have a point. She herself had just been wondering how she was going to pull off such a feat. A surge of determination ran through her, and she pushed those thoughts far from her mind. She knew that there was no alternative. She had to do this, and she was going to make it happen.

"Jason." She sat up slightly to look him in the eye. "My mom is not coming back. I have to find a way to deal with that. I know that it is not going to be easy. But I know what is right, and this is the way it is meant to be."

Jason smiled and shook his head. He helped her stand up the rest of the way into a tight hug and kissed her cheek softly. "If anyone can do it, its Clare LaFrace's daughter."

Gabriella nodded and began to cry again. She let Jason hold her as she tried to regain control of her emotions.

After fifteen minutes or so, Gabriella and Jason walked downstairs together, and to her dismay, Austin Knope was there. She marched right over to confront him. "What are you still doing here?" she demanded.

"We need to talk about the arrangements and the lawyer who is coming this afternoon," Austin told her. His eyes were red, and Gabriella recognized the same tear residue on his face.

She felt a twinge of guilt but quickly reminded herself of how many times he had been the cause for her tears. "OK, let's talk, then." She didn't give him a chance to say anything. "Robert and Cindy can help me with the arrangements, and since you have no legal obligation to me or my sisters— because you have made that perfectly clear over the last eighteen years— there is no need for you to be around for whatever lawyer is coming here." She put her hand up to stop Austin from speaking. "I am not done. We will let you know when the funeral is, and you can pay your last respects to my mother, something you failed to do during her life. Other than that, there is no reason for you be around." Her words were spoken so harshly that it was like the script she had memorized the first time he had disappointed her. She did not blink, for she would lose her composure, and she didn't want Austin to think that she was vulnerable or weak or that she could be taken advantage of. She continued her verbal assault. "This is a time for family grieving. As much as you have convinced yourself you are a part of this family, I am afraid you are mistaken. You are nothing more than a sperm donor." Gabriella's words were as sharp as jagged glass.

Austin held his head in dismay. He cleared his throat. "I know you are hurting right now," he said politely. It seemed hard for him to look at Gabriella. He turned to Cindy and Robert Throne. "I'll be in touch." He focused back on Gabriella. "I know you don't want to hear this, but I am going to say it anyways. I loved your mother very much, and I love you and your sisters very much. Whether you approve or not, it does not change the fact that I am your father. I have kept my distance your whole life, and I know that was a mistake. I will be back today around five. I hope that we can talk in a civilized manner, but until then, I want you to know if you need anything, I am only a phone call away." Austin picked up his keys, hugged Giuliana and Gemma good-bye, and walked out of the door.

Gabriella watched him walk away, as he had done so many times before; she felt everyone's eyes on her. She did feel a small amount of guilt for being so cruel to him. It was not like her to strike out so viciously even toward Austin, but he had gone too far on the wrong day, and that was that.

"Gabby," Cindy Throne called from the living room, "Jason is going to drive you to your house to pick up some clothes for you and your sisters. Your mother's lawyer, Mr. Morgan, is coming here at five o'clock this afternoon." She waited for Gabriella to acknowledge the information before continuing. "Robert and I will help with the arrangements if that is OK with you. And Gabby," she added, "Austin will be here for the meeting with Mr. Morgan, so please prepare yourself."

She thought about arguing with Cindy but decided against it. Gabriella nodded and gave Cindy a quick hug. "Thank you for everything you have done for us."

She hugged Gemma and Giuliana and assured them that she would be back as soon as possible. She grabbed her purse, stopped in front of the hallway mirror to adjust her hair but decided there was no helping it without a long shower, and then she followed Jason out the door.

3

Gabriella was getting settled in the front seat of Jason's ridiculous yellow Camaro. He had spent numerous unrecoverable hours on the car to
make it sound like a pissed-off bee stuck in a coffee can. She rummaged
in her bag for her phone, thinking about it for the first time in sixteen
hours—that had to be some kind of record—and at last, she pulled it out.
To her surprise, there was a little bit of life left in it. She pressed the
button that made the screen light up and saw that she had sixty-seven
missed calls and 138 new text messages, and her voice mail was full. She
rolled her eyes as she saw that at least thirty of the text messages were
from Alex Hickins. She had completely forgotten that she had ended
her two-year relationship with him. She had almost completely forgotten that he existed. She hadn't even told the story of her triumphant
victory over Danielle Dickert last night to her best friend—normally it
would have been something Jason would know mere minutes after it
happened—but now it all seemed so childish and immature. Her priori-
ties were different now, and she had a lot of growing up to do if she was
going to keep the promises that she had made.

Gabriella saw the passing trees, the cookie-cutter houses, the mail-
boxes with their own personalities—the world was still intact. The
sights of Laking were making her incredibly sad, so Gabriella turned
her head away from the window and tried her best to strike up a conversation with her best friend. "Hey, Jason, I didn't tell you; I forgot, but
I broke up with Alex last night."

He rolled his eyes and laughed.

"What?" She was a little surprised by his reaction.

"I already knew that," he said in an obvious tone. "Danielle Dickert went on a tirade blasting you in her status." He cleared his throat. "So how long do you think this will last?"

She half smiled. "How long will what last?" She already knew the answer.

"Have you guys picked a date to get back together yet?" His dimples were in full bloom, and the satisfied look on his face radiated from his entire body.

"Ha, ha," she said in derision. "For your information, I have been wanting to break up with him for quite some time now." She saw he wasn't convinced. "You know, since I am going to Brown—" She broke off. She wasn't going to Brown, she wasn't going anywhere, she was going to be that person she swore up and down that she would never be—a Laking citizen for life.

"Gab." Jason put his hand on her knee and massaged it gently.

Gabriella turned to face forward in the car. "Yeah, I guess it doesn't really matter anymore, given the recent event." She sighed in an attempt not to cry. She looked out the window as the same old town passed before her eyes. Nothing on the outside had changed, but on the inside, she would never be the same. Her entire life would change, and there was nothing that she could do about it. "Do you realize everything is going to be different now? I mean nothing is going to be the same ever again." Her eyes filled with watery tears once more.

Jason grabbed her hand and gave it a gentle squeeze. "I will help you get through this."

Gabriella knew that he was sincere, but this was not something that she could get through, with or without his help. She knew in her heart she would never truly be able to cope with the loss of her mother. The most important person in the world to her was gone—not willingly gone, just taken abruptly out of this world for no reason at all—and now Gabriella would never hear the sound of her mother's voice again. She let out a small whimper of despair as the tires of Jason's car left the smooth pavement to crunch on the gravel driveway that her mother had never gotten around to having paved, but it was on the list. Gabriella remembered the day five years ago when they had walked through the house for the first time, and the exuberant joy that radiated like the North Star from her mother's eyes as she knew that, that house was *the* house. Gabriella traveled back in time to let what were once joyous and precious moments, but were now painful memories, consume her.

Gabriella watched as Clare got out of the car and looked at the elegant gray house with white trim and four grand white pillars that held the roof in place, a house that welcomed you to the elegant cherry-oak front door, decorated with old-fashioned street lights that at one time held only candles but now served as decorative porch lights. And just above the door was a balcony that made them all feel like a princess. The porch stretched across the front of the house, not yet decorated, but many ideas circled their minds. The cherry blossom tree to one side and the oak trees to the other gave the house just the femininity that it needed. Gabriella could tell her mother was proud of herself as she slung a duffel bag over her shoulder and helped Giuliana out of the car. Gemma and Gabriella squabbled over who would have to carry what, but Clare didn't seem to notice; she was transfixed by what lay before her. It was their very own house, and she had done it on her own—a house that she could raise her children in, a house she could have the family Christmas at forever, a house that her grandchildren would be longing to come and visit in the summers.

"OK," Clare said, grabbing the keys from her pocket. "The furniture and the movers are coming tomorrow, so 1246 Willow Street is empty for the last time tonight. Tonight is just us; it's just our family."

Giuliana started a full sprint, basically waddling toward the door with her stuffed unicorn, which she had so cleverly named Sparkles, clutched to her side.

Gabriella smiled, watching her mother run to catch up with her. "So what do you want to do tonight?"

"Well, for starters," Clare said, a little short of breath, "go inside, order takeout, play some games—a slumber party in the living room." Clare pointed to the sleeping bags that Gemma was hauling inside.

"Games?" Gemma moaned. "What kind of games?"

"Only the fun ones." Clare ignored Gemma's protest and put the key into the keyhole of the red cherry-oak door and turned it until it clicked, and she pushed the door open into the foyer. One direction was the living room, the other the dining room, and in the center were the stairs that led up to the second floor.

Gabriella watched her mother as she moved gracefully throughout the empty house, running her hands over the untouched counters and bare walls. Her mother was taking in deep breaths to capture the essence of the empty house. Almost with every turn, she would close her eyes, breathe in heavily, and smile slightly. Gabriella saw her mother's golden chestnut hair flowing behind her with every step, she appeared to be in slow motion in Gabriella's mind, she could see her face so clearly; and the look of pure happiness and accomplishment, the spark in her light-sky-blue eyes glistened with small tears of happiness balling up in the corners, but Gabriella pretended not to see.

"All right." Clare put down the duffel bag, and it echoed throughout the entire empty house. "Let's get cozy. I'll order the food, and let's get ready to party *Full House* style."

They all laughed and did as they were instructed to do. They spent the night in the living room talking, playing games, and listening to their mother tell stories about far-off lands, which Gabriella secretly suspected were not exactly fiction but just a spin on her own experiences.

That night, the night before the furniture and movers came, had been one of the best nights of Gabriella's life. The happy memory caused her to fall back into uncontrollable sobs as the red cherry-oak door came into view, and she was forced to remember that her mother never again would be able to turn the key and open it.

Gabriella regretted all the time she had spent with her friends, all the times she had broken curfew, all the fights, and every time—it was rare, but it had happened—that she had told her that she hated her. Gabriella wished with all of her might for a redo. She had learned her lesson, she would appreciate her mother, she would not question or argue with her, she would respect her, never raise her voice, and she would make sure to tell her mother how much she loved her every day without fail. Jason was the clear sign that her wish had not come true, and no amount of wishing was going to change anything. She was going to have to learn how to live with being devastated and broken hearted for the rest of her life.

Gabriella tried to brace herself as Jason made his way to help her out of the car. She felt weak, as if she had been in an accident. She couldn't stand without some kind of support. Gabriella looked at the house that had been the statement that "Everything is great now," and now it said, "Nothing is ever going to be great again." Jason helped her out of the car, letting her lean on him for support. She was very grateful to him and didn't know how she could ever repay the kindness he had shown to her in the last day.

Gabriella looked around as she took her first step, crunching the gravel beneath her shoe. The flowers lining the path had wilted over-night; their color had faded as Clare faded from the world. They approached the porch where Gabriella had spent so many nights talking with her mother on the wooden swing that hung off to the side in front of the bay window. She could see a small trail of ants marching up and down the potted plant where Giuliana had dropped a cookie into the dirt, and no doubt her mother had told her at least four times to pick it up to keep the ants away. Her mother was everywhere, and they had only made it to the front steps of the porch.

Jason stopped her before she started up the steps and grabbed her hand. "We can drive around a little if you are not ready yet."

She smiled at him weakly but shook her head. "No, I have to do this. It will not be any different if we drive around the block a few times."

He nodded in agreement and put his hand on the small of her back to guide her in case she lost her nerve.

As they started up the stairs, she could feel the neighbors' eyes peering through the peepholes of their curtains at her, as if they expected some sort of press conference. She had not given much thought to the neighbors or the rumors, but she had no doubt that everyone in town was talking about it and just waiting for a glimpse of confirmation. With each step, Gabriella felt her mother's death become more and more final and real to her. She heard the neighbors gathering in a small, inconspicuous circle, chatting and deciding who would be the one to approach her first with their condolences. Gabriella considered turning around to flip them a universal sign that had a meaning no one would be able to mistake.

She took another step forward but faltered slightly. Jason was right there to catch her. He tightened his grip around her to make sure the potential fall didn't happen again. They made it to the front door and exchanged glances. The front cherry-oak door was a usually an inviting door, but today it might as well been taped off with police tape and quarantined because Gabriella did not want to go in there. She didn't ever want to go back in there. On the other side of the door was reality. Once the door was opened, there would be no more denying that her mother was no longer on this earth. The familiar tears were creeping back into her eyes. She gripped Jason's hand tightly and rummaged in her purse for her keys. She shuddered when the cold metal touched her hands. Part of her didn't want to pull out the key; she wanted to leave it there forever, hoping that it was all in fact a dream. Despite her best efforts, she pulled the key to the surface, and her hand trembled as she tried to put the key into the keyhole. Jason steadied her hand, and they turned the key together until it clicked as it had five years ago the night before the furniture came.

When the door opened, she hoped that her mother would come bustling out of the kitchen to greet her with a hug. This did not happen. In the picture in the foyer, a memory frozen in time from the first night in the house, they were all laughing, gathered around their mother, whom they loved so much. The only thing out of place in the house was the kitchen. It was quite obvious that they were in a hurry when they had left. Gabriella didn't really have to assume it had been upon the delivery of the horrible news of her mother's accident. She paused just beyond the foyer, and she wondered what the last thing her mother had touched was. If she could find that thing, she would just put her hand over it, and some kind of mystical power would connect her with her mother and provide her with some much-needed advice on how to get through the next few days. She cried loudly, and she did not try to fight the tears.

"Who cries this much?" she asked herself out loud. She covered her face with her hands. "Even if people lose someone they are really close to, do they really cry this much?" She was talking to herself. She was barely aware that Jason was within inches of her. She felt weak and helpless. She glanced up at Jason.

"Gabby, I know this is hard for you. It's hard for everyone," he said. "It is OK to cry, and I am here for you. My family is here for you." He wiped away some of her tears and pulled her into a tight hug.

"I know," she said through the sobs. She stood there for a moment in his arms, trying to gather her courage to make her way up the stairs. She did not know if she had the strength. She wanted so badly to wake up from this nightmare. She wanted things to be the way they had been yesterday.

"Do you want me to go with you up the stairs?" Jason asked.

"No, I think I should try to do this alone," she told him. "I'll call down if I need any help."

He nodded. "I'll straighten up the kitchen then for you," he offered.

She smiled toward him. "Thanks." She ran up the stairs faster than she had expected to and stumbled at the top. Gabriella stood at the top of the stairs looking around, wondering where she should start and what she should even grab. She tried to make a mental list of the things that she would need and made her way over to the hall closet to get a duffel bag big enough to hold everything. There were four bedrooms upstairs and one bathroom. It made the mornings interesting despite her mother's best attempts at a morning bathroom schedule.

Gabriella decided to start in Giuliana's room first. It was a typical six-year-old's room. She had dolls scattered from one end of the room to the other. Markers and crayons were strewn across her bed, and various toys and clothes were bulging from under it. The bedspread, decorated with unicorns and rainbows, was hanging halfway off the bed. The pillows were across the room; she probably had decided that her dolls needed them more than she did. Gabriella smiled, trying to remember how many times her mom had asked Giuliana to clean her room, and of course, Giuliana had failed miserably. Giuliana had once told her mother that the life of a kindergarten graduate was far too busy to be concerned with the silly task of cleaning a room. Giuliana was most definitely the comedian of the family. She had no filter, and whatever came to her mind, she said it out loud no matter how inappropriate it was. When she learned to talk, she started to repeat the words she had heard, and she was very honest about where the word had come from. Gabriella had gotten in a lot of trouble for the conversations she was having with her friends on the phone. So much so that it cost her a week of phone privileges.

Gabriella's heart broke at the thought of how little time Giuliana had gotten to spend with their mother. She tried not to think too much about it because Giuliana needed her, and she needed to know that Gabriella wasn't going anywhere—her role as older sister had just received a lot more responsibility.

She sighed and started to grab some clean clothes for Giuliana. She shoved what she thought would be pleasing to Giuliana to wear into the duffel bag. She saw Sparkles, Giuliana's favorite stuffed unicorn, and put her in the bag as well, and she took some coloring books to help keep her occupied. She tried to zip the bag and realized that she would need a bag for each of them at this rate.

Gabriella walked back to the hall closet to retrieve another bag and then went across the hallway to Gemma's room. Gemma's room was much different from any other room in the house. Everything had its place, almost everything had a label, her closet was organized by garment and then by color, there was a tall bookshelf stuffed to the max with books—however, it was not crammed or cluttered—and her bed was neatly made, with her pillows arranged just right, the biggest in the back and the smallest in the front. Gemma had a studious attitude that carried to all aspects of her life. She was consumed with getting good grades, and she could not be bothered with anything that might distract her. Gemma had a plan for her life, and she never let anything keep her from her goals. She had said on several occasions that she would be the first woman president, and she wanted to win a Nobel Peace Prize for curing an incurable disease. Gabriella thought that Gemma worked so hard partly because she too had been rejected by their father. She was always trying to impress or top the last thing that she had accomplished, possibly hoping to live up to the Knope name.

Gabriella's thoughts quickly started turning for the worst at the thought of Austin, so she hurried to distract herself to keep her mind on the task at hand. Gabriella gazed around the room, looking where to begin. Gemma's clothes were much easier to find, and Gabriella found it soothing to pick out her outfits for the coming days.

She tried to think of something to bring Gemma to comfort her, but nothing jumped out at her. Gemma did not have a precious stuffed animal or some sort of keepsake that she always kept close. Gabriella went over to the bookshelf to see if any book looked particularly worn, which would mean Gemma had spent a great deal of time reading it. She skimmed the books of Gemma's miniature library and stopped at *The Adventures of Huckleberry Finn*. Gemma had read this book a hundred times. Gabriella took it off the shelf and ran her hands over the worn cover. *The Adventures of Huckleberry Finn* was the first chapter book their mother had read to Gemma. Gemma had fallen asleep to the sound of Clare's voice. Gabriella carefully placed the book in the bag, making sure not to damage it at all.

She took a final look around, searching for anything else that would bring Gemma comfort. Gabriella saw her desk drawer labeled Do Not Open. Gabriella looked around to make sure that Gemma would not be jumping out of any corners or from behind any doors. She opened the drawer, and there was a sea of papers and pictures. There were pictures of her family and one particular boy she did not recognize, but Gabriella was sure it was Gemma's crush or longtime love. Gabriella was sure the boy had the same feelings for Gemma, but they were both too shy to do anything about it. Underneath the paper and pictures was Gemma's journal. Gabriella knew that a journal could be so precious. She knew that her mother had kept a journal, Gabriella kept a journal, and so did Gemma. Clare had always encouraged them to keep journals as a way to get the good and bad stuff out to make room for new memories, whatever they may be. Gabriella pulled out the journal, tempted to open it, but she resisted and put it in the bag. She left Gemma's room as she had found it—neat and tidy—and made her way down the hallway.

She passed her mother's room almost at a jog, not ever wanting to open it again, and she wondered how much it would cost to have it permanently sealed. Gabriella stopped at the hall closet one more time to grab a bag for herself, and then she went into her own room. It was not quite as messy as Giuliana's, but it was not as organized as Gemma's room. Her desk was that of a messy writer. She had notebooks, folders with papers sticking out of the corners, no sense of organization, sticky notes lining the top of the desk with different ideas that she had never managed to turn into anything other than an idea. Her room was as she had left it, but her life was in complete disarray, much like the papers on her desk. Her life had changed instantly, and now her dream of being a writer, an author, seemed just that: a dream much like the dream and hope of Santa Claus being real. She felt hopeless, with nowhere to really turn. Her mother wasn't there to give advice, she wasn't there to guide her, Gabriella had lost her forever. Gabriella's cheeks felt wet again; tears were escaping from her eyes once more. She wiped them away quickly, not wanting to fall back into the endless cycle.

She pushed the thoughts out of her mind and quickly began searching through her drawers for something to wear. She grabbed the first things she thought to be suitable. She grabbed her journal off of her bed, and she took the miniature photograph that resembled the gigantic family portrait that hung in the foyer. She lingered for a moment before carefully placing the picture into the bag.

She had everything she needed. And if she slowed down, the tears would come back again, and she was tired of crying. She stopped in the bathroom to grab some necessities for them all, and she then darted down the stairs as fast as she could without falling to get out of the house that was making her relive what she now considered to be very painful memories.

"Jason, I am ready to go," she called, looking for him in the living room. He wasn't there. She heard murmurs coming from the kitchen. Against her better judgment and knowing that Jason would not be alone, she went in there to hurry up whomever he was talking to.

Lee Ann Gable, Gabriella's neighbor from across the street, was in the kitchen chatting away with Jason. She was the gossip queen of Laking. If someone got sick, she was the first to know. She was the ringleader of the clan of ladies that roamed about town, hosting their garden parties, book clubs, and bingo nights. Lee Ann always took it upon herself to keep the town informed of anything that was going on, whether it concerned her or not.

Lee Ann stopped midsentence, catching sight of Gabriella. Lee Ann turned to face her and held out her arms. She clapped her hands together in a prayer style and began to weep. "Oh my goodness, you poor girl. You must be so sad." Lee Ann grabbed Gabriella and pulled her in for an uncomfortable hug.

Gabriella mouthed, "What the hell?" to Jason.

He shrugged and mouthed, "I'm sorry."

Gabriella could not be mad at him because she had lived next door to Lee Ann for five years. She had probably pushed her way in and convinced Jason that her presence was the only thing that could comfort Gabriella in her greatest time of need. Lee Ann was a plump woman, and she did her best to hide it, but the three chins she carried always gave her away despite her body suit's efforts. She had a tired-looking face that she tried to hide by wearing too much makeup, and her hair was something straight out of the sixties—big and full of hair spray. Gabriella managed to release herself from Lee Ann's clutches.

"Gabby, if you need anything at all, and I mean *anything*," she emphasized with her hands, "please do not hesitate to call." Lee Ann was waiting for Gabriella to divulge all of the details about her mother's untimely passing to confirm or disprove the rumors she had already heard.

Gabriella smiled politely, but she had no intentions of talking about her mother with Lee Ann, or anyone for that matter. "Lee Ann, I appreciate—"

"Gabby, now you must tell me when the funeral is and the visitations. Are you going to have people over here, or will it be at the Thrones', or will you be having the funeral reception somewhere else?" Lee Ann did not take a breath. She was barking out questions as if they were throwing some kind of party and she needed to square away the last-minute details. Her mother had not been gone a full twenty-four hours, and Lee Ann wanted to know if she could host the damn party.

Gabriella's face got hot, she balled her fists, she was ready to pounce, and she shot Lee Ann a warning look.

"Gabby, are you listening?" Lee Ann chuckled, not noticing the look on Gabriella's face. "I also brought a casserole over for you and your sisters. Which reminds me, I know a great realtor if you are going to sell the house. Oh, and if you ever need anyone to talk to about your father, you can come to me." Lee Ann stopped at the sight of Gabriella's scowl.

Gabriella felt Jason's touch, reminding her that she wasn't to haul off and slap Lee Ann as she had Austin. Gabriella's face was hot, and she was sure that Lee Ann could smell the anger pouring out of her. "Lee Ann, I cannot talk about any of this right now. Selling my dead mother's house is the last thing on my mind. So if you don't mind, Jason and I have to get going." Gabriella did not blink. She stared coldly at Lee Ann, who winced slightly.

"Well," she said, acting offended.

Jason stepped in. "Lee Ann, you need to go," He spoke softly as not to offend Lee Ann, but to make sure she knew that she had gone too far.

Lee Ann nodded toward Jason. "If you or your sisters need anything, you know where to find me." She turned around and walked—almost jogged—out of the house as quickly as possible.

As soon as she was out of earshot, Gabriella slammed her hands down on the counter. "The nerve of that woman," she growled.

"Did you really expect anything less, Gab?" Gabby could tell that Jason was amused, but she was not in the least, "Come on, let's go back to my house. My mom called while you were upstairs and said that the lawyer, Mr. Morgan, will be there at five. It's two now, so you will have time to shower and everything."

Gabriella nodded, and he took her by the hand and led her out the door. Gabriella closed the door behind her as she had done countless times, but this time, she was closing the door on a chapter of her life she was not ready to end. She knew once she got in Jason's car, there would be no turning back, and her life would be forever changed. The familiar tears she had grown accustomed to crept back into her eyes and fell slowly, one by one.

The drive back to Jason's seemed much longer, and it was silent except for the few poor attempts that Jason made at small talk. Gabriella was too consumed with her own thoughts to converse with anyone, even her very best friend. She thought of yesterday, when her mother had said see you later, but she did not realize how much later that would indeed be. How different things could have been if her mother had decided to spend the night down in Valley Mines because she was too tired to make the drive. How different things could be if the tractor-trailer had taken a different route instead of the fateful one that had led to her mother's death. Oh, how she wished she could have just one more moment with her mother.

She sighed deeply. "Wow," she said aloud, but mostly for own benefit. "It is crazy, the things you miss, and she has only been gone one day." She put her head back into the seat and thought, unknowingly out loud for herself and Jason to hear, "How am I going to do this? I need to go back in time and figure out a way to change what happened. I have to. There must be a way to change this." Sobbing once, she buried her face in her hands and whispered, "I miss her so much. I need her. I need her. I need you." She was consumed and couldn't control herself anymore. The uncontrollable crying came back. She was sobbing very loudly. She was gasping for a breath.

"Gabby, calm down, Gabby," Jason said, rubbing her arm.

She sobbed louder but turned her head to stare at him. She could feel the wetness of the tears on her cheeks, and her face was stinging hot.

"Gabby." He took her hand and placed it over his heart. "Babe, you are my best friend and the strongest person that I know. This is not going to be easy, even for you. It is going to be hard, and some days will be better than others, and some days will be worse. No one in their right mind expects you to be OK in five minutes." He looked at her, more serious than ever. "Gabriella, you need to cut yourself some slack."

"I know, I know." She sounded a bit annoyed. "It's just that I am now responsible for my two sisters. I am all they have left, and they are all I have left." She broke off, and the tears came again.

"You are not alone, Gabby, you're not alone." There were tears in his voice coming out now. "Gabby, you will always have me and my family, and your mom had a lot of friends who will help you; you know that." He looked at her as if he could see right into her heart. "Gabriella, your mother was a beautiful person, and I loved her like she was my own mother." He broke for a moment, choking back his own sobs. "I will help you get through this. I love you."

"Thanks," she murmured. "I love you too, Jase." She managed to smile at him weakly. She sat up to compose herself as they pulled into the drive of the Thrones' home. Her heart instantly sank into her stomach. Austin Knope's car was already there. She closed her eyes, hoping she had only imagined it in her exhaustion, but she had not—the car was still present.

"He is only here because he has to be here," Jason tried to reassure her.

She waved her hand at him to motion him to stop. "I know, I know." Why would he need to be there for legal proceedings? She could not think of anything that her mother would have left him in her will. He had single-handedly broken her mother's heart a dozen times. She jerked the bags out of the backseat. This brought the bags up harder than she had expected, and she hurt herself slightly. This only infuriated her more. She slammed the door shut, and she was ready to give Austin another piece of her mind.

"Gabby, Gabby," Jason said, panting. He had to run to catch up with her. "Whether you like it or not, Austin is your father and your sisters' father. So stay calm and try to be reasonable."

She knew Jason was right. She was praying that her mom would not want her to live with that man, knowing all the horrible things he had done to them, and she was praying that a judge would not make them live with him. She would indeed need to put her best face forward. She took a deep breath and entered the Thrones' home to find Austin Knope engaged in deep conversation with Gemma and Giuliana.

4

"Gemma, Giuliana," Gabriella called as she walked into the living room, "I have got clothes for you to change into if you want to run upstairs and clean up."

Giuliana ran into her sister's arms and gave her a hug. "I missed you, Gabby."

Gabriella bent down with a soft smile. "I brought Sparkles for you." She handed Giuliana the seasoned stuffed unicorn. Giuliana's face lit up with appreciation. "She's my favorite." She gave her sister another tight squeeze and ran up the stairs to get changed.

"That was very thoughtful of you, Gabriella," Austin Knope said as he walked into the foyer by the stairs.

"Yeah, I know my sister and what she likes," Gabriella snapped. "I don't expect you to understand that." She rolled her eyes like a defiant teenager as Gemma moved in between them.

"Thanks Gab," Gemma said, clutching *The Adventures of Huckleberry Finn* to her chest. "This was the first chapter book Mom read to me. Did you remember that?" Gemma asked, slightly surprised.

"Yes, it was the first one she read to me too." Gabriella smiled with soft tears in her eyes, thinking about the sound of her mother's voice.

"It's my favorite book," Gemma told her, holding the book tightly to her heart. "I better go help Giuliana get situated."

Gabriella nodded and turned her attention to Austin. She gave him a look daring him to say something to her.

"Gabriella, I know that you don't want me here, and I don't want to pressure you." Austin was sincere, but he wanted to talk.

"Good. Then don't." She was short and to the point. She decided that she didn't want to deal with him any more than she had to, so she ran up the stairs after her sisters without another word and without giving him a chance to say anything in response.

They had all finished their showers and were standing in the same bathroom, which was slightly bigger than their own, but they were still rubbing elbows. Gabriella, Gemma, and Giuliana stood in silence applying makeup and brushing their hair just as if it were a day of school and they were crammed in the tiny room getting ready. The only difference was that no one was fighting, there was no shoving, and there was no mumbling—just silence as they prepared to hear from a lawyer they had never met.

Gabriella looked at her two sisters as Gemma carefully twisted her hair up into a bun and Giuliana pretended to put on eye shadow. There they were, the same people she had spent most of her life with. Life goes on, but how do you manage, how do you move on? Gabriella stopped midline in her eyeliner, letting her thoughts run away. She had taken on so much in the last twenty-four hours, and at the same time, she had lost so much.

"Gabby, can you do this?" Gemma interrupted the silence. "I am fourteen, almost fifteen, so I am not completely useless or dumb."

"Gemma—" Gabriella tried to explain, but Gemma cut her off.

"Do you really think you can take care of us? I mean, you will have to give up everything. And you know that mom would not have wanted that," Gemma said.

Gabriella nodded, knowing that Gemma was right in a sense. "I know, but what other choice do we have? If I don't step up, we will be separated. You will be forced to live with someone we barely know. Mom wouldn't have wanted that."

"Probably not," Gemma agreed.

Gabriella didn't say anything else. They spoke with their eyes, both feeling the loss of their mother and the fear of the uncertainty of their future. Gabriella moved to her sister and bent down slightly to hug her. Giuliana, feeling left out, joined in, and they stood there with one another without saying anything until they heard Cindy Throne's voice calling them down.

A chubby man with a long face, stout nose, and old blue eyes shining out through his half-moon-shaped glasses was waiting at the bottom of the stairs rocking back and forth on his heels as if his favorite song were playing silently in his mind. His hair was basically gone, with a few strands still holding on not to be taken away by a gust of wind from a ceiling fan. He wore a brown suit with suede elbow patches and a whimsical sailboat tie, and his white shirt had a visible mustard stain that the tie was trying to hide unsuccessfully. And he held a tattered brown leather briefcase. The buckle had been reattached several times, and the tape from the last attempt was starting to peel. Gabriella thought that it must have been a gift from his wife or mother or something to possibly celebrate his first job in the legal profession.

"Hello, I am Jacob Morgan." He extended his hand to Gabriella. "I was Clare's—your mother's—lawyer."

She nodded. "I am Gabriella." She accepted his hand.

Mr. Morgan put up his hands to stop her. "Of course you are." He turned to Gemma. "You must be Gemma, the one on her way to becoming a highly regarded scientist, from what I hear." He beamed at her and turned slightly to face Giuliana. "And you, young lady...well, you must be the famous Giuliana." He took her hand very delicately to shake it and then turned back to Gabriella. "I have known your mother since she was sixteen. I was very fond of her." He grimaced.

"This way," Cindy Throne piped up to halt the coming sadness. She walked through the hall into the dining area, where Austin, Jason, and Robert Throne were waiting, seated around the table. Mr. Morgan sat at the head of table. Gabriella and her sisters took the open chairs on the right side of the table.

Gabriella grabbed Gemma's hand and squeezed it tightly, as if she were bracing for a shot or immediate pain.

Gemma whispered loud enough for only Gabriella to hear, "That hurt. Relax."

Gabriella nodded, but it was not an easy task. She was about to find out how hard her life really was going to be, in a legal sense. Would she not have any rights to keep her sisters with her as their guardian? Would she have to fight for everything for the rest of her life? How many jobs would she have to work? And how would she get the girls? She closed her eyes, prayed for the best, and took a deep breath. She looked up at Mr. Morgan to give him all of her attention.

"First of all," Mr. Morgan said, his voice drowning in pity, "I am so very sorry for your loss, and words cannot express my sorrow for you three young ladies." He paused to collect his thoughts. "Your mother was a wonderful woman, and she was a dear friend of mine. I know that she will be greatly missed." He took another moment before he continued. It seemed difficult for him to talk about Clare. "I would like to approach this matter with the utmost sincerity and caution. Clare LaFrace did not have a detailed will about certain subjects, but she did leave behind some minor instructions and personal items for each of you."

Gemma let out a whimper. Gabriella could see the tears falling from her sister's eyes freely. Gabriella put a consoling hand on Gemma's shoulder and pulled her close into her.

Mr. Morgan took out some large envelopes and a few folders from his worn briefcase. Everything had scribbling on the front, and Gabriella could make out her own name as well as her sisters' names. Her curiosity soared as she wondered what the contents were; they were bulging at the sides and looked to be full of something, whatever it was, and then she felt the color drain from her face almost immediately. Another envelope had Austin's name on it. It wasn't as full, but there was something there for him. What if it was instructions on how to take custody of them, how to sell the house, how to ruin their lives forever?

"Clare LaFrace updated these earlier this summer," Mr. Morgan said, pressing down on the large envelopes. "She has written letters to you throughout your whole lives. She gave me new ones almost monthly. She wanted you to have something to comfort you in case the worst happened." Mr. Morgan paused. "She wanted you to take her with you throughout your lives as well." A tear gleamed in the corner of his eyes.

"That woman, Clare—she was uncommonly kind." His voice choked. "You three were lucky to have her as your mother." He gulped and got up to hand out the envelopes. "Gabriella, this is for you; Gemma, this one is yours; and Giuliana, here you go." Mr. Morgan stopped behind Austin.

Gabriella could sense that Mr. Morgan's feelings did not differ too much from her own. He was hesitant about giving Austin the envelope. She could see the daggers wanting to break free from his old blue eyes straight into Austin. He was reluctant, but he didn't have much choice. "Mr. Knope, this is for you." He dropped it on the table in front him.

Gabriella, slightly angry that Austin had received any kind of closure, peeked inside her envelope and started to cry. She could not help herself, but the sight of her mother's handwriting, the mere thought that she had written those words, made her heart ache and feel joyous at the same time. She felt some certainty that her mother had left her mark on the world but the same certainty that she was not coming back ever again. The only things left were these letters, and Gabriella wasn't quite sure she understood what they were for. But her mother's handwriting was the most precious thing that she now possessed.

"Gabriella." Mr. Morgan interrupted her thoughts. "Clare's home is now yours, and don't worry about the mortgage. There isn't one. The deed and the paperwork are all in here." He passed the folder down to her.

Gabriella was flabbergasted, and problem number one was now solved. She had a home, a home where she could live with her sisters, a home that didn't come with a mortgage payment. "Wow," she said. "Thank you."

Mr. Morgan nodded toward her. "Now let's move on to the more pressing matter." He looked at Gemma. "Do you mind taking Giuliana into the other room?"

Gabriella could see that Gemma wanted to protest. She wanted to be a part of the pressing matter, but she knew that it would be pointless, so for the third time in her life, she did not argue. She grabbed Giuliana by the hand and led her into the living room.

Mr. Morgan continued as soon as they were out of earshot. "Clare didn't leave any instructions as to whom she wished to look after the two youngest girls." Mr. Morgan was careful with his words. "Gabriella, you are eighteen, so you are legally an adult." He looked as if he was waiting for them to respond.

Gabriella jumped in her seat as she felt a hand on her knee. She had been so fixated on Mr. Morgan's words that she had not noticed that Jason had moved over next to her. She wanted Mr. Morgan to say, "OK, Gabby, you are eighteen; you can have them, and there is nothing that Austin can do about it," but she knew that this was the least likely of scenarios. The lumps were piling up in her throat as she waited with stomach-turning anticipation for Mr. Morgan to finish his statement.

Mr. Morgan sighed at the lack of response. "This situation is very delicate." He spoke slowly. "I know that there is tension between the two of you." He gestured to Gabriella and Austin in case someone was confused as to whom he was speaking of. "I would really hate to see this go into a long, drawn-out court battle."

Austin spoke up. "No one wants that. I think that they should come and live with me. I am their father. It is the best solution." Austin's eyes were red and tired looking. He sounded sad but confident at the same time.

Gabriella grabbed Jason's hand, trying to keep her anger in control and to keep her mouth shut. Anything she would have to say would not be helpful; it would only be anger lashing out at the man who had abandoned all of them at one point or another.

"Well, in normal circumstances, that would be the case, Austin," Mr. Morgan replied.

Gabriella felt as if she was going to be sick. Mr. Morgan had taken a knife straight through her heart. Was he about to tell her that it didn't matter what she wanted, and there was nothing in her power that she could do to keep her family together?

"However…" Mr. Morgan began.

Gabriella saw a faint glint of hope. She wanted to grab it before it faded away.

"You are not and have never been legally obligated to your daughters. Your name is listed on the birth certificates, yes," he said before Austin tried to argue. "But you have never signed them. Also, you don't have any legal visitation rights, and you have been in and out of their lives since they were born." Mr. Morgan had something else to say but wasn't sure how. "And not to be too blunt, but these young girls have had enough heartache. I am not sure staying with someone they barely know would be the best for them."

Gabriella felt life move back into her face. Her heart swelled with joy, and she felt for the first time that everything might be OK. It was justice for all of the injustice that Austin had bestowed upon them, but most importantly, she was going to be able to keep her family together.

Mr. Morgan directed his attention to Gabriella. "Now, as soon as possible, you must file a petition for temporary legal guardianship, if that is your plan. I am assuming that is what will be best for all considered."

"No!" Austin shouted, refusing to be ignored any longer. "They are my daughters, and I will be damned if I am going to let Gabriella throw her life away."

Gabriella stood up at once. She wanted to reach across the table and slap him again. She could not understand why all of a sudden he had taken such an interest in her and her sisters. He had had plenty of time to make his presence known and respected, but now, when it best suited his reputation and hurt them the most, he was going to try to swoop in and be the hero.

"Mr. Knope," Mr. Morgan snapped at him, "calm yourself and let me finish." He turned his attention back to Gabriella. "Please sit down, and I will explain everything."

Gabriella glared at Austin from across the table. She felt Jason tug on her hand, and she sat down hesitantly to listen to what Mr. Morgan had to say.

"Now, as I was saying," he continued, "Gabriella, you must file a petition for temporary legal guardianship of your sisters." He put a great deal of emphasis on his next statement. "This will be approved right a way, and it will allow six months for anyone to come forward and contest the guardianship, and the process will go from there." Mr. Morgan nodded toward Austin.

Gabriella looked at the man who was her father, the man who had never wanted her, the man who had ignored her for most of her life, and the man who more than once had broken her mother's heart. His eyes were hers—the green eyes with the shimmers of amber, but that was all they had in common. He looked so satisfied, as if he couldn't wait to take control of everything and spilt them up as fast as possible.

"So," she began, trying to understand everything. "Let me see if I understand this. I can have temporary legal guardianship of my sisters, but only for six months?" She shot Austin a nasty look. "Let's be honest here. Austin will contest it, probably the day after I file, and what then? I lose because he's older." She felt her anger rise with every word that passed through her lips.

"Yes and no," Mr. Morgan replied. "I only recommend that you take your sisters first because it will be the easiest transition and there will be no chance for them to be placed into a temporary foster care. Now, for the six-month time limit, that is not necessarily true either."

Gabriella's expression was hopeful and excited, but she knew that whatever was to happen, there would be a long road ahead of them.

"If Mr. Knope feels that it is necessary to intervene, that your sisters will be better off in his care, he can file a petition to have custody change hands," Mr. Morgan explained further. "Let me give you some advice." He paused, looking between Austin and Gabriella. "Custody battles are ugly. No one really wins, and the children suffer the most. They are never cut and dry. Given this situation, no one would really win. I suggest you let the girls live with Gabriella in Clare's house, and you try among yourselves to reach some sort of agreement."

Austin spoke before anyone had a chance to. "Mr. Morgan, with all due respect, I think you are wrong for suggesting that Gabriella take on this task. She is supposed to go to Brown in a few weeks, and she can't give that up. I know that I have not been a good father, but I am not going to continue on the same pattern. I think that the girls should live with me, period, and Gabriella, you are more than welcome to come along." Austin knew that he was on the verge of creating World War Three.

She stood up again, slammed her hands down on the table, and let her bottled rage come to the surface. "You have got to be fucking kidding me." She laughed haughtily. "You want to rip this family apart, and we just lost our mother yesterday?" She was so angry that she couldn't control her volume any longer. "I get that your first choice is the wrong one because when it comes to being a dad, you suck! And another thing: how dare you come in here and try to act like you have all the answers. You don't this time, Austin. Your answer for everything is walk away, just ignore them, they don't exist." Tears started streaming down her face.

"Gabriella, I know you are angry with me," he began.

"Really," she screamed. "What was your first clue? Let's see, you ignored me pretty much my whole life, you broke my mother's heart a dozen times, you only come around when it is convenient for you, you never wanted me. Or is it my friendly tone that tipped you off?" She had never in her life felt so much rage pass through her.

"Gabriella, please. I only want to make up for all that and do what is best for you." Austin's voice was verging on desperate.

She was close to jumping across the table. "You don't get to decide what is best for me," she screamed at him. "You don't know me. You do not know my sisters. You can't fix this. Unless you can bring her back, you can't fix this. No one can." She had lost control, and the uncontrollable sobs came back. Jason forced her to sit down next to him. He put his arm around her, brushed the hair out of her face, and tried to wipe away the tears.

"This is what I was afraid of," Mr. Morgan said with the deepest regret. "Gabriella, if you need my services, I will be more than happy to address the tension. Oh yes," he said, pulling a folder from his briefcase, "I almost forgot. There is something else that your mother left you and your sisters. It is all listed in this folder; she did not want to make the amount public." He handed the folder over to her.

Gabriella took the folder, trying to stop crying. "Mr. Morgan, thank you. Will you be at the wake tomorrow?"

"Of course." He nodded and bowed to them as he left the room. Cindy and Robert Throne followed him out.

"Gabriella, I need to speak with you, please." Austin's tone was soft but firm.

Gabriella did not want to speak to him; she had nothing to say. She turned to face him. She could feel her face getting hot and her temper flaring up again. "What?" she snapped.

"Can you at least pretend to be civil with me?" he pleaded with her. Catching her glare, he knew his request would go unfulfilled. "Can we be honest? Gabriella, you are only eighteen years old. You are not old enough to care for two young girls."

Gabriella rolled her eyes, determined to disprove him. "Let's be honest. You are not a good father, but I don't want to point out the obvious." She was like a combative fifteen-year-old. "I am their sister, and I am the only person left who knows them."

"Gabriella, you cannot put your life on hold. Your mother would not have wanted that. She would want you to go to Brown. She would want you to follow your dreams. Let me step in and take this burden off you. After all, I am their father." He was imploring her to see reason and not be blinded by the hate she felt for him.

Gabriella's temper boiled over; the urge to cause him bodily harm was taking over. She raised her hand and pointed aggressively at him. "Don't you dare pretend you know what my mother wanted. You never cared enough to stick around for her. She was only interesting to you when things were not perfect in your cookie-cutter life." Her voice was starting to crack. "You never wanted me—I mean her. And I am not going to let you hurt my sisters like that." The tears came back once more. She stopped speaking at once so as not to appear weak. She did not want to let that man see any emotion from her. He had caused her too much pain, and she would be damned if she would let him do that to her sisters. They had already been through too much.

There were tears in the corners of Austin's amber filled eyes. "Gabriella, I am sorry." He was sincere with his words. "I know I did not make the right choices when it came to you, but I have always wanted you and your mother. Just other things got in the way. I thought I was doing what was best for both of you."

"What? By ignoring me? By ignoring her?" she screamed. Her emotions and hidden feelings were emerging from their vault inside of her.

"I know that I have made mistakes." He sighed, knowing that there was no end in sight to this argument. "I just want to make up for all the wrong that I have done to you and your mother. I have been trying to ever since Giuliana was born, but you will not let me get close."

She rolled her eyes and allowed her hardened shell to close over her again. "If you want to make up for everything, then leave us alone. Don't you think losing our mother was enough?"

He shook his head in dismay, and a few tears rolled down his cheek. "I am so sorry that Clare is gone. It is killing me. You have no idea how I felt about your mother." He was yelling at Gabriella now. "I loved her very much. Whether you believe that or not makes no difference to me. Now I am not going to walk away like I have in the past. I am going to do right by you girls, and I am going to step up and be a father." Austin wiped his face of the tears that had drenched his own face the last few days.

Gabriella's mouth gaped open at him. "Are you fucking kidding me?" She was pissed off and ready to explode. "Now you want to be a father?" Her thoughts were spinning out of control, and she didn't know what to say or do. She let her anger take over. "Austin, you cannot just decide to be a father after the fact and whenever it is the best for your image."

"Gabriella, having three children while I am married to a woman who isn't their mother isn't good for anyone's image," he yelled back at her. She could tell that he hadn't meant to say it aloud. He looked confused and tried to recover. "Gabriella, I meant that is not exactly traditional, but it does not change the fact that I am your father."

She looked into his green-amber eyes, which were exactly the same as hers. She let the crying come back. "You are not my father. You have never been one to me, and you never will be." She was done arguing with him. "Please leave. I have no use for you, and I have too much to deal with right now." Her eyes were piercing straight through him. "I guess I will see you in six months in court."

"Gabby, please, just talk to me," Austin pleaded.

Jason answered before Gabriella could. "Mr. Knope, I think that is enough talking for today." He stepped in front of Gabby. "I think she has dealt with enough today. Give it some time and try talking again without lawyers and ultimatums. Maybe you can reach a compromise."

Austin nodded. "You're right, Jason. That is enough for today." He peered behind Jason to make eye contact with Gabriella. "Go ahead and file for the six-month temporary custody, and then we will go from there." He looked at her and waited for a response.

She said nothing.

Austin turned to Jason. "Take care of her." He hung his head down and walked out of the room.

Gabriella heard him saying his good-byes to Gemma and Giuliana in the other room. She heard the door closing behind him as he left. She fell to her knees, shaking and sobbing uncontrollably. "Jason," she said through the sobs, "I cannot lose my sisters. Please don't let that happen." She knew that there wasn't much that he could do, but she wanted him to comfort her and make promises that he could not keep.

He bent down next to her and rocked her back in forth in his arms. "I know, I know," he whispered in her ear. "I will do whatever I can to help you. I promise." He kissed her forehead, and she continued to sob quietly on the dining room floor.

5

Gabriella had holed herself up inside of Jason's room for the remainder of the night. She needed to be alone, she needed to process all of her thoughts, and there was only one way she knew to do that. She had retreated into the safe haven of the pages of her journal and began to write with the most emotion she ever had in her life.

I cannot believe that man would even have the nerve to come here. I mean, come on, why? Why now? He has had 18 years to be a part of my life, and now that my mother is gone, he thinks he can swoop in and be some kind of hero. I miss her so much. I want her back. I don't think I will ever be able to deal with this. Why did this happen? She was only 33. People don't die at 33. She should have stayed home. I should have stayed home, and maybe we could have had a family night and played games. She had been begging me to do that. Why didn't I do that? Because of my meaningless night with my now ex-boyfriend, who probably never cared about me anyways.

How am I going to be able to take care of my sisters? How can I keep that promise? I don't even know where to begin, but what choice do I have? I could let them go and live with Austin, but he might just decide to walk away one day when he is tired of them or because Giuliana refuses to clean her room and Gemma throws a fit about him ruining her life. I know that will happen. I can't lose them. I can't lose anything more than I already have. I think I might literally break in half.

I guess I don't get to be eighteen anymore. I have to be the person my mom would have wanted me to be in her absence. I have to grow up. I have to do this for my mom. God, I miss her so much. All I can do is cry. My eyes hurt, and my face feels chapped and dry. I don't know how to stop the tears. I need to be strong for my sisters and encourage them that we can get through this. But how am I supposed to do that when I feel so broken and weak? I would give anything to talk to her one more time, to say good-bye, to hear her voice.

Gabriella looked up from her journal and let the tears fall onto the pages, smudging the ink. She closed her eyes, hoping the day would disappear and she could rewind time to save her mother's life. But her stomach grumbled, reminding her that she was very much alive, and there was no way to get the time machine she desperately required. Gabriella pondered her hunger for a moment, and it only caused her more pain realizing that her mother would never feel hungry again, that death was so final and absolute and sudden. There had been no warning, no sign, it had just taken her mother away in mere seconds. She began to weep once more as the image of her mother started to fade from her mind.

There was a knock at the door. She sat up and tried to wipe her face and wipe away her smudged makeup as the door creaked open. Jason entered the room cautiously, holding a few bags. He smiled at her and walked toward the bed. The smell of grease-soaked French fries and a cheeseburger filled her nostrils, and she couldn't help but smile.

"Hey," he said casually. "I figured you were hungry, so I stopped on my way home and got you something to eat." He handed her a bag. "By the way, it's kind of weird knocking on my own door."

She laughed. She thought it might have been her first genuine smile all day. "Where did you go?" she asked, plunging face first into the juicy burger he had brought back for her.

"I went to your house," he told her. "I noticed that you only really brought what your sisters needed for the next few days. Your bag had some slim pickins." He smiled slyly at her.

Gabriella laughed, and she thought Jason had a point. By the time she had come to her room, she was ready to get out of that house. "Let's see what you brought then, Mr. Know-It-All."

Jason gave her a self-satisfied smile. "Well, for starters..." He opened the bag and pulled out a few of the items. "Your hair straightener, because we both know why you always really wear your hair up. And your makeup bag with all your goodies in it." Jason winked at her, outlining his dimples. "And I stopped at the store and got you some waterproof mascara. I thought you could use it." He tossed the unopened package to her.

She laughed, seeing that he had drawn a sad face with tears running down it. Even though some might consider it rude, she knew that he was joking, and she appreciated it more than all of the "I am so sorry for your loss" words. Jason had always said that he would be there for her no matter what, and until the last two days, she didn't fully understand what that meant. He had shown her an unconditional love that no man had ever bestowed upon her.

Gabriella looked up, and he was smiling at her as he had done a thousand times before. But this time, she felt flutters in her stomach. She started blushing and feeling embarrassed and unsure of what to say. The feeling scared her somewhat. She looked up at the guy who had been her best friend since grade school. His handsome face, his hazel eyes that were almost green glimmered down at her. She thought briefly of what it would be like to be his wife, to be in love with him, how it would feel. There was silence in the room, but it wasn't awkward, it was understood.

"You OK?" Jason asked, noticing Gabriella's reddening cheeks.

Gabriella smiled timidly at her best friend. "Jason," she whispered, "you have been absolutely amazing during all of this. There is no way that I could have made it through today or yesterday without you."

Jason put his finger against her lips. "Shh. There is no reason to thank me, Gabby. I know that you would be there for me in an instant. I am just trying to do what little I can to make it a little bit easier on you. You are my best friend, and I love you. And Gabby, I am so sorry that you have to go through this." His voice cracked a bit. "I wish I could bring her back and take away your pain, but all I can bring is cheeseburgers, fries, and waterproof mascara." He slipped his arm around Gabriella as the familiar tears crept back into her eyes.

She didn't want to cry anymore, but she couldn't help it. She put her arms around Jason and hugged him tightly, almost as if she were a small child begging him not to go. He brushed her hair with his hands, murmured soft whispers of comfort to her, and held her until the tears had dried and she had nothing left to pour out.

Her face was burning from crying. She sat up and just stared down at the floor, unsure of what to do or what to say.

Jason pretended to be tired and stretched out his arms and let out an overdramatic yawn. "Well, it has been a really long day, and tomorrow is going to be even longer. I am going to let you get some sleep. You can stay in here if you want, and I will sleep downstairs." When she didn't reply, he got up and started to walk toward the door.

"Jason, wait." Gabriella's confidence surged. "Do you think it would be all right if you could just..." Her confidence had faded as quickly as it had come. She knew that Jason would understand that she didn't want to be alone, but she felt awkward asking. Gabriella rolled her eyes at herself. "Jason, could you...I mean, do you think it would be all right if you just slept in here with me?" She didn't want him to think that she was coming on to him, as absurd as that sounded, so she quickly added, "I just don't want to be alone."

Jason smiled, amused by how she had stumbled over her words. "Sure." He walked back toward her but took a right and headed to his dresser to begin his nightly routine.

"And you don't think it's weird?" Gabriella said, feeling unsure of herself. She had just had some new, unfamiliar feelings for him, but Jason probably just looked at her the same way he always had.

He laughed. "Gab, its fine." He walked toward her and bent down where she was sitting on the bed.

She could feel his cool breath on her face. She could smell the intoxicating cologne that she had always thought was off putting, but it was now quite pleasant. She wanted to grab him and pull him into a deep, passionate kiss.

He kissed her forehead. "I don't mind sleeping next to the most gorgeous girl in Laking, Ohio." He winked at her.

She shuddered with unanticipated pleasure. She felt her cheeks turning red, so she jumped off the bed and headed out of the room to get changed and ready for bed. Gabriella fussed over her appearance for bed more than she ever had before. She looked up in the mirror and splashed cold water on her face to wash away the residue that she was sure would be like a permanent birthmark for the next few days no matter how much she scrubbed. Her brown hair was pulled back into a ponytail, her cheeks were red, her eyes were red and sore, and she was fretting over feelings that she had no business having. "Relax, dumbass," she whispered to herself in the mirror. "It's just Jason. He's my best friend, nothing else." She rolled her eyes and decided it would be best just to go to sleep as soon as possible. As she was heading out of the bathroom, she stopped and quickly put on a dab of perfume before she went back into Jason's room.

She knocked before entering the room.

"Come in," he called from the other side of the door.

They both stopped in their footsteps and stared as if they had never seen each other before. She was eyeing his sculpted shirtless physique, which she had never paid much attention to. She never understood why girls always went so crazy over it, and girls never understood how Gabriella could be "just friends" with Jason Throne. Realizing she was staring, she quickly darted her eyes to the floor as casually as possible.

Jason smiled and continued to be his usual self. "I can put a shirt on if this makes you uncomfortable." He pointed to his well-outlined, almost perfectly toned abs.

Gabriella rolled her eyes at him, trying to act normal. "Don't flatter yourself." She laughed. "I have seen better." Gabriella tried to avoid his eyes at all costs. She hurried and got under the covers. She could feel Jason hesitating, not sure whether he should lie next to her or perhaps on the floor, or maybe at the opposite end of the bed. After struggling with his position, he finally lay next to her on the bed. She could feel the mattress move as he did, and she could feel the heat from his body. He too had put on quick spritz of cologne, and for the first time in her life, she was understanding what all of those girls saw in Jason Throne. But he was only her best friend and nothing more.

Gabriella turned to lie flat in the bed, and she stared blankly up at the ceiling. Jason had the same stick-on stars that Alex Hickins had left from his childhood, which still were a luminous green. "Jason," she said, letting the day slip away from her, "do you think tomorrow will be any better?" She already knew the answer.

He turned propped up on one arm to face her. "No."

They both laughed.

"Do you think my mom is here with me?" she asked.

"Without a doubt." He stroked her cheek.

"Yeah, I think you're right," she replied. She sighed loudly, not wanting to go to sleep. "Jason?"

"Yeah?"

"Do you think everything is going to work itself out?"

He kissed her forehead. "Yes. No matter what happens, everything will work out for the best." He wrapped his arms tightly around her until she drifted into an uneasy sleep.

The next morning, Gabriella awoke alone in Jason's bed. She let the light in, squinting to get a look at her surroundings. She grumbled and rolled over to find a note in Jason's handwriting on the pillow.

Clean yourself up. You stink. And come down for breakfast.

Love ya,

Jason

The smile that Jason's note had created quickly disappeared as she realized today was today. The day when it all became too real. Her mother's wake was today, and tomorrow the funeral. The first steps in moving forward in her new life without her mother. She would have to face all the awful realities today. People would be paying their last respects, and people would be offering an overwhelming amount of sympathy and more burned casseroles than she would know what to do with. No amount of effort from her would make the day disappear as easily as her smile, and there was nothing she could do to change the past. So with that, she got up and headed to the bathroom to take a shower.

The hot water felt soothing as it washed away the dried tears and some of the sadness that had been caked onto her body. She stood under the hot water cascading over her as if she were just a rock in the stream, and it didn't matter where she stood, but it was going to get around her, and that was how she had to face the day. She just needed to get around the sadness and put on a smile and a grateful face because no matter what she did, it was going to come.

Gabriella got out, dried off, and dressed in a blue blouse and black slacks. She put on makeup, which she considered to be pointless because it would be off in a matter of hours, considering she cried at least five times an hour for ten minutes at a time. She smiled again as she carefully opened the package of waterproof mascara so as not to destroy Jason's artwork, and she wondered if it would indeed be waterproof enough to last the whole day. She took a final glance in Jason's dingy mirror and decided it was as good as it was going to get.

Gabriella walked down the hallway and peered into the guest room, where she had left Gemma and Giuliana the night before, but the bed had already been made. Cindy Throne had already neatly arranged the pillows with her signature mints. Gabriella thought that Cindy was living out some fantasy of having her own quaint bed-and-breakfast whenever she had overnight guests. Gabriella was impressed with Cindy's decorating skills and how she made everything look so easy. She always had breakfast waiting and made sure the house was neat and everything was in place. She was really the perfect housewife. Gabriella's thoughts went back to her own mother and how everything was clean, but it was never tidy unless you were in Gemma's room. There was nothing that could be done about it; there was always something somewhere out of place. The beds hardly got made, and they didn't have a guest room.

Gabriella was proud of herself. She had thought of her mother without crying. If she were to accomplish nothing else the rest of the day, that would be OK.

As Gabriella made her way down the stairs, she heard the sounds of laughter pouring from the kitchen, followed by the indistinguishable voice of Giuliana telling a dramatic story from kindergarten.

Jason came jogging out of the kitchen and kissed her on the cheek as if it were becoming a habit. "Good morning," he said cheerfully. "There are a few people already here." He was smiling as if he had just heard the concept of the tooth fairy.

"Who?" Gabriella realized then that she wasn't even sure what time it was. She had abandoned her cell phone, which was usually attached to her hand. She wondered if she had slept in late, and she searched for a clock quickly.

Jason read her mind. "Don't worry; it's only nine."

Gabriella felt relived but even more confused. "Who would be here this early?"

Jason was bobbing back and forth with a stupid grin on his face, barely able to contain his excitement. "Alexis Jackson is in my kitchen!"

Gabriella nodded, but she wasn't surprised. Alexis Jackson was a reporter for an entertainment show that her mom had placed. Her mom had discovered a lot of talent and a few notable names, but Alexis Jackson wasn't really one of them.

"And"—Jason's eyes grew bigger and his face went red—"Jenna Fox."

"Seriously? Jenna Fox?" That surprised Gabriella. Jenna Fox was a very famous actress, singer, and writer. Anything that would put her in the public spotlight, Jenna Fox could do it and do it well.

"Yes, and she is so hot!" Jason whispered loudly.

"Keep your pants on." Gabriella felt a spasm of jealously. She didn't know why the feelings for Jason were coming out now. Was she just very vulnerable, and he had been incredibly nice to her? Whatever the reason was, she wished at that moment that she had taken a little more time with her hair.

Gabriella followed Jason into the kitchen. There stood two real-life Barbie dolls within five feet of her. Jenna Fox—tall, long blond hair, long legs, perfect skin, perfect body, perfect smile, and the perfect life—was talking to her younger sisters like the family she only saw on Christmas. Jenna had always been very gracious to Gabriella's mother. In every award speech, Jenna would thank Clare for leading her down the road to stardom. Alexis Jackson, equally as pretty, was talking to Cindy about some upcoming auditions that would change her career's trajectory.

Gabriella made herself visible to everyone in the kitchen only to be nearly knocked over and mauled by Alex Hickins. He wrapped her up in a tight hug, as if she were just learning the terrible news for the first time. She shot a look to Jason that said, "I might just strangle you."

"Oh yeah, Gabby." Jason had a sheepish grin on his face. "Alex is here as well." He didn't waste his time trying to save her from what was going to be an awkward conversation. Jason marched straight over to the breakfast bar and plopped down by Alexis Jackson and Jenna Fox.

Gabriella was more than annoyed; she was verging on anger. "Alex."

Before she could begin, Alex cut in and tried to kiss her. "Baby, I know we had a fight, but that doesn't matter. I love you; I am here for you."

"Alex, we did not have a fight. We broke up," she reminded him. "And we are not getting back together. If you want to pay your respects to my mother, that is fine. The wake is at five o'clock tonight at Mount Pleasant Funeral Home in town."

"Gabby," Alex said, not fazed by bluntness, "I have tried to call you a thousand times. Don't shut me out, OK? I can't imagine what you are going through, but I can help you. I love you."

She didn't want to deal with him right now. She was well aware of how many times he had called her, and she hadn't called him back for a reason. "Alex—"

"I really think you need me. We both know how stubborn you can be. Just let me help you, and then we can talk about everything else later."

Frustrated, she raised her voice to try to make him and everyone else in the room understand. "I am not trying to be mean, but this isn't about us. It isn't about you. This is about my family. This is a difficult time for us right now. Can you just respect the situation?"

He sighed. "So we are really over?"

She accidently laughed. "Yes. We have been for quite some time. We both know that."

He nodded in agreement and knew that it wasn't time to argue about that. "I just don't want you to be alone. You shouldn't be alone right now."

She kissed him softly in appreciation for how well he knew her. "I know, but I am fine, and I am not alone."

Alex looked around the Thrones' kitchen and nodded in agreement. He kissed her cheek. "Gabriella, I am really sorry for your loss, and your mother was a great woman. I will see you tonight at the wake with my parents and brother. If you decide that you need anything from me, just call, and I will be there. My family loves you, and I love you too." He was sincere.

Gabriella knew that he was telling the truth. "I know." She hugged him and held on a little longer, feeling good in his familiar arms. "I'll see you tonight."

Alex nodded, and Cindy Throne walked him to the door.

Cindy walked back into the kitchen and prepared to scold her only child. "Jason, I thought you ran out of the kitchen to tell Gabby that Alex was here."

Jason's face turned pink. "Well," he stuttered, not able to think of a reasonable explanation—mostly because, Gabriella thought, there wasn't one.

Gabriella waved off Jason's poor attempts. "He told me that Jenna Fox and Alexis Jackson were here. He must have been too excited and forgot to mention Alex." Gabriella smiled at him as if they were even now.

Jason buried his head in embarrassment, and everyone in the room laughed at his expense.

"Gabriella Knope, I have not seen you in years," Jenna Fox said, emerging from behind the breakfast bar. "Look at you and how beautiful you are." Jenna approached her with open arms. "Oh, you are the spitting image of your mother." She was looking Gabriella up and down. Jenna had always been very humble and kind to everyone.

"Thanks." Gabriella blushed. "It means a lot."

Jenna had tears welling in her eyes. "I can't tell you how sorry I am. It is so tragic and unjust."

Gabriella only nodded, not ready to test out her waterproof mascara quite yet. "Jenna, it was very nice of you to make the trip to Laking from Los Angeles."

"Gabby"—Jenna put her hands on Gabriella's shoulders—"I owe your mother my career. If it weren't for her, I would still be living in Marshall, Missouri. I can't believe she is gone. You know your mother and I stayed in touch."

Gabriella nodded again, recalling stories. "I know. Mom always used to tell us when you would call. I know she loved hearing from you, and I know that she was very proud of you." Gabriella hoped to offer some comfort to Jenna.

Jenna beamed at her. "Thank you." She excused herself from the room.

As the morning wore on, everyone sat around the table talking about their favorite moments with Clare. Gabriella felt minor comfort in everyone's words, but mostly it was just a painful reminder that her mother was not coming back. Gemma had already had enough and excused herself for the bathroom, and that had been over an hour ago. Giuliana had escaped to the living room, and she had fallen asleep with Sparkles clutched tightly to her chest.

Gabriella was exhausted as well, and she needed time to be alone. She excused herself from the table, saying she needed some fresh air. She got in her car and drove to city hall to file for temporary custody of her two sisters. She had hoped that it would be a simple process, much like applying for your driver's license, but the forms alone proved to be difficult to fill out. She didn't know the answers to half the questions, and she began to question whether she could indeed provide the care that her two sisters needed. She knew the only alternative was no alternative at all but a cop-out from the responsibility that her mother would have wanted her to take on, and Gabriella wasn't going to disappoint her mother no matter what.

Gabriella solved her own problems and called Mr. Morgan to help her fill in the missing information, and as she filled in the blanks, she understood that she would be taking on the role of mother. She would be the sole caretaker for them. They would come to her for more than just an older sister's advice; they would expect her to have all the answers. And she would be setting the curfews and taking care of the meal planning, all of the tasks that their mother had always asked for a little appreciation. Gabriella would now be doing those same tasks.

Gabriella returned to the Thrones' home to find Jenna Fox telling everyone how her mother had talked her out of a career in politics. Gabriella laughed at how everyone was eating out of the palm of her hand, and knowing that she didn't want to be asked for her opinion on the matter, she left the kitchen as fast as she had come. No one but Gemma seemed to notice. Gemma politely excused herself and followed Gabriella into the living room. Gabriella sat down on the couch, leaned her head back, and allowed her eyes to close.

"Hey." Gemma sat next to her. "How are you holding up?"

"Fine." Gabriella shrugged. "You?"

"OK, I guess," she replied in the same unconvincing tone. "Can I ask you something without you biting my head off, or just ignoring my question completely?"

Gabriella opened her eyes halfway to acknowledge Gemma. "What?"

Gemma cleared her throat. "Well," she began, "how do you think you are going to be able to take care of us?"

"Well..." Gabriella thought seriously for a moment to come up with an answer to put her sister's worries at ease. "Mom has left us some money." Gabriella had in all honesty forgotten about the money. She couldn't remember if she had even looked at the amount.

Gemma gave her a questionable look. "Really? How much? I didn't even know Mom had any money to leave us."

"I don't know exactly," Gabriella admitted. "I guess I should be on top of that stuff."

Gemma changed the subject. "Did you read your letter from Mom?"

Gabriella had forgotten about the letters that had brought her so much comfort. "No." She felt guilty that she had not read them, and even worse that she had forgotten them.

"You didn't?" Gemma gasped. "I would have thought you would have ripped it open right away."

"Well I didn't," Gabriella snapped at her sister.

"Sorry," Gemma said, backing off the subject. "You should at least read the good-bye letter she wrote you."

"Yeah, I will." Gabriella was trying to end the conversation.

"Gabby," Gemma began, "I don't want to live with Austin, but he is our father and the only parent we have, and the courts will side with him. You know that. I don't want to see you get hurt because of him. We both know that it will go to court. You shouldn't have to put your life on hold. It isn't fair to you." She spoke quickly, as she had been holding it all in the last two days.

Gabriella shared the same concerns that Gemma did, but she refused to let them deter her from her goals. "Gemma. Don't worry about any of that. I can do my two years here, and then we will figure it out. People go to school, have families, and work all the time." She saw Gemma wasn't convinced. "I know that this is what I am supposed to do. I know that it is the right thing to do. And it may be an uphill battle, but it will be worth it in the end. I know it."

"Gabby, just don't put it on your shoulders alone, because you are not alone." Gemma put her hand on her sister's knee and gave it a squeeze. "I will do what I can to help and support you. Just be careful."

Gabriella nodded, relieved that Gemma did not want to argue any longer.

Cindy Throne came into the room. She cleared her throat to make her presence known. "Hi, girls." She was overly enthusiastic, and she must have heard herself speaking because she quickly changed her tone to a sympathetic one. "Are you ready to go?"

Gabriella and Gemma exchanged looks of confusion.

Cindy nodded, picking up on it. "To the funeral home. It's time for the wake to begin."

"Oh, right." Gabriella tried to smile but failed. The lumps in her throat rose up, trying to escape. She didn't want to go. She didn't want to be strong. She didn't want to face the truth. It didn't matter what she wanted because she was no longer a child, but an adult who had to grow up literally overnight.

Giuliana came barreling out of the kitchen toward Gabriella. Giuliana threw her arms around Gabriella, crying, "Gabby, I don't want to say good-bye to Mommy."

Gabriella's heart broke all over again. "Honey," she said through the sobs. "You never have to say good-bye to Mommy." She pulled Giuliana close to her.

"Gabby, I don't want to go," Giuliana pleaded.

Gabby brushed the hair out of her face and wiped the tears away. "It's going to be OK, I promise." She looked at Giuliana's heart breaking and decided to be straightforward. "Gemma and I don't want to go either, and we aren't ready for Mom to be gone where we can't see her, but sometimes we have to do what we don't want to do." She took another breath in and let out a whimper. "Giuliana, Mommy is watching us from above, and someday, long from now, we will be able to see her again. I promise." She wrapped Giuliana in a tight embrace. Gemma moved over to join them.

Cindy Throne stood in the corner crying, and she cleared her throat, signaling it was time to go. They got up, interlocked hands, and walked out to the door to their mother's wake.

6

The next morning, Gabriella woke up with her sisters on either side of her, the same way she had the night after she found out the tragic news that changed her life forever. Her head throbbed from the incessant crying, her cheeks were chapped from the endless tears, and her eyes burned, feeling as if they had not slept in days. Yesterday had not gone as well as she had hoped; she was dealing with Austin Knope in a confined space with everyone watching her every move, Alex Hickins was grasping at straws to rekindle their relationship, and Lee Ann Gable was trying to solicit the services of her real-estate brother. Today was the actual funeral, and she would be giving the eulogy, which she had not written yet, wearing high heels that she could not walk in, and she would have to appear appreciative of the statement, "I am so sorry for your loss and what you are going through."

Gabriella had been broken. She was lost without her mother, and she could no longer go to her for any kind of advice. Her mother could no longer offer comforting words, and her mother would never be able to say "I love you" to her again. She started to dive into self-pity, with her tears building up their forces again in the corners of her eyes.

Something on the guest-room nightstand caught her eye. It was the bulging envelope with her name scribbled across it. She had been so comforted by the sight of her mother's handwriting, yet she had not opened the letters. She had told herself that she had forgotten about them, but perhaps she was scared to see her mother say good-bye to her. But today was that day that she would be saying good-bye, and she could not do it without her mother's help. She carefully maneuvered out of the bed without disturbing her sisters. She grabbed the envelope off the night table and tiptoed out of the room.

She stood at the end of the long hallway, realizing she was not in her own home. She did not have a place to go to be alone. She glanced at the oversized clock that hung in the hall; it was six o'clock in the morning. Gabriella tried to think quickly before everyone started moving about to prepare for the day ahead of them. A sudden rush of logic and clarity washed over her, and she knew exactly where to go. Jason and his father had spent a summer building the ultimate tree house, which in its prime was envied by every child in Laking. Gabriella would come over occasionally and help as much as she could, but when it was finished, Jason and Gabriella had their freedom, or at least the freedom that a house in the trees provides. She spent her time at the Thrones' inside of that tree house. Jason and Gabriella had adventures and camp-outs, and Gabriella had divulged some of her darkest secrets to Jason there. If she could not be in her own room to read her mother's good-bye words to her, the only other place she would accept was that tree house.

She crept down the stairs, ensuring not even a squeak escaped the old wood flooring. She did not want any questions, she did not want to be bothered, and she did not want to be followed. She closed the door behind her carefully so as not to make a sound, and as she walked around the wraparound porch, she took in a deep breath of the crisp morning air and looked into the sky hoping for a glimpse of something proving that there actually was a heaven and that her mom was now living there. But there was no mystical light or funny-shaped cloud. All she had was her faith, and she hoped that would be enough.

There, within her sight, was the tree house where she had shared so many wonderful memories with Jason. It was missing some boards on top, the railing was sinking slightly, and the blue paint was chipping, but it still looked marvelous, a place for adventure to be held. She climbed up the rickety old ladder, and fresh pine filled her nostrils.

The inside was not as big as she remembered. She could feel the pressure of the boards against the trees with each movement she made. Gabriella was no longer small enough to walk around inside, so she crawled carefully to what so long ago she had claimed to be her side of the tree house. It was decorated with her favorite pictures, including one of her whole family when Giuliana was a baby. There they were a happy family, with a new sister and a new outlook on life, only to be taken away six short years later. Now she had to say good-bye to her mother. She wasn't sure if she was ready, but she knew that she never really would be.

She took in a huge breath and opened the envelope very carefully. Dozens and dozens of letters spilled out. Each one had a different title scribbled on the envelope. One said, "First day of college." Another said, "Wedding," and one read "Jason," and another read "Austin Knope." Gabriella was sure that the lawyer must have mixed up the envelopes, and the letter was meant for Austin. She picked up the letter with every intention of reading it, but underneath was the one that read "Good-Bye." She put Austin's letter down and with a shaky hand picked up the "Good-bye" letter. She started to cry before she could even open it. This was it, this was the end. She looked down at the words written in her mother's handwriting; they were so beautiful. She felt as if her mother were there with her, and the comfort that her handwriting provided was all she really needed. She was scared to read it, scared of what it might say, scared that she would tell her to give Austin a chance and let him take her sisters. She let the tears fall one by one, dripping, streaming down her cheeks, and she began to read:

Dear Gabriella,

As cliché as it may sound, if you are reading this, then I am gone. I hope that you are not in too much pain, and I am sorry that I left your life so soon. I rewrite this letter to you each summer, so it is fresh in my mind and more current. Brown University. That is huge. I am so proud of you! You are an amazing young woman with a talent that you have to share with the world. I know that if I am gone, you are very confused. I know you will feel compelled to do what you think is right. I am not there to guide you in the right direction, and all I can tell you is to follow your heart. I will let you figure out what is right and what is best; I know you will make the right decision because neither decision is wrong. I know that I wasn't the best mother in the world, but I promise you were the best daughter. I learned how to be a mother as I went, and I kind of grew up with you. I have learned so much from you. I have to tell you how much I admire you and respect the person you have become. You have so much in the world going for you, and I don't want you to think about how I am not going to be there. I want you to think about how I will always be with you wherever you decide to take me. I have left you the house and enough money so you won't have to worry too much—in the short term, anyways. I am sure that you will keep your sisters with you as long as you can. I don't expect you to raise them as your own, but I do expect you to be in their lives. I don't worry about them as much, knowing that I have raised you to be so great. You need to remember that you do not need to take on the world alone. Let others help, and don't shut yourself off. Please, Gabby, do not give up on your dreams. You are still there. My life has run its course, and I would not change anything—nothing at all. My beautiful, sweet daughter. I love you, and I will be looking down always to keep an eye out. Always carry me in your heart. I know you will be in mine.

PS: 1.) Don't read the letters until they are meant to be read. Each title means something different. If you haven't experienced it or it hasn't happened, don't cheat. Don't sneak the way I know you did with the Christmas presents in my trunk in my room when you were six.

2.) You are a great writer; I spent many years reading your journals and diaries. You can't be mad; I am your mother, and it is my job.

3.) Look at Jason. He will have a lot of your answers...

Love you always and forever no matter where I am,

Your mother, Clare Marie LaFrace.

Gabriella's tears were a mixture of sadness and happiness from the comfort brought by reading the words her mother had written for her. It was almost as if she could hear her voice in her mind, and she really hadn't gone that far. Gabriella hugged the letter close to her heart. She felt a new surge of energy, of power flowing through her. She took a final look at the precious paper, kissed it, and carefully put it back into the envelope. She put the letter back with the rest and started to sift through all of the contents inside the envelope.

She was surprised to find that her mother had thought of every big event in her life that she would go through, from graduating college to getting married to pregnancy. Everything that Gabriella would experience, her mom would be right there with her, giving her much-needed advice. Instantly the fragile paper became her most priceless possession. She tried to think of places where she could store the envelopes, so they would be safe from every possible event that might damage them. Gabriella thought a safe inside of a safe might work, but she might need to have a fireproof box inside the second safe.

She noticed that the folder with the legal documents were on the floor of the tree house.

She opened the folder to find boring house deeds and documents and forms that she still needed to fill out. There was another form that had a list of all of her mother's possessions that were left to her to divide among her sisters. She scanned the sheet and stopped and reread the same line four times to make sure she had read it correctly. There wasn't any way the amount could be correct. Her mother had been doing very well for the last five years and she had always been a saver, but this—Gabriella seriously wondered if it was a typo on Mr. Morgan's part. Gabriella thought back about how many times her mom had told her no about getting some piece of clothing because it was too expensive, and every Sunday morning, her mom would clip coupons for the groceries and whatever could be used to save money. Gabriella remembered that Clare had a couple of lucky breaks in her career. Perhaps she did not realize how lucky. Clare LaFrace had left Gabriella and her sisters a little over one million dollars. Gabriella was absolutely flabbergasted. Her mother was gone, but she had made everything better for Gabriella. Gabriella felt so much relief and certainty take hold of her, and she knew that she would still have to work, but things would not be as difficult as she had previously expected. Austin would lose the leverage that Gabriella would not be able to provide financially for her sisters. It would come down to who was fit to raise them, and Gabriella had no doubts that she would win that battle.

She climbed down the rickety old ladder with her precious cargo clutched tightly to her chest and headed back inside. It was the day of her mother's funeral, and oddly, today was the best she had felt since the tragic news. For the first time, she thought she might be OK. She walked through the door and heard everyone beginning to stir. She glanced at the clock in the living room. It was already eight in the morning. She thought that she had only disappeared for fifteen minutes, not two hours.

Jason was in the kitchen helping himself to a bowl of cereal.

"Hi." She walked in quietly.

Startled, he spilled a little bit of his Cocoa Puffs on the counter. "Oh, hi. I didn't know you were up yet."

"Couldn't sleep," she replied causally.

Jason nodded understanding. "So"—his tone was a little more serious—"are you ready for today?"

"Yes." She was surprised at her own confidence, and she could see that Jason was too. "I read my letter," she added.

Jason nodded again and sat down on the stool closest to her. "What did it say?"

She wasn't sure she wanted to reveal the details of the letter. The letter from her mother was so precious and private. It was the only thing that had made her see the light at the end of the long tunnel she was in. "Well," she began, unsure, "no offense, but I don't think I really want to tell anyone. But I can tell you that she has put my mind and worries at ease. And everything is going to be OK." Instead of tears of sadness, it was tears of relief that started to fall.

Jason smiled and put his hand on top of hers. "I am glad that she can still help you. That's why she wrote the letters. Did you just read the good-bye or all of them?"

"Just the good-bye letter for now." She thought of the countless letters that her mother had written, and she wondered about what each of them said, how they would make her feel. Would it be easier as time went on to read them? "She made me promise not to look before I am supposed to. I guess I really will be able to take her with me wherever I go." She looked up from the floor and saw that Jason was giving into the tears that he had made scarce that he had hidden for her sake.

He shook his head, trying to appear strong, as he had the entire week. "You know your mom was a great woman, and..." His voice trailed off. He covered his face with his hands and began to weep.

Gabriella felt guilty watching Jason cry. She felt somewhat selfish because she had failed to realize that he must be grieving the loss of her mother, and she had not once asked him how he was doing. He had been close to Clare, and he had looked to her as a second mother. "Hey." She reached out to grab his hand. "You know my mom loved you very much, and you meant a great deal to her." She squeezed his hand and gave him a heartfelt smile. "You know, I don't think I have told you how much I appreciate everything you have done for me."

He wiped his eyes. "You might have mentioned it." They were intertwined in each other's arms. Jason pulled back slightly and kissed Gabriella on her lips.

Gabriella was unsure of how to react. She knew the kiss wasn't meant in a romantic way, but part of her wanted it to be just that. She smiled to Jason and left the kitchen to go ready herself for what she thought was going to be the most difficult day of her life. But now she knew that it was going to be all right.

Gabriella, Gemma, and Giuliana piled into a black car that was waiting outside to take them to the funeral home. Gabriella looked out of the window at the Thrones' home as the car pulled away. She was saying good-bye, and there wasn't any turning back. She knew that things would never be the same. She knew that she was going to have to strive to become the selfless person her mother had been. She would have to put her sisters' needs above her own, and Gabby knew it was the right thing to do.

"Gabby." Gemma snapped her fingers in Gabriella's face trying to get her attention. "Did you write a speech?"

"What?" Gabriella was lost in her own thoughts.

"Did you write a speech?" Gemma sounded annoyed with her older sister.

"What? Oh, yeah. I have something planned," she lied. Gabriella did not have anything planned. She had not given it too much thought, but she assumed that when the time came, the words would come.

"That is always like you," Gemma muttered, under her breath but loud and clear enough for Gabriella to hear.

Gabriella knew today was going to be hard for them, but she was surprised by Gemma's attitude. "What are you talking about?"

"You always wait until the last minute to do something important, or you just bullshit," Gemma said in a harsh tone. "This is for Mom. You should be prepared, and you should not disappoint her."

"Gemma, I have got it under control, I promise." Gabriella tried to brush her sister's arm, but Gemma jerked away.

"Gabby, it has to be perfect." Gemma began to cry.

"OK." Gabriella didn't know what else to say, and she didn't know how to make it perfect even if she had written something down.

Giuliana piped up from in between them. "Gabby, Gemma is just jealous because she wants to say something."

Gemma let out an aggravated scream. "God, Giuliana, why can't you mind your own damn business?"

"Gemma," Gabriella snapped, "you don't talk to her like that." Gabriella slipped her arm around Giuliana to assure her everything was OK. "Now, Gemma, you are more than welcome to say something at the service. It's up to you," Gabriella said calmly. Gabriella didn't know why Gemma just didn't come to her and ask her, why she thought that she wasn't allowed.

Gemma looked up with tears drenching her face. "I just wanted to be able to say good-bye to her like you are." She cleared her throat, trying to control her sobs. "The letter mom left me really made me think a lot, and it made me feel great inside, and I want to say something at the service."

"Well, I want to say something too then," Giuliana protested.

Gabriella nodded. She had forgotten that her sisters had received their own letters as well. She realized just how selfish she had been the last few days, and she had to change, she had to put her sisters' needs before her own. "Gemma, I know what you mean, and that is fine. You can say whatever you want." They exchanged understanding glances. "And so can you, Giuliana." Gabriella gave her sister a quick squeeze. The car returned to silence except for Giuliana humming a song she did not know. Gabriella had too much on her mind to make small talk, and she was sure that Gemma felt the same.

They arrived at Mount Pleasant Funeral Home before anyone else. Gabriella thought that Mount Pleasant was an odd name for a funeral home. There was not anything pleasant about it. It was a place that no one wanted to visit, people would fear it, and people definitely did not want to be the subject on the outside sign.

They piled out of the car and walked up steps of what Mount Pleasant called an inviting entrance. The smell of decayed tears and a distinct aroma of death greeted them as they walked through the doorway into the chapel hall. She saw the white coffin with brass handles and intricate designs on the sides that held her mother's lifeless body. There were rose wreaths, houseplants, bouquets of lilies, and potted orchids placed around the casket, and they were indeed breathtakingly beautiful, but they were not powerful enough to bring back her mother. Flowers and plants are supposed to offer comfort in someone's time of need, but why? Was it so that Gabriella and her sisters could appreciate the marvel of nature, which had created such beautiful petals, or that the scent of a rose was supposed to remind them of the way their mother would smell right after she took the towel off her freshly washed hair? Gabriella felt the pain of loss balling inside of her like a cannonball that was ready to explode.

Gabriella thought of other families when they suffered a great loss. They normally had another parent to turn to, the grandparents, or maybe even an aunt or uncle, but they only had one another and some close family friends. Clare had been abandoned as a baby and never knew her real parents. She had bounced from foster home to foster home throughout her life, but she never seemed to be angry about it. She always told them that she would never change anything because she wouldn't have been the person or the mother she was without the experiences.

Gabriella's thoughts were broken up by the arrival of Cindy, Robert, and Jason Throne. They were all dressed in traditional black, and Gabriella never understood why everyone always wore black to funerals. She knew it was a tradition, and she herself had on a black dress with a cardigan, but why? Weren't funerals dark enough? Would it not make more sense to wear vibrant colors to lighten the mood? People were already depressed enough when they had to say good-bye to a loved one, but if they could bring themselves to put on a piece of brightly colored clothing, it might be the extra push they needed.

She looked at Jason from across the room. She thought that he looked sleek and very grown up in his suit. Some of the feelings she had been having crept back into her heart. She had told herself that it was just because he had been so nice to her and she needed him as a friend, and that was it—he was her best friend and nothing more.

Jason looked up and caught her staring at him and smiled. She blushed slightly.

He walked up to her and hugged her. "You are beautiful," he whispered in her ear.

"Thanks," she murmured, becoming intoxicated from his fresh rain scent.

He gave her a reassuring look. "You going to be OK?"

She nodded, kissed him on the cheek, and took her position with her sisters at the front of the chapel to greet the mourners. Gabriella was astonished at the number of people who came in support for her mother, but although her heart was truly touched, she had no real desire to talk to these strangers. Gabriella put on a good face and appeared to be appreciative, but the truth was that to her knowledge, they did not know her mother or her sisters. She began to consider how much she did not know about her mother's life. She had not realized that she had touched the lives of so many.

And then it happened. The person she had been dreading the most appeared with his perfect wife, his perfect children—the keepers, as Gabriella called them. Biologically, they were her half sister and half brothers, but she did not care. To her they were aliens from another planet on dangerous ground, and they should be banished. They walked in perfect formation, as if they had practiced. No one stepped out of line.

They all smiled at the appropriate times and to the appropriate people. They were the town celebrities. Everyone gawked over how beautiful they were, how wonderful their house was, and how lucky they were to have Austin Knope as their father.

Alice Knope, Austin's wife, and his daughter Audrey were both wearing black dresses with only slight differences in the sleeves and the neckline. They both wore a single strand of pearls complemented by pearl earrings, and they looked as if they had had their hair professionally styled.

"Gabby," Audrey Knope said as she walked up to her, "I am so sorry for your loss. I cannot imagine what you are going through." Audrey was a few years younger than Gemma, and she had often tried to be close to Gemma and Gabriella, only for Gabriella to turn her away. Audrey always tried to push and push until Gabriella would explode, and then Audrey would run off and whine to her mother. Her mother would then call Clare and tell her that she needed to control Gabriella.

Gabriella rolled her eyes at Audrey, and Gemma stepped in. "Thank you for your condolences."

Giuliana caught a glimpse of Austin and ran over to him at once. He scooped her up in a big hug. This seemed to bother Alice, whose expression faltered for few moments. She composed herself and turned to Gabriella and Gemma. "I know that you and I are not on the best of terms." Alice was treading lightly to avoid an explosion of hatred from Gabriella. "But I wanted to pay my respects to your mother and support my"—she put a great deal of emphasis on the word—"*husband* during this difficult time."

Gabriella's face warmed promptly, and she wanted to slap Alice as she had Austin for disrespecting her mother. Gemma touched her arm to remind her where they were, but Gabriella did not care. She smiled through her gritted teeth. "I guess 'your husband'"—Gabriella used air quotes—"loves you so much that that's why he needed my mother to remind him of that." She stepped in a little closer and spoke barely above a whisper. "Do not disrespect my mother ever again, especially today. She was a better woman than you will ever be, and you and I both know that. Hell, even Austin agreed."

"God, Gabby," Audrey snapped, "why do you always have to be so mean?"

Gabriella smiled maliciously at her. "Well, that's that," Gabriella said loud enough for the entire room to hear. "Thank you for coming; please take your seats."

Alice and Audrey were not trying to hide their uncomfortable expressions. They stomped off cursing under their breath, causing other people in the room to stare. Gabriella caught a glimpse of Jason from the corner of her eye staring and shaking his head at her. She smiled back and shrugged.

"Gabby"—Gemma was forceful and pinched her arm—"you shouldn't have done that."

"I know, I know." She motioned her sister to calm down. "She shouldn't have said anything to us given the circumstances, so maybe she just won't talk to us anymore." They both laughed a little too loudly. "All right." She composed herself, and Gemma and Gabriella started to make their way to their seats.

"Gabriella, may I speak with you before the service starts?" Austin asked hopeful.

Gemma nudged her sister to oblige, but Gabriella was resistant until Gemma gave her another painful pinch. "Ouch," she said, rubbing her arm and glaring at Gemma. "I suppose."

He tried to lead her by the arm, but Gabriella did not want him to touch her. She followed him out to the corridor, where not even Lee Ann Gable could eavesdrop. "I wanted to apologize about the way things happened the other day and some of the things that were said." He paused. He was looking at her deeply, trying to figure out what she was thinking. "I wanted to see if we could take some time to get to know each other." He had put on his charming political face for this conversation.

Gabriella knew there had to be some sort of catch, and she had no intention of letting him get the best of her. "I think I know you well enough."

"Gabby—" Austin sounded sincere, but Gabriella had learned at a young age that his words were hollow.

"No," she said sternly. "This is not the day to talk about it. Today is about her." She pointed in the direction of the beautifully decorated casket in which her mother had lain down to sleep, "And you cannot replace her."

"I know," he admitted. "No one ever can, but that's not what I am trying to do."

"Enough." Her heart had once been full of hope when it came to her father, but now it was shattered, and the pieces were scattered from one end of the world to the other. It would be impossible for her to ever give him another chance. "I don't want anything to do with you."

Austin smiled at her and shook his head.

Gabriella felt a little insulted by his reaction. "What?"

Austin put his hand on her shoulder. "You are just so much like your mother." He smiled at her again. "I am glad that you are. Just remember that she is always with you, and I hope someday that you will let me in."

"Austin." She jerked away. "I did, and you walked away without even saying good-bye. My mother—she died. She's dead, and she still said good-bye." Her anger began to boil along with her broken heart. She desperately wanted to know what a hug with her father felt like, but Gabriella pushed that all out of her mind and walked away.

She felt her face get hot. She didn't know why she let him affect her so much. She had always been particularly talented when it came to shutting out any emotional attachment to her father, and most of the time she didn't even think about him. Gabriella tried not to let the bitter thoughts take over her mind. Today was not about Austin Knope or her feelings toward him, but about her mother, Clare, the most beautiful person inside and out that she had ever known.

"Gabriella," Father Patrick Morton called from the hallway, "are you out there?"

"Oh yes, Father Morton," Gabriella responded politely. "I am just trying to collect my thoughts before I give the eulogy."

He nodded in understanding. "We are ready to begin."

"Father Morton," she called after him, "Gemma would like to say a few words, and little Giuliana says she wants to say something as well." Gabriella thought with reading her mother's good-bye words to her that she could handle anything, but she was quickly discovering they were only words, and all she had left was the memory of her voice, not the actuality of her presence.

"That will be fine, Gabriella." He motioned her to follow him into the chapel. "They are waiting."

She nodded and followed him to the chapel with a stream of tears starting to trickle down her face. Gabriella took her seat between Gemma and Giuliana and took their hands for support and comfort. This was it, the funeral was going to begin, it was the closest she would ever be to her mother's body again.

"Please bow your heads in prayer," Father Morton commanded.

Gabriella obeyed, but her mind was not focused on the words. She had to come up with her own words, and she had not written anything down. She knew that she had to stand up there in front of what seemed to be more than a hundred people and talk about her mother. She could barely think about her mom without crying. She wished at that moment that she were more like Gemma, organized and prepared. Instead, she was about to let her mother down again by stumbling over her words and crying like a scolded toddler.

Gemma nudged her hard in the ribs.

"What?" she snapped, rubbing her side.

"Sorry." Gemma noticed the grimace on Gabriella's face. "You go first. I am too nervous."

Gabriella nodded, not feeling any less nervous than Gemma. Father Morton called Gabriella up to the podium. As she walked to the front of the chapel, she saw her mother's face in the flames, smiling, telling her she could do anything. She remembered the pep talk Clare had given her before she gave her valedictorian speech.

Her mother had said, "Don't imagine everyone in their underwear because that is just silly, but imagine it's me and your sisters only looking up at you, and we could not be more proud of you if we tried. You earned this, they didn't give it to you, you earned it, remember that. And I took a peek at your speech last night, and you have nothing to worry about. I love you, Gabriella."

Gabriella smiled at the sound of her mother's voice in her mind. Those words had given her the courage and confidence to deliver her speech at her high-school graduation, and now, moments like that were her own private treasures that only she had the map to. She glanced at her mother's lifeless body, and the tears came once more. She gripped the podium for support and put her head down for a brief moment. She heard everyone whispering about her, but she did not care. She was going to pay homage to her mother. She didn't have any notes, but only a small picture of her mother that she laid in front of her on the podium. She smiled down at her mother's beauty, stood up straight, and took in a heavy breath.

"Thank you all for coming." She looked around, and instead of familiar and unfamiliar faces, she saw her mother's face in everyone in the crowd, smiling up, giving her the words that she had been searching for all of her life. "I know it would mean a lot to my mother to know that she touched the lives of so many." She wasn't scared anymore. She smiled up at the crowd. "I was dreading making this speech today, given the circumstances, but this morning, Mom helped me with that. Even when she was alive, she was preparing for a time when she would no longer be able to comfort us with a long talk or a simple hug. My mother wrote my sisters and me letters that we will be able to take with us for the rest of our lives. She will always be present in all of our lives for our big moments that, when you dream about them as a little girl, your mother is right there with you. We will always have her voice and her pure, pure heart. This morning I chose to read my good-bye letter from her, and she made me realize that I cannot be afraid of the uncertainty in our future, but I have to leap forward with faith. She reminded me that the words live inside of me, and I am the only one who can make them count. So here it goes." She took in a deep breath, pushed aside the tears, and cleared her mind, and she felt as if her mother were standing next to her holding her hand whispering, "You can do this." That was all Gabriella needed.

"Clare Marie LaFrace was my mother. I am a lucky girl to have had such a mother. She was only sixteen when she became pregnant with me, and despite the advice she received to not keep me, she did. She kept me, raised me, and loved me. I know that she struggled, but she never let it show. She never let me go without. She taught my sisters and me that life is hard, and you must work for everything you have and always be grateful for the things in your life no matter how small the good may seem. And that is exactly what she did. No matter how much life pushed her down, she always got right back up. She had this unbreakable spirit about her that inspired everyone around her. She was an uncommonly kind woman, and she had this special talent for seeing the good in people even when everyone else had lost hope." Gabriella paused and looked around the room. Her eyes saw strangers crying and people holding one another, trying to cope with such a great loss. And her gaze stopped with Austin, whose tears had soaked his face as if he had been caught in a torrential rainstorm. Their eyes were connected, and she felt his pain, and for the first time in her life, she felt compassion for her father. She knew what she had to say. "My mother taught me that life is not always fair, and it does not always turn out how we expect it to, but I think her life was better than she expected it to be.

"She led a life full of love, hope, and happiness. She had passion for love, and no matter what public opinion is or was, it was her dream to hold on to it. As far as I know, she loved only one man. She loved him the way we were taught by our favorite fairy-tale characters. She would have done anything for him, and I know he loved her back. He was the father of her children whom she always held a dear place in her heart for." She looked directly at Austin. "Thank you for showing my mother that kind of love and for filling her life with it."

People gasped loudly at the surprise of Gabriella mentioning her father in her speech. It was public knowledge that she despised him and the nontraditional relationship he had shared with her mother, but Gabriella didn't care. Today was not about her, it was about honoring her mother's memory, and she could not deny the fact that Austin and her mother had loved each other deeply.

Gabriella smiled and took in another deep breath. "I know that it sounds cheesy and cliché, but I think that my mother was really happy. She was a great, humble, honest person. She did the best and made the most of her life with the hand she got dealt. She never regretted her past or the people in it. She always said that without failures in your life, you will inevitably be the weakest person around. I know that she was taken from us too soon, but I know that she lived a full and happy life. My sisters and I appreciate your support at this difficult crossroad in our life, but we ask you not to feel sorry for us and treat us as if we are going to shatter in a million pieces at the slightest tap. Envy us because our mother was a truly wonderful and one-of-a-kind person. Every second that we were able to spend with her is precious and treasured. Remember her beauty, grace, and poise. Laking will never be the same. There will be a void that will not ever be filled, because Clare Marie LaFrace was and is irreplaceable. I am honored to be her daughter." Gabriella turned to the casket. "We love you, Mom, and we will see you someday in the far-off future." Gabriella walked back to her chair, and as soon as her back was facing the crowd, she let the tears flow freely. She could not stop them, and she did not want to.

"Thank you, Gabriella, for that beautiful eulogy," Father Morton said. "Gemma and Giuliana Knope, would you like to say a few words before we conclude our service today?" He motioned the girls to come up front. Gemma helped Giuliana out of her oversized chair, and the usher ran a stepstool to the podium so Giuliana could reach the microphone.

Giuliana had very little fear inside of her. A crowd of people gathered for a reason she didn't quite understand, and it did not faze her. Gabriella looked at her sister's golden locks tied up in a ponytail with the fancy barrettes that she had bought with Clare the week before and her black ruffled dress, which Cindy Throne had gone to the mall to pick up for them. Giuliana peered over the podium, barely able to see even with the step stool to assist her, and began to speak. "I just wanted to say"—she had a slight squeak in her voice—"I loved my mommy very much, and I know that she loved me and Gabby and Gemma and Daddy. But I learned a couple of days ago that I don't have to say good-bye. I can see her every night when I go to bed and dream, and she will be there waiting to hear about my day. I will miss her and our Saturday morning cartoons, but it will be OK because I have the best sisters in the world." Giuliana got down with Gemma's help and walked over to the casket and kissed the top of it. "Love you, Mommy. See you in heaven." And with that, those who had been fighting back their own sobs lost the great battle.

Gabriella let out a loud cry as Giuliana climbed on her lap. Now it was Gemma's turn to say her final good-byes.

Gemma was shaky, and the tears were barreling down her face. She stood in front of everyone and choked on her sobs. She bypassed the podium and walked over to the long silver casket and whispered, "Good-bye. I love you, Mom." To Gemma, no one else was in the room. She had a moment alone, and the people in the crowd had faded away. She bowed her head for a moment. Her chest was moving up and down at a heavy pace. She closed her eyes one more time to gather her strength, took a final moment to look at her mother, and then walked over to the podium.

With trembling hands, she took out a folded piece of paper that did not contain her handwriting. Her voice was barely over a whisper, but everyone could hear and feel her pain, especially Gabriella. Gabriella had the urge to get up to help and protect her sister from her own agony, but she sensed that this was something Gemma needed to do on her own. She wanted to say good-bye in her own right.

"As Gabriella told you, my mother was so thoughtful that she wrote us letters to help us cope with her death and to take her along in our lives." Gemma sobbed through the words. She gulped loudly and took in another deep breath. "I want to share my letter with you today. This is very personal, but I think my mom would have wanted me to." Gemma looked at Gabriella for her approval, and Gabriella nodded toward her sister.

"OK, here it goes," she began. "Dear Gemma, as cliché as it sounds, if you are reading this, I am gone, and I am so sorry for that." It was at that moment Gemma's voice faded, and it was Clare's soothing tone that filled the room.

"I hope you are not in too much pain and remember that I love you very much. I try to rewrite this letter every year so they are current with your life. These letters are hard for me to write because it is my greatest fear to say good-bye before you are ready, and I would like to be there in person to go through all of your life's events. But we can be prepared for the worst, and I can always be there with you as long as you take me. Life is beyond our control in most instances, and sometimes things happen like that. And it may seem they are not fair, but it is no one's fault—it

just is. Gemma, you are my second-born child and proof that there is such a thing as true love no matter how hard you try to fight it. I think it is important that you know how much I love your father, and I always will. We just never got the timing right. I know that probably doesn't make sense to you, but someday it will, and I promise that your father has always loved you and felt what he did was for the best. Your sister Gabby will help take great care of you and Giuliana. I have no doubt in my mind of that.

"Now, Gemma, as for you, you need to remember that there is a life outside of books, and it can be just as great as the books you love. There is life outside of grades and accomplishments. I know that even minimal effort on your part will result in the greatest achievements. You are so brilliant; don't ever doubt that. You need to live your life, love your life, and make it a great experience. You and only you can make it memorable. I know that you are scared to make mistakes, and you are scared of failure, but I will let you in on a little secret: so am I. But if I had not lived my life to the fullest and took the chances I did, I would be without the three most amazing daughters in the world. I would not trade you for anything in the world. And I would not trade the unorthodox love that I share with your father for anything in the world. Gemma, I will always be with you, in your heart, breath, and life. I love you, and I will miss you more than you will ever know. But someday in the far-off future, I have faith that we will be together again. I will love you forever and always.

"Your mother, Clare LaFrace."

"My sister was right." Gemma carefully folded the precious paper and put it back into her pocket. "Anyone who knew my mother was very lucky. And my mother was right—my sister will take very good care of us." She turned to look at the casket once more. "I love you, and I will miss you more than you could ever have known." She lingered for only a moment before taking her seat next to her sisters, and they bowed their heads in prayer.

7

They arrived back at their mother's home for the repast after the funeral. It was going to be the first time that her sisters would be back in the home together since the night their lives changed forever. The sound of the crackling gravel beneath the tires created an uneasy feeling in the car, a frightened anticipation of walking up the path they had so many times before. It wasn't the fear of the unknown; it was fear of the inevitable that when they opened the door, their mother wouldn't be there to greet them as she had done so many times before.

Gabriella's earlier confidence from her mother's good-bye letter had faded as quickly as the day had passed. She had just spent the last hour trying to calm Giuliana, who was crying hysterically and telling her how much she missed their mom and wanted her to come back home now, and despite Gabriella's every attempt to calm her, Giuliana only cried louder. Gemma was edgy, and her manners had long since disappeared. When Gabriella asked Gemma for help with Giuliana, she rolled her eyes and walked away. Gabriella hadn't had the six years or fourteen years of mom practice leading up to the difficult ages they were both at, but it didn't matter. Gabriella would have to learn at an accelerated pace and keep it together no matter what.

The car halted and no one wanted to be the first to get out, so they sat in silence for a few moments, staring up at the house that should have been quarantined or have yellow tape strewn across the door to give warning about the loss the home had just suffered. After much hesitation, they finally got out of the car and walked up the path surrounded by wilted flowers. The bushes weren't as vibrant green; the door wasn't as cherry red as it had been a few days ago. The house had suffered the loss of its heart and soul. They all took a deep breath and joined hands as if they were bracing for whatever evil had taken up residence since they had been gone, and Gabriella pushed open the door, which felt heavier than normal. The air in the home was stale, stagnant. It did not possess the charm it had the night before the furniture came. It was now an awful reminder of how wonderful their life use to be. Gabriella caught a small glimpse of her mother's picture hanging in the foyer. They were all laughing, gathered around the woman whom they all admired dearly.

They moved into the living room, and it was obvious that some-one had been there to clean and set up for the repast after the funeral. Gabriella wanted nothing more than to be alone with her sisters and not have to deal with people on their way over at that very moment, but she did not have a choice.

She started up the stairs with her sisters to get ready for the repast, but there was a knock at the door. She motioned her sisters to go on without her. Gabriella was sure it was the caterer or the Thrones. Gabriella opened the door, and to her surprise, it was not the caterer or the Thrones, but Austin Knope alone. His face was red and tired and his eyes were swollen from the crying that never seemed to stop, but he just stared at her without saying anything. Before Gabriella could make any kind of remark, he hugged her. Gabriella thought that it might be the first time that he had ever hugged her that she could remember. She didn't know how to act or what to do. It was as if a complete stranger off the street had walked up to her and wrapped her in an awkward embrace. Gabriella had always imagined what it would be like to have a dad who loved her without question. There were no words between them, nor was she hugging him back. She stood there like a statue for at least five min-utes until he finally released her.

"Gabby." He looked at her as if it were the first time that he had ever met her. "You have my eyes." He was silent again.

Gabriella didn't know what to say or how to react. Part of her felt the need to comfort him. But she could never look past what he had done to her and her family, and she was silent.

"Gabby, I love you and your sisters so much." He was sincere in his words. "I know that I haven't been the best dad in the world to you three, but that changes from this moment on." He buried his hands in his face. "I miss her. I love her."

He didn't have to name names for Gabriella to know whom he was talking about, but it didn't change the past. "Austin, I know that you are hurting." She spoke softly. "And I am sorry, and I even understand, but you can't just pick a day eighteen years later to be my dad, and you can't expect me to forgive you overnight."

Austin looked into her eyes. She could see the pain he was feeling, and she wondered how much of it was guilt.

"Gabriella..." His voice trailed off.

"What?" She wanted to hear what he had to say.

"I know that you are not going to forgive me overnight, but I need you to know that I am not going to walk away this time. I have never been far from you all. I know that you don't understand that, but I have always been there in some way." Austin's lip was quivering, and his voice was shaky, trying to conceal the pain he was in.

Gabriella did not know what to say. The simple truth was that he had never been there for her. She could not forgive Austin for not wanting her, and the fear of opening her life up to have him walk away again was far too great.

"Would it be OK with you if we came today for the repast here?" he asked, knowing that Gabriella did not believe him. "We can talk about the living situation later."

Gabriella was put off a little that Austin still thought there was anything to discuss about the living situation. She was more than confident that her sisters should remain with her, but nonetheless, today was not the day. She nodded toward him and stepped aside so he could come in.

"No." He put his hand up. "I have to go pick up my wife and your brothers and sister." He turned around and left as suddenly as he had appeared.

As soon as Austin pulled out of the drive, the Thrones pulled in to begin the casserole exchange and the endless looks of "Oh my gosh, you poor thing." She smiled, waved toward them, and left the door open for them to let themselves in. She headed upstairs to freshen up.

As she got closer to the landing at the top of the stairs, she heard Gemma yelling at Giuliana in her room. Gabriella knew this was the first of many fights that she would have to mediate, and she hurried toward the room before things got completely out of hand.

"Hey," Gabriella yelled over her sisters' own screaming voices, "what is going on in here?"

"Giuliana will not cooperate at all with me!" Gemma screamed. "She is being a selfish, spoiled brat!"

Gabriella was not going to tolerate that tone, not today. "All right, that is enough." Gabriella gave Gemma a look saying that she should know better. "Today is difficult enough without the two of you bickering." She turned her attention to Giuliana. "What is wrong?"

Giuliana sniffled. "Gemma won't let me change out of my clothes. I just want to put on my favorite dress." Clare had had a special way of dealing with Giuliana when she got in one of her moods that both Gemma and Gabriella had never fully grasped or appreciated.

She looked at Giuliana very seriously. "OK, Giuliana, we don't always get our way, and today you have to wear what you have on." She put her up on the bed to stop her from talking back. "I promise you can change by seven o'clock tonight," she said in a firm tone.

Giuliana looked at Gabriella for a sign of weakness, but with no sign in sight, she nodded and apologized to Gemma.

"Gemma, why don't you go ahead and freshen up. I will help Giuliana." Gabriella gestured to her sister and gave her a warm smile. Gemma stomped off out of the room. Gabriella sighed and started helping Giuliana finish up her hair. As she ran the brush through her tangled golden hair, she realized that Giuliana was only six years old. It wasn't a secret or anything, but Gabriella understood what that meant in that moment. She would have to help her get ready for school and teach her all of the moral guidelines that their mother had taught her and Gemma. Giuliana had so much growing up to do, and it was up to Gabriella to guide her young sister in a way a mother would.

Cindy Throne poked her head into Giuliana's room. "Are you girls ready to come downstairs? There are quite a few people here already."

"Oh yeah, in a couple of minutes." Gabriella had almost forgotten that people would be at their home today to talk more about the life of Clare LaFrace and how devastating her loss was. "All right, you ready?" she asked Giuliana in a cheerful voice.

"Yep." Giuliana jumped off the bed.

"Gabby," Gemma called from the hallway, "come on, let's get this over with."

Gabriella pushed herself up from the bed and followed her young sister to the hallway.

"Ready?" she asked Gemma.

Gemma nodded.

They started down the stairs, one behind the other. The house was swollen with people consumed by their own menial conversations, but to Gabriella's horror, silence instantly fell upon the room as they walked into the living room. Everyone peered around as if they were elusive royal people who never went out in public. Gabriella nudged Gemma to find refuge among the people they actually knew. Everyone was hoping they would be the first to console. After whispers of how sorry they felt for the sisters, the room returned to lively chatter as they huddled around the Thrones for protection.

"How are you guys holding up?" Cindy Throne took a cocktail shrimp from a passing tray.

"I am OK," Gabriella and Gemma said at the same time. They exchanged glances and giggled.

"Gabriella, your eulogy at the service this morning was beautiful," Robert Throne said. He was a tall man with a face one would expect a dad to have. He was middle aged, and it showed. He had brown hair with gray visible throughout, but he was a handsome, older version of the very dreamy Jason Throne. "Gemma, your speech was very moving as well," he added, nodding his head toward her.

"Are you ready to make your rounds?" Jason asked.

"Are you ready to come along?" Gabriella quipped back.

He smiled at her. "You know I would not miss it for the world."

Gemma rolled her eyes at them. "Why don't you two just get married already."

Cindy and Robert both laughed loudly. "We were thinking the same thing."

Jason laughed and rolled his eyes, but Gabriella felt a twinge of hope at that statement and turned slightly pink. No one had ever really understood their relationship, but it had made sense to both of them until recently, when Gabriella started to notice what all the other teenage girls raved about. Jason was handsome, funny, smart, and so caring. He was what every girl would ever dream up in a perfect match.

"Well, my future wife," Jason said sarcastically, "are you ready?"

"Well of course," she replied playfully, trying not to be too excited at the thought of marriage. She grabbed Giuliana's hand, and Gemma followed. All Gabriella wanted to do was to say thank you for coming and be done with it. She did not want to listen to all of the wonderful stories and memories of her mother. She really just wanted today to be over with, but alas, everyone wanted to pay their respects and talk until they became tired of their own voice.

"Gabriella, Gemma, and Giuliana." Lee Ann Gable cornered them first. "You girls must be so heartbroken." She clutched her heart. "I am right across the street, so is there anything I can do?"

Gabriella may have been too quick to answer. "No."

Lee Ann looked offended. "Well, I enjoyed your mother's company very much, and I will miss her stories a great deal."

"So will I," Giuliana piped up.

"Oh, honey," Lee Ann whined.

"Lee Ann," Gabriella said, stepping in before she could say another word, "we appreciate your condolences and your enthusiasm to help our family during this difficult time. I promise if I need a cup of sugar or milk, I will call on you first."

Lee Ann gave her a disappointed look. "So you are not selling the house?"

"No," Gabriella replied. "We are staying in our home."

"Oh." Lee Ann looked puzzled and surprised. "I am not trying to pry." And by that she meant she wanted every tidbit of information that Gabriella was willing to share.

Gemma and Gabriella shot her warning looks to back off.

But Lee Ann continued, unfazed. "I thought that your father would care for you, and you would move in with him."

Gabriella felt her temper rising, and she did her best to contain it. "Lee Ann, I am trying to be polite." She spoke through a fake smile. "Don't make it more difficult than usual. And thank you for your fake sympathy." Gabriella hurried her sister to the next set of condolences and thank you for comings before Lee Ann Gable could say another word.

It had been a long day already for Gabriella and her sisters. They had talked to friends of their mother's and Gabriella's friends who were so shocked about her decision not to leave for school, and they did not seem sure what they should be sorrier for. She had tried to avoid the Knopes as much as possible. Gabriella had made a small effort to be nice to Austin. She did not want to argue—she did not have the energy—and she did feel a bit sorry for him, but it didn't change how she felt about him.

"Gabby." Alex Hickins approached her from a corner of the room she was near. "Can we talk?"

Gabriella looked at him, not really wanting to agree, but she decided that she had better get this over with too. She looked at Jason, who read her look, and he took Giuliana over to the food table to help her get something to eat.

Gemma laughed under her breath and muttered, "Good luck with the idiot."

Gabriella shot her a warning look. "What's up?" She followed Alex over to a private corner at the opposite end of the room. Alex tried to take her hand, but Gabriella used it to brush some invisible hair out of her face as casually as possible. Alex was very handsome, and she had always had weak spot for him. He was well dressed and groomed, he smelled of his own love potion, and he could always make the but-terflies in her stomach take flight.

"I heard you weren't going to Brown this fall." He was fidgeting with his sleeves.

"Yes," she replied. She had already had to explain her decision to so many people she had lost count.

He looked at her unsure if he should continue. "Well, I think you are making a mistake."

She chuckled. "What makes you think you can tell me you think I am making a mistake? You are not my boyfriend anymore."

"Gabby." He reached out to grab her hand, but she jerked away. "I love you and I know I messed up, but it doesn't change the fact that you were leaving in the fall. And the Good Lord knows that you would not have been back except for major holidays. So we would not have worked out anyways. We know that. But I am telling you because I love you, and I care about you. You should go to Brown." His intentions were sincere, but it did not matter. She had already made her decision.

She looked into those forest-green eyes that made her melt inside. Her hard exterior was peeling away, and it took some self-control for her not to throw her arms around him. "Alex," she began to explain, "you just don't understand. My family needs me right now. I want to go to Brown, yes, but I can't leave them. Brown will always be there, and I guess I will just have to go later than expected." She rubbed his shoulder to reassure him. "I am doing the right thing."

He pulled her in tight for a hug. "Gabby, just think about it before you go through with anything. And Gabby, I am really sorry about your mom. She was an awesome lady."

She laughed. "Yeah, she was pretty awesome." For the first time that night, she succumbed to her tears and let them fall freely. She allowed Alex to wrap his arms around her one last time. She knew that things were over with him, but there was something about him that made her feel comfortable and at ease.

"Are you OK?" He stroked her face with just one finger, sending a warm, tingly sensation through Gabriella's body.

She blushed. "Yeah, I will be fine." She stared into the eyes that she was leaving behind. They had shared so much together, but she knew it was time to move on. "Well, I have to get back to my sisters and say hello to everyone else." She turned to walk away.

"Gabby, wait." Alex grabbed her arm to stop her. "Can I call you? Maybe we can work things out."

She smiled at him and thought it would be the easiest thing to do, but she realized the easiest thing wasn't always the right thing to do. She turned to face him. "Alex, I don't want to be with you anymore. We can try to be friends in the future, but that is it. I have to move on, and you need to move on. It would be best for both of us." She was sincere and felt a stitch of guilt seeing how hurt Alex was by her words. "I am not saying this to be mean, but honestly, we both know that we were over a long time ago."

He looked deep into her eyes and nodded. "I suppose you are right. Friends, then."

She nodded and kissed him on the cheek. She walked away, and she was proud of herself for not falling back into his arms no matter how much she wanted to at that moment. She was staying in Laking for the time being, but that did not mean that she had to lead the same life.

Before she could make her way back to her sisters, Mr. Morgan was approaching her. She decided it would be most polite to accept his condolences and listen to whatever story he felt necessary to divulge.

"Gabriella, may I have a quick word?" Mr. Morgan barely waited for her to respond and started moving toward the kitchen.

"Certainly," Gabriella said as she trotted to catch up with him.

"Gabriella, I know that this is not the proper day to speak about this, but I needed to speak to you as soon as I could." Mr. Morgan's voice was rushed. He was looking over his shoulders and all around to make sure no one was in sight to overhear their conversation. "I received a call that you filed your temporary custody papers yesterday," he said, barely over a whisper.

Gabriella was starting to worry as well. "Is everything OK?"

"Yes, yes, for now," he reassured her. "But..." his voice trailed off.

She could sense that he was unsure of how to break whatever bad news he had. "Mr. Morgan, please, what is it?"

"Austin, your father, has already contested custody of your sisters. I was able to stop his paperwork in time. So it will not go through until Monday." He saw Gabriella was about to burst into tears. "Do not worry, Gabby. Your sisters will remain with you, but I have to warn you as I did before, no one wins in custody battles. Not really. You are in for a long haul, young lady."

Gabriella was speechless. "How could—" she started to say, but Mr. Morgan put his hand up to stop her.

"Gabriella, I am sure you are going to retain my services, correct?" he asked, and then waited for her to nod in approval.

She did not know anything about lawyers, and she felt betrayed again by Austin, who had gone behind her back to take her sisters away from her. And just today he had cried on her shoulder, and she had let him. Gabriella felt as if she had been used, and she felt like a fool. She nodded at Mr. Morgan, realizing she had no other choice.

"Gabriella," Mr. Morgan said, whispering loudly to ensure she understood the seriousness of the matter at hand, "you need to be prepared. The case is unusual, but I will be honest. Your chances are slim, but that does not mean that there isn't a chance. There will not be a hearing or anything official for at least three months—possibly even six." He glanced up to make sure no was listening in. "Do you have a boyfriend?"

Gabriella's thoughts were going a mile a minute. She was trying to hang on to every word Mr. Morgan was saying, but did he really just ask her that? "What?" She was confused.

He asked the question again at a slower pace. "Do you have a boyfriend?"

"Um..." She could not think of what her having a boyfriend had to do with her sisters. "No, I don't." She had to ask, "Why does that matter?"

"Let me explain, Gabriella." Mr. Morgan looked up to ensure they were still alone. "You are only eighteen, but if you were to marry, it could possibly help your case."

"Married," she shouted in disbelief. She spoke so loudly that people in the other room were now causally moving closer to the kitchen to see what all the noise was about. "Married," she whispered to Mr. Morgan. "I am not seeing anyone right now, and I am not ready for marriage."

Gabriella was shocked by the idea, and she wasn't sure she would retain Mr. Morgan if he had any more ideas like this.

"Gabriella, may I be frank?" he asked.

She nodded, hoping he would give some sort of insight to his insanity.

"Austin is very well off. I do believe he is the wealthiest man in town, and perhaps even in the state. He can afford the best." Mr. Morgan was stating the obvious. "Now, what we have on our side is the years that he spent ignoring your family. The fact he was never married to your mother. The fact that he never signed any of the birth certificates. But I am afraid that will not be enough. I know that your mother left you some funds, so that won't be a major problem. But it isn't the kind of security that Austin can provide." He paused, giving her some time to comprehend the situation. "The judge is going to see you as an irresponsible teenager who is angry at her father, and with your openness of how much you do not like him, that will work against you." Mr. Morgan gave her some more time, and then he said what he had pulled her aside to tell her. "Perhaps if you could find someone from a suitable family with a promising future, and someone you care for, you could have an arranged marriage of sorts. I hope this isn't too presumptuous of me, but Jason Throne would be a good match. You two are incredibly close, and it could be a good solution until you are both, say, twenty-five or so. And if you are not happy with each other, get divorced and marry for love."

Gabriella was flabbergasted. She did not know what to say. She first lost her mother, she had to give up Brown for her family, and now she was supposed to give up her chance at love so it would look better to some judge. Her life was unraveling faster than she could find the loose thread. "Mr. Morgan..." She wasn't sure what to say, but she knew he expected her to reply. "What are my chances of keeping custody of my sisters if I do not get married?" She feared that she knew the answer, and she wanted to shut off her ears, not wanting to hear the answer.

He shook his head in dismay. "Very slim."

"And if I get married?" she asked.

"Not one hundred percent, but I would say seventy-five percent. If you were to marry someone responsible, it would look much better on your part. It would show how serious you are." He looked at her, imploring her to consider his suggestion.

Gabriella was at a loss. "Any other advice?" She was sarcastic without really meaning to be.

"Gabriella, I understand that you have to make choices that are way beyond your years, and I do understand if you do not want to make them. I am just trying to give you a head start because unfortunately, time is not on our side. Austin has already put steps into action to take custody away from you," he explained.

She nodded. "OK, I will do what I have to do. This is not about me anymore. It is about the well-being of my sisters. How long do I have before they start reviewing our case?" She wasn't sure where the confidence was coming from. She knew that she did not have a choice, and her sisters' interests were her number-one priority. "Mr. Morgan, I have lost my mother, and I am not going to let my family fall apart just because some idiot had a change of heart."

Mr. Morgan gave her an approving look. "Your mother would be so proud of you." Mr. Morgan squeezed her hand. "You probably have three weeks at most before they start the review."

Gabriella smiled back and left the room. The house was beginning to clear out, and only the people who mattered were still around. She glanced around the room to see the people she truly did care about, and she pondered the decisions she would have to make. Gabriella was not going to let Austin Knope tear her family apart, and she would not let him take the last thing in the world she had left to hold on to.

8

Over the next few days, Gabriella and her sisters tried unsuccessfully to settle into some sort of routine, and it was hard for Giuliana and Gemma to accept the fact that Gabriella was indeed in charge. They had gotten so many phone calls that they had taken the phone off the hook, and what seemed to be an ingenious solution to the phone ringing was replaced with the doorbell ringing incessantly with people they really did not want to see, people they barely knew, and some they didn't know at all, each more anxious than the last to drop off their condolences layered in an oven-ready dish. Their refrigerator was jammed full of lasagnas, casseroles, and other concoctions that just required Gabriella to preheat the oven. She was slightly relieved that she had not had to test out her cooking skills quite yet, but eventually, the casseroles would run out or start to mold, and she would have to try her best not to burn their dinner nightly.

Gabriella had been trying to keep busy by canceling her enrollment at Brown, paying bills that she had never known existed, consoling Giuliana and her nightly nightmares, and, in a small space at the very back of her mind, trying to come up with a way to bring up the idea of marriage to her best friend, Jason, without sounding as if she were completely off her rocker. She wondered how he would react. She wondered if he in any way had feelings for her. Everyone had always said that they would end up together. But it was now or never, because if he wasn't receptive, she would have to crawl back to Alex and make him marry her. She grumbled at the thought of Alex and how many people would say, "I always said that Gabriella Knope would never amount to anything." Frustrated and wanting nothing but to scream and let everyone within a three-block radius know how she was really feeling, she managed only to slam her fists into the couch, hoping that her sisters upstairs couldn't hear.

She longed for her mom to be the one causing the vibrations on the ceiling, but it was only Giuliana jumping on and off her bed pretending to be an Olympic diver. Gabriella wished that there were a special emergency telephone number that could connect her with her mother in heaven. She had no one to seek advice from on this subject; she was on her own. Jason was the only one she could talk to about any of this, but this time, he was the last person that she could ask. He was coming over later in the afternoon, and she was about to get up to go get ready when Gemma came into the living room.

Gemma grumbled inaudible words under her breath and plopped heavily onto the couch, causing the entire couch to shake.

"You OK?" Gabriella knew the answer, and she knew that she should continue with caution because Gemma had been ready to fly off the handle at the slightest irritation.

Gemma gave her sister a look of disgust and rolled her eyes. "Whatever."

Gabriella held her own attitude back. "What's wrong?"

"Nothing you can fix," Gemma snapped.

"Gemma." Gabriella tried to remain calm and to slide her arm around her sister's shoulders, but Gemma pulled away. Gabriella wasn't sure how to comfort her. She didn't want to make it worse. They sat in silence for a few moments until Gabriella attempted to change the subject. "So, you go back to school in two weeks. When do you want to go shopping?"

Gemma shot another look of disgust toward her sister. "Thanks." She started to get up and head back upstairs.

"Come on." Gabriella pulled her back down. "Things are not going to get better unless we make an effort. Just talk to me."

"God, Gabby." Gemma jumped up again and started screaming. "You just don't get it."

"Then explain it to me," Gabriella yelled back.

Gemma folded her arms in a defiant manner against her chest and said nothing.

"Gemma..." Gabriella stood up next to her sister and hugged her, trying to break away all of her defenses.

"It's just that..." Her words began to jumble, and the familiar sobs started to take over. "It's just that people are going to know about what happened and be all like, 'Oh, I am so sorry,' and 'Oh my goodness, I cannot imagine what you are going through.' And I honestly can't take any more of that crap." Gabriella helped her back to the couch. "I can't get over this if people keep reminding me." She looked up at Gabriella for comfort. "It is bad enough this house smells like her." She buried her face in her hands. "I don't want it to quit smelling like her. Then she really would be gone."

Gabriella had fears, but she had to do her best to be the strong force that her sister needed. "Gemma, she is never going to be gone. Look in the mirror. You are like her twin." Gabriella smiled. "And just tell those people thanks but no thanks."

"Yeah," Gemma sobbed. "That easy?" Gemma said in a sarcastic tone.

"No, I suppose not, but we have to try," Gabriella said truthfully.

"You think we will ever stop being crybabies?" Gemma managed a weak smile while trying to dry her eyes.

"Well, I will, but you have always been a crybaby, so good luck." Gabriella laughed, and she hoped Gemma would respond the same way.

Gemma laughed. "About the clothes," she said, making an effort, "how about this afternoon?"

"Well, Jason is coming by this afternoon. How about tomorrow? We will make a day of it. We will get Giuliana's stuff and your stuff. Sound good?" She hoped it would be what her sisters needed to get out of their funk somewhat.

"Great." Gemma seemed to be excited.

Their conversation was interrupted by a knock at the door.

"Another casserole," Gemma said, rolling her eyes once more.

Gabriella laughed and got off of the couch. "Yeah, probably." She walked through the foyer to answer the door.

"Hey, I know I said I would not be here until later, but I got a date tonight," Jason said before Gabriella could even open the door all the way. "I wanted to stop by and spend some time with you guys." Jason walked inside before she could invite him.

Gabriella was sure the horror of embarrassment was wearing on her face. She had not even showered yet. She had planned on looking her best in two hours when he was supposed to be there, but now she looked as if she had been living in the woods for a few days—her hair greased back in an unbrushed ponytail, her clothes stained from the constant wear, and a smell that she was sure wasn't that of fragrant roses. "Oh." Her hands were trembling, and she wondered for a brief moment whether he would notice if she were to dart up the stairs, slip into the shower, and come out as if she had been at a beauty parlor all day, as they do in the movies. "I wish you would have called." She tried to straighten herself up as much as possible.

"I did, but you did not answer your phone, and your house phone is always busy," he replied in a casual tone.

Gabriella blushed. "Well, let me go change upstairs." She tried to rub off the various stains that were basically neon signs flashing, "Look at me! I am such a slob."

He waved his hand at her. "Gabby, you look fine." He looked her up and down. "Besides, it's just me." He smiled at her and sat down next to Gemma and gave her a hug.

"Right, Right." Her words were sputtering out like a water hose with a few kinks in it, causing Gemma to eye her suspiciously. "So, who is your date with?" She took in a deep breath and told herself silently to pull it together.

"Ashley Barton." Jason drew the name out, as if he were surprised she didn't already know.

"Oh, she is really pretty." Gabriella felt a ball of jealously swirling around, and she was trying to quickly devise a plan to keep Jason from his date.

"I know." Jason was now looking at her in the same suspicious manner. "You know we have been seeing each other for a couple months now."

"Oh yeah. That's right. I completely forgot." She laughed awkwardly.

"Are you OK?" He had known her long enough to know when something was off.

She didn't answer him, but instead turned to Gemma. "Hey, Gemma, could you give us a moment alone?" Gemma rolled her eyes and walked upstairs. Gabriella listened for the closing of her door before she continued. "Well, there is something I do need to talk to you about."

"OK," she thought. "The hard part is over. Now, how do I tell him that I want and have to marry him within a few weeks? Oh my God, how stupid am I? I can't ask him this. There is no way, no matter how understanding and great he is, that he will understand this. I can't put him in this kind of position. I can't, I just can't."

"Are you going to tell me, or are you going to make me guess?" Jason asked.

Gabriella could not ask that of her best friend. It was too much. "Nothing, forget it." She looked away, trying to act as natural as possible. "I hope you have a really good time on your date."

"Gabriella"—he never called her that—"you aren't getting off that easy!"

She knew that he wouldn't give up the challenge to retrieve the information that she had just decided to lock away. "It's just," she began timidly, "I thought..." Gabriella thought that maybe she could be honest with him about everything—the marriage and her newfound feelings for him—and he might understand, but something was still holding her back. It was the fear of the unknown. The fear of losing him forever over some silly schoolgirl crush. The fear of losing him forever because of the enormity of what marriage would entail.

He looked as if he wanted to shake the truth out of her. "Gabby, just tell me!"

It was now or never. Gabriella gulped and went for it. "Mr. Morgan told me at the funeral that I would have a much better chance of keeping the girls if I got married. And lately I have had feelings. I don't know if it's because of everything going on, or because I have had them for a while but kind of always put it on the back burner."

"OK." He was trying to process what she had just sputtered out. "Let me try to understand. You have to get married." He held up one finger.

"You have feelings." He nodded again, holding up a second finger, and his look of clarity faded. "Who?"

Gabriella's face turned red, and she looked away, unable to face him. She had spilled her guts, but he had not grasped that she was talking about him.

Jason let out a loud gasp of air. "Me?"

Gabriella was too embarrassed to say anything. She only nodded.

"Why?" he asked in disbelief.

Gabriella didn't have to hesitate to answer his question. "I think I have always had feelings for you, but you are my best friend, so I sort of just blocked them out. You have been there for me through everything, and this last week, you have been so great, and my whole life, you have been amazing."

Jason was quiet for a few moments, surely replaying what she had just told him over in his head. He looked up at her. "You have feelings for me?"

Gabriella began to panic. "Don't feel like you have to say anything back. I am not asking for anything. I just wanted you to know."

Jason was silent once again. He stared down into the floor, kicking the invisible air over his shoes.

She assumed that he was trying to figure out how to let her down easy. He had always been very sweet to any girl whom he didn't feel the same about. Gabriella didn't want to be in that category. "Jason, just forget I said anything, please."

Jason turned his eyes toward her. He placed her hand inside of his and moved closer to her, so that their knees were touching.

Gabriella felt as if she were in one of her dreams that she only ever revealed to her journal, and in about five seconds, when his face came toward her, she would wake up with disappointment and confusion.

Jason smiled his weak-at-the-knees smile and cupped her face with his hand. He moved a strand of her hair from her face and tucked it behind her ears. "Gabby, I have always had feelings for you."

She wanted to shriek in excitement. She could feel his breath on her face. She could feel the tension building between them. He started to turn his head, and he flashed a half-sexy smile at her and looked down into her eyes once more. He pulled her lips into his. Their lips connected as the piece of the puzzle they had both been missing. He kissed her softly and romantically, anticipating every move she made. He was caressing her face as he kissed. His lips were soft, as if no one had ever kissed them before. Kissing Jason did not feel awkward or forced. It felt natural. It felt right.

He pulled away, just enough to stare into her eyes. "I have wanted to do that for so long."

She nodded in agreement. She rested her head against his. "Jason," she whispered, "what are we doing?"

"Well, I don't know about you, but I am sitting on the couch with the most beautiful girl I know." He pulled her over to sit on the couch with him.

For a brief moment, Gabriella felt like a normal teenager about to embark on a new relationship, but then the needs of her sisters came rushing back into her mind like a charging bull after the red cloth, and that was where her focus needed to be. "Jason, I need to be honest with you." She took in a deep breath. "I have to get married."

He scooted away slightly but still held her hand.

"Jason," she began.

He put up his hand up to silence her. "Gabby," Jason began, not sure where his words were going to take him, "I have been in love with you since we were kids, but I never thought you felt the same way about me."

Gabriella's jaw dropped. She quickly closed it and tried to wrap her head around what he had just said. "He loves me. Oh my God. He loves me. I love him, but I can't say that to him. I don't think it's the right time. Everything will be too complicated. Are we even old enough to know what love is? I thought that I loved Alex, but that was a joke and a waste of time. I know he's staring at me, waiting for me to say something. What? What should I say?"

"I am pretty sure you are feeling the same way I felt when you said you have to get married." He laughed.

She laughed awkwardly, but she didn't know how to respond.

"Gabby, forget about everything that I just said." He pulled her face closer to his. "What you are willing to do for your family is amazing.

I know everything that you have been through the last week. You are not ready to go down that road, and that's fine. I don't need that from you." He stopped for a moment to think about what to say next. "I will do whatever you need me to do, and if you need me to marry you, in a heartbeat, I would be honored." He gently kissed her forehead.

Gabriella felt the all-too-familiar tears creep back into her eyes, but this time they were not tears of sadness, but tears of great appreciation. She brushed the stray hairs that hung over his eyes away, grasped his face with both hands, and pulled him into her lips. The kiss was electric, time was frozen, the only thing able to move was their lips interlacing, and from that moment on, she would no longer be able to deny that she was indeed in love with her best friend, Jason Throne.

9

The next day Gabriella drove her sisters to the neighboring town of Pranch, Ohio, to participate in some retail therapy where no one was likely to recognize them. Her hopes were high, possibly too high, that they would behave and their moods would be unusually pleasant. Gabriella still had not told her sisters about her unofficial engagement to Jason or the fact that they were no longer "just friends." Somewhere in the back of her mind, Gabriella thought that if she bought Gemma and Giuliana a slew of new clothes, school supplies, and a few odds and ends they didn't need, they might not care about the sudden change and they would be onboard with whatever she had to say.

Gabriella imagined the possible reactions in her mind, none of which gave her the courage to make her announcement. Giuliana would most likely not understand and only accuse them of sitting in a tree and k-i-s-s-i-n-g. Gemma, on the other hand, was likely to have a fit of rage, as if she were suffering from a mental disorder. She could quite possibly try to inflict some sort of bodily harm. She might throw things or maybe just stomp her feet and pout like a two-year-old. No matter what way she decided to break the news to Gemma, there would be a heated discussion even if she had just gotten a whole new wardrobe. Gabriella wished that she and Jason could just go to the courthouse and get married. Then she could tell everyone like a normal eighteen-year-old.

The grumbling in her stomach reminded her that they hadn't taken any time to eat, and it was almost three o'clock. Gabriella decided it was time to take a break and grab some lunch in every parent's nightmare—the food court. The place with choices that made it impossible to come to any kind of agreement. Gabriella decided to let them each decide what they wanted, to avoid any battle of wills. She was sure that it was the easy way out, but what was she to do? She was a teenage parent of a fourteen and six-year-old, so despite what it may seem to people who didn't know her, experience just wasn't on her side.

Her sisters seemed content, so it was now or never. She spoke as if she were to give a speech before a class that she was not prepared for. "I need to tell you guys something."

Gemma stopped eating at once. "We have to live with Austin," she blurted out.

"No," Gabriella snapped. She tried to recover with an awkward smile, but then a sudden relief washed over her. Living with Austin would be far worse than her getting married, and this just might be what she needed to soften them up for her news.

"What is it, then?" Gemma was becoming impatient.

Gabriella looked back and forth to Gemma and Giuliana. She was starting to understand that this rash decision would not only change her life but the lives of her sisters as well. She had to do what she thought would be their best chance of staying together, no matter what it meant. "There is no easy way to tell you guys this." Her voice started to trail off as she wondered if she was making the right decision. "But I think it will be for the best, and I think it will make everything work out the way we want."

"Gabby." Gemma seemed to think that Gabriella was being overly dramatic, and she went back to eating. "Will you just tell us already?" she asked with a mouth full of rice and chicken.

Gabriella gulped. "Jason and I are getting married." She closed her eyes in an attempt to make Gemma's reaction imaginary, but there was only silence. She peeked through the bottom of her eyelid, and Gemma's mouth was hanging open. Shock had taken over. Gabriella would take silence over an arm-waving lunatic any day.

Gemma was checking out her surroundings, and her expression faded from shock to pure anger. "Are you insane?" she snarled through her gritted teeth, well aware of how out of control her temper could become. "Have you completely lost it?" There were daggers swimming in her eyes, but they were trapped in the endless ocean of blue that surrounded them.

Gabriella knew that the question was rhetorical, but she had to make her sister understand. "Gemma, I have to."

Gemma did not give her a chance to speak. "Gabby, this is not the solution. You cannot marry Jason. I don't care what problem you think you are solving. You are only creating more. I know that even you are not that stupid!"

"Gemma!" Gabriella snapped. "I will remind you that I am in charge, and my decisions are what they are: my decisions." She was unaware of her voice rising and gaining attention from the strangers at the neighboring tables, and frankly, she did not care. "Gemma, I have to do what is best for you and Giuliana. I know that you don't understand, and I really don't expect you to, but it is the only way we can stay together as a family. I am not going to let Austin Knope pretend that he gives an actual shit about us!" Gabriella felt her face getting hot, and her voice was cracking at the mention of his name.

Gemma was unfazed. "Gab, this is not the way to keep us together. If anything, this will be the thing that separates us." She shook her head ferociously. "Who said that you need to get married?" Gemma didn't give Gabriella a chance to answer. "Mr. Morgan?" She looked to Gabriella for her to confirm her suspicions. "Who cares what he says? He is an old man full of old-fashioned traditions. You are only eighteen years old. You are not mature enough to get married." Gemma paused for a moment and reached across the table and put her hand on top of her sister's. "Gabby, fight Austin as yourself. That is more than enough. Don't lie. You are better than that. You will just be giving him things to use against you in court. You don't need a sham marriage to prove that you are the better person to take care of us."

Gabriella couldn't remember the last time her sister had been so nice to her or said anything so kind, but Gabriella still thought that she was right. "Gemma, please understand. I have to do this for what is best for you guys, and it wouldn't really be a sham wedding. Jason loves me, and I love him. It just all unfolded sooner than everyone thought it would."

"No!" Gemma screamed. "I won't let you do this!"

And there was the reaction that Gabriella had tried to mentally prepare for but had not so secretly hoped would not come to this. She noticed the crowd was no longer trying to be cautious of their staring but was full on watching, debating on whether to grab popcorn for the rest of the show. She sighed and said in a loud whisper, "Gemma, that is enough. This is not the place." She gestured with her eyes to the people who were watching them.

Gemma muttered a few inaudible words under her breath and slammed some chicken and rice into her mouth, which caused her to choke slightly.

Gabriella was slightly amused, but she did not laugh, knowing that it would most definitely create a screaming match on the car ride home. Giuliana was mindlessly playing with her chicken nuggets, which she had no intention of finishing. She didn't bat one lash at their heated argument.

After they had finished, Gabriella cleared their table, Gemma helped gather their purchases, and they headed toward the car. Gabriella's mind was far away and consumed with guilt. She thought that Gemma might be right about Jason. Gabriella had never found the idea of marriage at eighteen appealing, and she had just told herself that it was the only solution. But maybe Gemma was right. Maybe it would just create more problems. She was hurting and ter-rified, and the thought of losing her sisters consumed her mind and made her so nauseous that on the way to the car, she had to stop by the bathroom.

Gabriella started to wonder how any legal authority figure would give custody to an eighteen-year-old girl who was very angry with her father. A judge would see that because it was the truth, but Austin in her mind was no father. He had abandoned them. He had not given them a second look, and he acted as if they did not exist. Gabriella had wrestled with the question for most her life as to why she wasn't good enough for him, but she had just allowed herself to become indifferent to him. Gabriella only returned the courtesy she had learned straight from him—she pretended he didn't exist.

She felt confused and lost, and the person she would go to for advice was no longer an option. And if she were still here, Gabriella wouldn't be in this situation. Gabriella felt a tear slide down her face, but she quickly brushed it away, pretending it had never happened. Marrying Jason would create tension between her and Gemma, and Gemma would not understand. Perhaps she was still too young to fully comprehend the magnitude of the situation, or maybe she was wiser than Gabriella gave her credit for.

Gabriella reached the car, and as she was loading Giuliana in, she realized again that this would be her life for the next twelve years. She would have to come to terms with raising and molding Giuliana into the person she would eventually become. She really would be giving up everything to be a parent. Giuliana would look to her more as a mother than a sister. Every decision she was to make would affect her family.

Gabriella and Gemma, though sitting only inches away from each other, did not say a word. Giuliana carried the conversation on the hour-long drive home. She was excited about her new outfits. She was rummaging through the bags and holding up each one to announce what day she planned to wear it. Gabriella smiled in the rearview mirror at her to encourage her silliness, and she was sure she saw Gemma concealing a small smile and quiet chuckle.

They pulled into the drive, and what looked like packages and flowers were waiting on the front porch. It was not unusual; for the last week, they had been getting condolence gifts daily. They had enough flowers in the house to start their own shop. Gabriella was beginning to despise the smell. They were an all-too-real reminder that loss was a very real thing, and no matter the beauty of a flower petal, it would not bring back her mother.

They piled out of the car with their hands full of bags. It took Giuliana longer because she had taken it upon herself to organize her new clothes into daily categories, and she put "the spares," as she called them, on the floorboard of the car. Gabriella, becoming more annoyed than amused with Giuliana's antics, grabbed the empty bags to start putting the clothes back inside. She stopped at the sound of crunching gravel coming from behind her car. Gabriella looked at the approaching car, expecting to see Jason or Lee Ann Gable. Lee Ann had been making regular visits, saying she was on her way home or she was just going for a walk. Gabriella thought Lee Ann's unannounced visits would be less annoying if she were honest about the reason for them, but Gabriella was sure that Lee Ann had her own definition of honesty.

Gabriella did not recognize the car, a red sports car, nor could she make out who it was, with the blinding sunlight bouncing off the windshield. It was an expensive car, too expensive for Jason or Lee Ann to be driving. Then the car door opened, and a man stepped out. Gabriella dropped her bags.

"What are you doing here?" she asked.

"I need to speak with you." Austin Knope walked over to help her with her dropped bags.

"Don't." She immediately snatched the bags back and motioned her sisters inside quickly. "Go on; I'll be in, in a minute," she told them.

Gemma did not question for once and took Giuliana inside quickly. Gabriella turned her attention back to Austin after the front door was firmly shut. "What?" Her tone was harsh.

"Gabriella, I want to talk about the upcoming custody hearing," he told her.

She laughed haughtily. "Do you want to talk about how you lied about waiting to file your appeal?"

Austin nodded. His appearance wasn't as well kept as normal. His eyes were glazed with burning red over the soft embers of amber peeking through the emerald. His blue T-shirt was neither tucked nor collared, his jeans were faded, and his shoes were old and tattered and stained with grass all around. He wore a baseball cap with a small faded tiger on the front; the stitching had long since passed.

"Gabby, please understand that I did what I know I need to do." His tone was sincere, and his eyes were hurt.

"STOP," she screamed. She wasn't about to fall for an "it will be different this time" speech. "Just stop coming and going. Just go, and stop pretending that you give a shit about us. Maybe you do feel guilty, and you should, and you think this will make things right with mom." She looked into the sun, hoping it would conceal her tears from him. He wasn't worth it.

"I am not going ever again." His voice cracked, and his eyes started to fill with water. "I know that you are angry with me, and you have every right to be, but I am going to spend the rest of my life making it up to you. I know that this will be the best for you, and in the near future, you will see that, I promise."

"Wow." She nodded her head and smiled angrily. Her mind swarmed with thoughts and memories of Austin's taillights, which she had seen so many times, and now, now he wanted to stay, and now he wanted to be the hero. Gabriella wasn't going to let him infect her family anymore. "Austin, how can you tell me that you want to make it up to me? Don't you think it is a little too late for that? You are the one who chose to walk away, and in case you haven't noticed, our mother is no longer here for you to screw around with. She never gave up on you, and look where that got her." Gabriella couldn't fight back the sobs when the image of her mother came to her mind. The moving memories in her mind—she could see Clare walking down the street, happy, laughing, all to be ruined by the sight of Austin and Alice doing the same thing. Clare would always say that she understood and it didn't bother her, but each time, a little light left her eyes, and her heart was broken a little more with each giggle, hand holding, and simple kiss on the cheek that Austin gave to Alice. And it only made Gabriella's hatred for her father root into the furthest reaches of her heart.

Austin, visibly stung by Gabriella's words, could not look her in the eye. He stared at the ground and kicked the gravel back and forth over his shoe. He took off his tattered old cap, ran his hand through his sandy-blond hair, and looked up slightly. "I am sorry, Gabriella." He was silent, barely looking at her, waiting for her to respond.

That was it, she thought. She was genuinely surprised that that was all he said after all of the cruel things that she had thrown at him. He didn't even try to defend himself.

Gabriella asked something that she had always wanted to know the answer to but was afraid of what the answer might be. "Why?" He had her eyes—or she had his; he was her father—but he had never cared. He always left. She wanted to know, but then the anger and hatred consumed her once more. "Why did you file for custody?" Her tone was even, unemotional, controlled.

The first why was the softest Gabriella had ever spoken to him in recent memory, and he wished that he could have replayed her gentle voice, "the real Gabriella," not the angry girl who hated him with no lack of cause. He cleared his throat, knowing that she wasn't ready to understand everything yet. He lamely said, "Because I had to, and I think if you give me a chance, you will understand."

Gabriella rolled her eyes in a true rebellious fashion and laughed. "Austin," she said, barely blinking as she gathered the remaining bags still on the ground, "I am only going to say this one time, and then I never want to speak of this again. I am eighteen years old; I do own this house, so I am old enough to make my own decisions. You did not want me. You did not want Gemma. You did not want Giuliana. You wanted my mother only when things were bad in your perfect life." She saw the hurt in his eyes, but he had hurt her one too many times for her to care. "You chose your 'real family' over us. You live five minutes away, and I don't know you because you didn't want to know me. You didn't give us the chance to get to know our brothers or our sister. You chose to break our hearts over and over again." Gabriella felt tears swelling up in her eyes, and her voice began to crack. She took a deep breath, and she let the anger take control. "You are a horrible father. You cannot decide after eighteen years that you want to be a part of our lives and expect that door to be swinging with a huge welcome sign. It closed the day you broke my mother's heart the first time." Her voice rose at a steady pace. "You only care about yourself! And I refuse to let you poison Giuliana with your vile and your way of life. Gemma hates you as much as I do, and we want nothing to do with you." She composed herself once more. "If you want to make amends, then drop the case. And drop it today." She did not want to give him a chance to respond. She turned around and headed to the door.

"Gabriella," Austin called after her, "I am not going to drop my petition for custody because everything you said is true."

Gabriella stopped and turned to face him. The little girl inside longing for her daddy wanted to hear what he had to say.

He took a couple of steps closer, but not close enough where he could reach out and touch her. "You are right, I am not a good father. I know that. I have to live with the mistakes that I have made, and I have to live with the fact that I waited too long to admit that your mother was the one for me. But I am not going to give up. I love you and your sisters. I always have. I am going to make up for every mistake I have ever made when it comes to you. I understand that it will take you a long time to forgive me, but I am never walking away again." He wiped a few tears from his face. He held his hands out, pleading for her to understand. "I am not taking you to court to be a jerk. I am trying to be a good father. Please understand." He sighed and barely whispered. "I will not let you sacrifice your life for my mistakes."

The little girl inside of her wanted to believe him, but the young adult remembered all too well the pain that he had caused. He had left one too many times. And after all, he was a politician, and she was sure he had mastered the art of heartfelt, meaningful speeches. It was probably how he had gotten her mother into bed on so many occasions. Gabriella refused to repeat the mistakes of her mother. She was not going to fall for his act, but something inside made it hard for her to turn her back to him and walk inside. She looked at Austin long and hard. He was waiting for her to say something, but there were no words to express her hurt and anger. He wanted her to run into his arms and let him be the swooping hero, but it was too late for that, and any chance he had died along with her mother. "I am not paying for your mistakes. I am learning from them. I am taking responsibility for what you deemed unworthy of your time." She didn't allow another word to be spoken. She turned away and hurried inside.

She peered out the window so that Austin could not see her. She saw him wipe his eyes, shake his head, and get into his car. Gabriella thought that for a brief moment they made eye contact as he sat in his car. But then Austin pulled out of the drive, and Gabriella made another memory of her father's taillights in her eyes.

Gabriella sat down on the couch, replaying what had just happened in her head. She felt the balling knot in her stomach, her lip started to quiver, and her eyes started to swell with water, and at that moment, Gemma walked into the living room and sat down next to her. There wasn't any need for words or tension. Gemma started stroking Gabriella's hair as her mother used to do whenever she had had a bad day or a fight with a boyfriend, or just needed someone to talk to. Gabriella laid her head down in Gemma's lap and let the tears come as they sat in complete understanding of each other.

10

Several days passed, as uneventful and slow as grains of sand passing through an hourglass. Gabriella and her sisters had not had any outside contact for three days, and it was nice. She wanted to spend as much time with her sisters as she could and relish the fact that they were the only things keeping her from turning into a zombie stuffing cheese puffs into her mouth. Gabriella and Gemma mutually agreed to turn off their cell phones and the ringer on the house phone, and they spent most of the day playing board games, looking at pictures, talking, and watching their share of chick flicks.

Gabriella tried to make Giuliana stick to a schedule for bedtime and chores, but Giuliana was certainly testing the boundaries with Gabriella, as any child would do with a new babysitter, and Gabriella was quickly realizing that she was going to have to tighten up her easygoing attitude. Gemma was trying to be somewhat accommodating, snapping at her older sister only a few times a day and allowing Gabriella the time to take a shower. Gabriella gestured to Gemma that she was going upstairs so Giuliana wouldn't hound her with a thousand "Can I go with?" and "Why not?" questions.

She entered her room, which was messier than usual, and rummaged for some clean clothes. The selection was scarce. She realized that she would have to start the housework chart again that hung on the fridge and had her mother's fading handwriting and gold stars to signal that Giuliana had done a good job. The thought almost made her cry—a lot of things almost made her cry—and instead of time healing the wound it, it was only deepening it. The unpleasant stench in her room brought her back to her dismal domestic skills. The dishes were piling up along with laundry, and there had been no real cleaning done for a couple of weeks. Gabriella told herself starting right then and there that she would start trying harder, and implicate a plan into action.

Gabriella's eyes scanned her room and landed on a picture of her and Jason framed in a "best friends" frame sitting on her desk. It brought her back to the idea of marrying him and the amazing kiss they had shared, and he told her that he had always thought that they would end up together. It was something that she had always secretly dreamed about, but the only soul she had ever revealed that to was her journal. Her journal. She had last written in it the night after her mother's accident. She had never gone this long without updating the events that seemed as if they happened a lifetime ago, when in reality it had only been a few weeks of radical change every day. Everything had happened so fast, and then after her encounter with Austin, she just pushed everything far from her mind, and she and Gemma hadn't discussed her marrying Jason at all. It was a taboo subject— no one brought it up, and no one wanted to bring it up.

Gabriella had been so sure that marrying Jason would solve all of her problems, but would it really? Or would it just be another disaster? If they did go through with the wedding, would Jason expect her to be intimate with him? She had never been intimate with anyone before, contrary to what most people assumed. Would it be a normal marriage, or was that something else she had to give up? Her mind swelled with doubt and worry. And then a small amount of clarity showed itself in the frozen memory of Jason's smiles and his eyes looking at her while she was laughing uncontrollably. She couldn't remember what was so funny, only that Jason always made her laugh. Clare's voice filled her mind as she drifted back in time to one of her precious memories:

Gabriella was pacing back and forth in front of her mother's door. She felt she was getting too old to go in and lie in her mother's lap and whine to her about how pathetic her life was, so maybe if she forced her mom to force her to tell her what was wrong, then she wouldn't be so lame.

"Gab," Clare LaFrace called from the bedroom, "is that you?"

Gabriella poked her head in sheepishly. "Yeah."

Clare turned around to face her daughter. She looked like a soap star ready for bed; the only difference was that her look was natural. Her hair fell, bouncing with just the right amount of curl, and her skin shimmered with the right amount of glow. In Gabriella's eyes, she was flawless, and there would never be a woman who could compare.

Gabriella walked in and sat down on the white satin bench at the foot of the four-poster bed.

Clare walked over and sat down next to her. "What happened?"

"What makes you think something happened?" Gabriella asked, trying to come off cool.

Clare eyed her, knowing better. "Well, let's see. Your eyes are red, your face is splotchy, and you were pacing outside my door." She smiled. "Now, I can draw one of two conclusions: you've been smoking pot and you stayed outside too long, or that a boy made you cry. Which is it?"

Gabriella laughed. "Pot?" she repeated. "You know better."

"The boy then." Clare said. "All right, what happened?"

"That's just it. I don't know. Everything was going fine. He was asking me out over and over again all last year, and I finally said yes, I would go out with him. But two weeks later, he's bored, and he dumped me." She sighed, exhausted from her incessant and needless crying that had taken place for the last few hours.

Clare wrapped up her daughter in a tight hug and stroked her brown locks tied in a ponytail. "Honey, did you love him?"

"Who knows what that is?" Gabriella said bitterly.

"Well, I do," Clare quipped back. "It's beautiful. It's wonderful. It's worth fighting for, and when it happens to you, you will know what I mean."

"How will I know?" Gabriella asked, as if she were six years old again and her mother were telling her the story of a princess and how she fell in love with the most handsome prince.

"Well," Clare said, getting a far-off look, as if she were remembering her own past, "when someone makes you want to laugh and cry at the same time, that's pretty special. That's when I knew."

Gabriella came back to reality, and there was an image of Jason, and she imagined being in a floor-length wedding gown, staring at her own reflection in a mirror. She imagined the happiness she would feel on that day, and then she thought of the sadness that would come. It would be another place that her mother wouldn't be and another thing that her mother had been robbed of by a careless driver. It didn't matter when her wedding was, it would be the same: her mother would not be sitting in the front pew.

Gabriella wiped away the tears once more. "I have to stop this," she said aloud. She knew at that moment that she couldn't wallow in her own depression if she wanted to move forward. And she had to, whether she wanted to or not. She took the first step and picked up her phone, which she had disregarded for the last few weeks, and started to sift through the contents. She had twenty-five voice mails and over a hundred texts to sort through. Voice mails first, she thought, and she started to scroll through them. "Jason, Alex, Lindsey, Lee Ann, Cindy Throne, Elise, Jennifer." She scrolled to the end of the list and dropped her phone, unsure of what she had just read on the screen. Gabriella had a voice mail from her mother. It was the voice she had so longed to hear, the voice that filled her mind, the voice that was in her dreams, but it was so far out of reach there was no number to call. Now she had been given another chance, one last message from her mom, one last "I love you." Gabriella brought the phone to her ear and pressed play.

"Gabby"—Clare's voice was clear as day and as normal as she had heard it that morning—"I am leaving Valley Mines, and I should be home in a couple of hours. I lost track of time. The talent was a bust, but when I get home, try to be there because there is something I need to talk to you about. I love you so much, proud of you. Give your sisters a kiss for me, tell them I love them, and I will see you soon." Clare's message ended.

"Talk to me about what?" Gabriella started to fall into anguish once more. "I'll never know." The tears started to fall again like rain from the sky. They were endless, soaking, and burning. Her life had been so clear three weeks ago, and now it was all in shambles. She had no one, and at that thought, her phone started to vibrate.

Jason's name flashed across the screen. She looked at the phone vibrating across her desk as if it were doing a small dance moving closer and closer to the edge, and then she laughed, thinking that he was always there. And she began to cry, thinking how grateful she was to have him in her life. Gabriella hesitated only slightly and then answered the phone. She could hear Jason's voice before she had brought the phone all the way up to her ear.

"Gabby." He sounded worried. "Gabby, are you there?"

"Yes," Gabriella replied.

"Are you OK?" Jason asked, catching her somber tone.

She had been ready to move on five minutes ago, but now she felt empty again. She felt the gaping hole inside of her, and there wasn't anything she or anyone could do to fix it. Her voice cracked with pain. "Jason, I heard her voice." She felt weak, breathless, and helpless.

"Whose voice, Gabby?" Jason asked, more worried than before.

Gabriella knew that he would understand once she could put a coherent sentence together. "Jason," she said, her voice still shaky, "on the night of mom's accident." She stopped and buried her face in her hands. The thought of her mother's accident still made her stomach twist and turn, and all that was keeping it steady was a knife ready to pierce her heart. The memories, the shock, the ingrained memory of that night would never go away. It would replay in slow motion over and over again until she took her final breath.

"Gabby." Jason sounded almost frantic now. Gabriella had been silent for at least two minutes. "What about it? Are you OK?"

She let the oxygen fill her lungs and hoped that the breaths would make her pain subside. Her voice still shaky but controlled, she began to explain. "On the night of the accident, she left me a voice mail. I remember seeing it when I left Alex's house that night, but I forgot about it because you called me and sounded all worried. And after I found out why you were so worried, I didn't really think about my phone." She started to cry more. "And I heard her voice, I heard her say I love you, I heard her. It was normal, like it had been every day. She was on her way home, but God didn't care. He killed her, he killed her. Why? Why?" Gabriella fell to her knees so hard the floor shook. She barely had a hold of her phone anymore. Nothing mattered. She began to weep uncontrollably. Everything she had been holding inside rushed to the surface.

"Gabby," Jason shouted, realizing that she had dropped the phone. "I'm coming over," he shouted into the phone.

Gabriella barely heard him, and it didn't matter; she had forgotten about the phone. She was left in a spiraling sadness that saw no end in sight. There was no dim light at the end of any tunnel. She was alone; it was dark. She closed her eyes and saw Clare's face within inches of hers, just staring, no words, just looking at each other. Gabriella wished with all of her might that she had the strength and the power to bring her back. But reality took over, and she was lying on the floor curled in a ball, soaking the carpet with her tears. Gabriella wasn't sure where she found the strength, but she got up.

"Baby steps," she said out loud. She walked back over to her desk to set her phone down, and under the corner of a legal-sized envelope, something caught her attention. She felt so dumb that she had not thought to look to her mother for the help and comfort that she needed. She had almost forgotten about the letters. A part of her wanted to rip each one open to cherish each word that her mother had written. Knowing that Clare had touched the same envelopes that Gabriella was holding in her hands made her cherish them that much more. She rummaged through them, reading the titles on the outside. Gabriella stopped when she saw one labeled Coping. Her mother had truly thought of everything.

Gabriella carefully opened the envelope so as not to tear it. There it was, the only thing she had left of her mother that no else could have: her handwriting. Gabriella took in a deep breath and began to read.

Dear Gabriella,

I sincerely hope you never have to read this letter, and if you are reading this after my passing, I am so very sorry to have caused you that pain. Dealing with loss or any kind of sadness can be difficult and sad, but you must find the silver linings. Look for the good that is all around you and know that no matter how alone you feel, you never are. For one, you will always have me. That is the main point of all these letters—to let you take me with you and remember me and let me guide you the best way that I can, by letting you make your own mistakes. And I'll be there in spirit to catch you if you fall. No matter what has brought you to search for answers from me, remember how smart, strong, and amazing you are. You have the world at your fingertips. And if it is letting go of me, know that you and your sisters made my life great. I feel I got four lifetimes of happiness. Don't feel sad, because I haven't gone anywhere. I am right where I belong—in the hearts of my daughters, and I wouldn't have it any other way. I'm always watching over you, that I promise. Write it down, Gab, then chin up, smile, kiss your sisters for me, and remember that I love you so much. And I miss you just as much, but someday we will see each other again; I am sure of it.

Love you always and forever,
Your Mother, Clare Marie LaFrace

Gabriella looked up and smiled through the tears. She knew that the next year would probably be the most difficult of her life, but she would make it through, and she wasn't alone. It was OK to cry and be weak at times, but in the end, what mattered was keeping her family together, and that was what she had to focus on.

Her thoughts were interrupted by the doorbell, and then Jason's voice traveled up the stairs, reminding Gabriella of what had just taken place. She had had a minor meltdown while she was on the phone with him.

She quickly put away her letter and secured her envelope in her desk drawer. Her face was stained with tears, blotchy and red all over. She looked as if she had not slept for days. Gabriella did her best to make herself look somewhat presentable. She heard Jason's footsteps racing up the stairs. Gabriella swung open the door, causing him to almost fall over. She couldn't help but laugh a little at him.

He gained his composure as if nothing had happened, leaped toward her, and wrapped his arms around her. "Are you OK?"

Gabriella felt her worries wash away with just his touch. She was desperately wishing she would have had a breakdown after the shower. "I'm fine. Just a minor breakdown."

Jason knew better. "Are you sure?"

Gabriella beamed at him. "Yeah, at least I will be."

"You really scared me," he admitted. "I thought that you had a nervous breakdown or something. I have never heard you like that before."

She looked at him and knew that this was the time for therapy. She knew that she could tell him exactly what she was thinking and feeling, and he would understand. She pulled away from his embrace and walked back over to her desk. "Jason, I'm not OK." It was the first time she had said that out loud.

He nodded and sat down on the bed and gave her his full attention.

"But I am going to be," she continued. "I heard my mother's voice today. And when I saw the message was still there, I was beside myself. I think the anticipation, the not knowing what it would say, or the simple fact that it was her voice...I don't know, but I was really happy for the first time since the accident, you know." She closed her eyes and replayed her mother's message in her mind. "She said that she loved me, and she wanted to talk to me about something. But I will never know what that was, and when I realized that, I started to crumble." She took in a deep breath. "She is really gone. She isn't in the next town, she is just gone. Most of the time, I can't sleep, eat, or move because the pain is too much. But then I look at Gemma and Giuliana, and I am responsible for them, so I get up, force myself to eat, and force myself to fall asleep, or I count sheep all night." She smiled at him. "She's still here, though, with me, and she always will be if I let her. It's up to us to keep her memory alive and be the best that we can." Gabriella moved over to the bed and sat next to Jason and peered into his hazel eyes. "I love you, but I can't marry you."

"I know." He nodded.

Gabriella was relieved that he didn't seem to be hurt. "I'm glad we are on the same page."

Jason smiled, intensifying his adorable dimples, and took her hands in his. "Gabby." He brushed the side of her cheek with two fingers so gently it was like a light, passing breeze that sent a shiver from her head to toe. "I want to be more than just your friend. I can't stop thinking about that kiss, and—"

Gabriella blushed, but she held up her hand to stop him from going any further. Part of her wanted to pull him in closer and recreate the moment, but then, another part of her was pulling away, scared of what else she might lose. "Jason, part of me wants to see where things could go with us, but the other part—"

"I knew there was going to be a but."

Guilt consumed her; she didn't want to hurt his feelings. "I need to focus on my sisters right now. I need to focus on keeping them with me."

He pulled her chin up slightly and gently kissed her lips. "I know."

Gabriella forgot about the time, day, and all of her problems for a brief moment. She was hypnotized by his seductive kisses. She didn't want them to stop, "So what now?" she murmured.

"I think"—he trickled small kisses up her neck—"you need to spend some more time with your sisters today. I will come over tomorrow, and we can all spend the day together."

"OK." She didn't want him to leave, but he was right. She needed to share the voice mail with her sisters and be with them. She had to inform Gemma that she was in fact, for the first time in her life, right about Gabriella's decision. It was a mistake.

Jason stood up and pulled Gabriella by her hands up to him. He pressed his lips against hers softly and brought her into a tight embrace. "I love you, Gab. See you tomorrow." And with that, he walked out of her room and down the stairs. Saying small good-byes to Gemma and Giuliana, he left their house.

Everything in her mind was clear once more. She didn't need a husband to fight Austin for custody; she had had everything all along. She had her mother's words of encouragement, Jason's love, and her sisters by her side, and that was all that she needed. She felt happy for the first time since the accident, and the fear of the unknown that had consumed her earlier that day had disappeared and turned to excitement and anticipation.

11

The next morning Gabriella tried cooking a nice breakfast for her, Gemma, and Giuliana, the way their mother, Clare, used to do on Saturday mornings. However, the end result wasn't exactly what Gabriella had imagined. Everything was going along well—the smell of French toast and pancakes drifted through the house; the kitchen was filled with laughter and love. It was picture-perfect until Gemma had a fit of rage surge through her, resulting in a few broken plates, a crying Giuliana, and an emotionally exhausted Gabriella. The last Gabriella had heard from Gemma was the sound of her slamming her door, which she was sure that the hinges had popped off and the whole neighborhood had heard. Gabriella had spent a good portion of the morning trying to pinpoint what had set her off in the first place. Nothing stood out of the ordinary in her mind, and Gemma was certainly not offering up any information to help solve the mystery.

Gabriella did her best to put the outburst in the back of her mind and give her attention to Giuliana as best as she could, but something told her not to disregard Gemma too much. She needed years of parenting experience to come wrapped in a bow, but then again, it didn't take a genius to figure out that Gemma was struggling more than she was letting on. She had been too moody lately, but Gabriella didn't know what she could do to reach her or make her feel better.

Giuliana was humming a song that Clare used to sing to them when they were young, no words, just a simple, soft melody. Giuliana stopped what she was doing, put down her crayon, and looked up at Gabriella. "Did Mommy write me letters too?"

Gabriella's eyes widened, and she snapped her crayon in half. "What?" Shocked and guilt-ridden, she didn't know what else to say.

Giuliana stood up and placed her tiny hands on her tiny hips. "Well, Mommy gave Gemma and you letters. And there was an envelope with my name on it, but I never got to see inside of it."

Gabriella and Gemma had been so consumed with their own grief and the problems that arose shortly after her mother's passing with Austin that she had kind of neglected Giuliana. "Of course you do," Gabriella told her.

Giuliana threw her hands up in the air with excitement. "Yay! Do you have it?"

Gabriella felt the guilt wash over her once more. "No, I don't." Gabriella tried to think long and hard about where they could be, but she couldn't remember seeing them after they got them. She truly hoped that they had not gotten lost in the commotion of things, but there was a lot going on, and they could have easily been misplaced. Gabriella felt like crying. How could she have been so thoughtless and careless to lose such a precious gift, which wasn't even hers to lose?

"Do you think Gemma still has it?" Giuliana asked, hopeful.

"Oh, thank God, yes. I am sure she does." Gabriella took her little sister by the hand and practically pulled her up the stairs two at a time.

"She had it on the day we got them, but she was too busy reading hers that she forgot about mine," Giuliana added.

"I'm sorry." Gabriella would not be able to forgive herself if Gemma didn't have the letters. She hurried her pace with each passing second, hoping that she would be able to make the situation right.

Gabriella started to turn Gemma's door handle, but remembering her volatile mood, she stopped in midturn and knocked instead. Gemma did not answer. Gabriella put her ear up to the door to see if Gemma was just ignoring her as usual; she thought that she heard the faint sound of the shower running down the hall. Gabriella cracked the door, but Gemma was nowhere to been seen, and Gabriella could not wait. She entered, jumping back at the overpowering smell.

Gemma's room was a disaster. There were papers crumpled in the corners and scattered all over her desk, clothes scattered from one end to the other. It smelled like something had died in here two months ago, and there would be no amount of air freshener that could help. Gemma's room was usually the tidiest room in the house with labels and places for everything. The only time Gabriella had ever seen anything in her room not in its proper place was when Gemma had been secretly been keeping a pet turtle that she "rescued" from the side of the road. Well, the turtle escaped from the shoebox it had been living in, and Gemma had torn apart her room looking for the turtle, who had managed to find its way to Clare's bathroom. And that morning their mother was not too thrilled when she found the escapee in her shower.

Gabriella held her nose as she stepped inside, but her mouth dropped open at the sight of Gemma's bed. Gemma had ripped open the letters that their mother had left her. It looked like they had all been read several times, examined for any hidden meaning, and held close. Gabriella felt an urge to pick up a letter to read, but she had to stop herself. She knew that someday, if Gemma wanted her to know what their mother had said to her in the letters, she would let Gabriella read them. Gemma was hurting, there was no more denying that, and Gabriella would have to find a way to comfort her.

She had to remind herself why she had come into Gemma's room in the first place, and that was to find Giuliana's letters. Giuliana deserved the same type of closure they were both given, and Gabriella was determined not to disappoint her. She started rummaging through Gemma's things. She was not being nosy or particularly taking note of what she saw; she just wanted to find the legal-size envelope with Giuliana's name. Old Gemma would have labeled it and put it somewhere easy to find, but it was quite obvious that Gemma wasn't herself, and Gabriella thought it would be a while before Gemma was able to return to normal. Gabriella told herself that she would do what she could to help Gemma, and she would be willing to get her any kind of help that she needed. It was insane to think that they would be okay after a few weeks of their mother's passing. Gabriella had found a way to somewhat cope, or at least a way not to cry every time she thought of her mother's face. Maybe if Gemma would let her, she could help her start to move on with her life.

Gabriella's searching was interrupted by ferocious screams of anger. "What the hell are you doing in here? Get out now!"

Gabriella felt responding anger rising up inside of her, but she didn't have time to fight. "Giuliana wants her letters that Mom left her, and she told me that you had them. I knocked, but you were in the shower."

Gemma did not say a word. Glaring at her sister, she stomped across the room and pushed Gabriella so hard she had to fight to keep her balance. Gemma moved a few things around on her desk and thrust the envelope into her hands.

Gabriella gave her a concerned look. "Gemma." She wanted to offer some kind of advice, but Gemma did not want any part of it.

"Don't," she screamed. "GET OUT NOW!" Gemma pointed angrily to the door.

Gabriella clinched her fists and her jaw to fight the urge to strike back at Gemma for her inexcusable behavior, but she had other things to do, so Gabriella walked out of the room without saying another word to her sister.

Gabriella took a few deep breaths before she walked into Giuliana's room. Gabriella was going to be reading Giuliana the good-bye words that their mother had left, and she knew that she had to get her emotions in check. She could not get through her own letters without shedding annoying tears, and what would their mother say to Giuliana? Poor Giuliana, she was only six years old, and she had been robbed of her mother. Gabriella felt the tears creeping into her eyes already. She took in deep breaths over and over, trying to calm herself. Deciding now or never, she knocked on Giuliana's door.

Giuliana leaped up at the sight of Gabriella. "Did you find it? Did you find it?" she asked excitedly.

Gabriella nodded. "Sure did." She held up the envelope. "I can read it to you if you want, or you can read it yourself."

Giuliana looked to be thinking it over pensively. "You read it this time, please." Giuliana put away her coloring book and hopped onto her bed. She cleared a spot for Gabriella by banishing all of her stuffed animals to the floor in one clean sweep.

Gabriella snuggled up against her, and Giuliana rested her head on Gabby's shoulder. "Are you ready?" Gabriella's voice cracked a bit as she sifted through all the sealed letters in the envelope, until she found the one that was labeled *"Good-bye for Now."*

"Yes," Giuliana cooed.

"Okay, here we go." Gabriella unfolded the letter carefully so not to tear it and began to read her mother's words to Giuliana:

My Dearest Giuliana,

My baby, the light in my eyes, the joy that makes my heart swell with pride. I am sorry that I am gone at your young age, and I am so sorry that I am going to miss out on so much of your life. You have to know that you are one of the greatest joys of my life. You are a beautiful young girl, and I know you will be in great hands. Your sister Gabby will make sure you are well taken care of. And if you let him, your daddy will be there for you, and he loves you very much. I know that Mommy not being there will not make any sense to you, but you need to remember I will always be with you. When you need help that your sisters or daddy cannot provide, just look inside of your heart and you will be able to hear my voice guiding you in the right direction. I won't be there to teach you all the things that I want to, but you have two amazing sisters who can fill in the holes that I left. I want you to know that I love you and I will miss you dearly. I have written a lot of letters for you to read later on in your life so you can take me with you on your journey. You have such beautiful qualities that have taught me so much, like your honesty, beauty, and love for life; it has inspired me beyond anything I could have ever dreamed of. Giuliana, you are only six years old, but you have taught me so much about life. You made me realize that it is never too late to go after what I want. You and your sisters are the reason I smile in the morning. You and you alone have taught me the value of honesty. You are so pure at your young age, but I think you will always be as honest as you are now, and I want you to know how important of a quality that is to possess. Never be afraid to tell the truth, and never be afraid to ask for help. And never forget that I will always be there for you even if I cannot physically be in your life. I know that you will keep me in your heart so I can remain by your side. I love you more than you will ever know. It is not fair that we got to spend such a small amount of time with each other, but the time that we did have is a blessing I am forever grateful for. You changed my life for the better. Giuliana, you take care of your sisters, keep your head up, and never give up on your dreams. I love you, and I will miss you.

Love always and forever, your mother, Clare LaFrace

Giuliana had small tears streaming down her face, but she was smiling brightly like she had just spotted a rainbow on a sunny day. "Mommy changed my life too," Giuliana said, staring at the words written by her mother. "She loved me better than anyone ever will, and I know that not all kids get that."

Gabriella couldn't help but weep at Giuliana's wise nature, which was way beyond any six-year-old she had ever encountered. She pulled Giuliana in tight and hugged her as if they hadn't seen each other in quite some time.

"What's wrong, Gabby?" Giuliana asked.

"Nothing," Gabriella said through her sobs. "I am just really proud of you."

"Oh," she said, unsurprised. "Well, I am proud of you too."

Gabriella laughed. "For what?"

Giuliana smiled. "For not burning the breakfast."

Gabby smiled down at her sister and kissed her on top of her head.

"Gabby, thanks for reading it to me," Giuliana said. "Can we go eat lunch?"

"Sure, Giuliana, sure." Gabriella found a safe place, up out of Giuliana's reach, to store the remaining letters, and they headed downstairs for lunch.

Gabriella was making lunch when the doorbell rang. She looked at the time and knew it had to be Jason. She had completely lost track of time, and again she was not as ready as she had hoped to be, but at least today she had taken a shower, brushed her hair, and applied some makeup. It was a few steps up from yesterday when she had not showered for three days, her face was stained with tears, and she was pretty sure her hair was ready for a bird to build its nest in, but today Gabriella was in a better place. There was finally a dim light at the end of the tunnel.

"Gabby, are you going to answer the door?" Giuliana asked when the doorbell rang for a second time.

"What—oh, yeah." Gabriella shook her head back into reality, trying to dismiss any apprehension she was feeling at the moment. She walked out of the kitchen into the foyer. The oversized picture stared at her as she approached the door. She turned to face the mirror that hung in the foyer and started to straighten up a bit before she opened the door to her future boyfriend, or perhaps he was already her boyfriend. She wasn't really sure; they had not really talked about it, and every time they'd kissed, she was usually in tears or feeling vulnerable about something. She was feeling very grateful that she had taken the time to put on a little makeup—even though Jason had seen her numerous times without it, she didn't want him to look at her as a friend any longer. She wiped away the invisible imperfections and tried to fix her hair. Deciding she could do no more without a full beauty team, she answered the door.

Jason stood holding a bouquet of red, purple, and yellow tulips, which happened to be some of her favorite flowers, and he was looking as handsome as ever. It was obvious that he had taken the time to make sure his appearance was up to par. Every hair on his head was strategically placed to highlight his cheekbones, he looked freshly shaven, and he had taken the time to pick out something nice. And he was wearing what Gabriella referred to as his "butt pants," which cupped his bottom perfectly, accentuating all the right places. Gabriella felt her knees buckle slightly as his oceanic scent filled her nostrils. She felt like she had been staring for hours before he gave her that sly smile that defined his jawline and made his hazel eyes turn a shade of forestry green.

"Hey Gabby," he said. "Are you going to invite me in?"

She couldn't speak; she felt so nervous, but nothing was out of the ordinary. Jason had come over to her house more times than she could count, but everything was different now, and no matter what, it would never be the same. Her face was pink; her heart swelled with excitement and worry at the same time. What if nothing would ever be the same again, and what if their relationship blew up in their faces? Gabriella couldn't imagine her life without Jason. Her face went from pink to red, realizing the awkward silence was still there and he was waiting to be invited inside. As she stepped aside to allow him to enter, her hand brushed his arm, and a new flock of butterflies took flight.

"My mom sent these for you." Jason handed her the flowers.

"Oh." Gabriella couldn't hide her disappointment. Maybe she had misread the signs, and nothing was really going on between them, and Jason was just being nice to her after everything she had been through. "Well, tell her I said thank you." She hurried into the kitchen before he could say anything in response.

"Looks like I am just in time for lunch." Jason stuck out his nonexistent gut and patted it, making the sound echo through the house.

Gabriella went back to making their grilled cheese, "Do you want one?" Gabriella asked, Jason, holding up the cheese.

"Sure." Jason sat down next to Giuliana as she was coloring away. "All right, what do we got here? A purple lion?" He made his voice sound excited to humor Giuliana. "You know, if I had a lion, I would want it to be purple."

"I hope you know lions aren't purple," Giuliana told him frankly. "Lions are usually a tannish yellow with a big golden-brown mane!" Giuliana's eyes grew bigger as she described the physique of lions and how they weren't friendly or to be tampered with.

Gabriella smiled at the sight of them. She admired how good Jason was with her, and it gave her small glances into the future of what it might possibly be like if she were to end up with him. She could see him being a caring and devoted father, and not one who would pick up and leave at the first scent of difficulty.

"Where is Gemma?" Jason got up to give her a hand.

"She is holed up in her room." Gabriella's thoughts went back to this morning's fight and what she'd found in her room.

"Everything okay?" Jason asked, catching Gabriella's troubled gaze.

Gabriella shrugged her shoulders, knowing that Jason would get the hint that she really did not want to talk about it in front of Giuliana.

He nodded and changed the subject quickly. "I'm starving; thanks for lunch, Gab." He gave her hand a quick squeeze and carried the plates over to the table.

She felt her face turn pink again and warmth surge through her at his touch. "No problem."

Gabriella sat down at the table with them and began to eat slowly. She wasn't sure what to say or how to act. The awkward energy that she had feared soon made its presence known so much that even Giuliana had noticed. She looked back and forth between them.

"Gabby," Giuliana piped up. "Did Gemma dig a hole in her room?"

Gabriella laughed and choked at the same time. "No, why would you ask that?" She tried to recover quickly from the food that had inadvertently escaped her mouth.

"You said that Gemma was holed up in her room," Giuliana replied in a squeaky voice.

"Oh, well, that's just an expression." Gabriella chuckled. "I just meant that she hasn't come out of her room much lately."

"Why don't you just say that she is mad that she caught you going through her stuff?" Giuliana's voice was even and flat.

"Well." Gabriella laughed again. "I wasn't really going through her stuff. I was looking for your letters, remember?"

"I know that, silly." Giuliana rolled her eyes. "But that is why she is so mad right now."

"Okay." Gabriella knew that there was no sense in arguing. "You are probably right."

"Giuliana, you better remember that forever," Jason told her.

She looked confused. "What?"

"That your sister told you that you were right, because that might not ever happen again in your life." He gave Gabriella a sly look out of the corner of his eye.

"Hey." Gabriella pretended to be offended, but she knew that he was kind of right. "That is not true at all."

"Yeah, yeah." Jason waved her off. "So what have you two been doing all day?"

Giuliana did not give Gabriella a chance to answer first. "Gabby read me Mommy's letter that she left for me."

"Oh really," Jason said. "What was it about?"

Gabriella started to speak up to tell Giuliana that she didn't have to share the letters with anyone if she didn't want to, but Giuliana did not give her a chance.

Giuliana did not mind. "It was about how much she is going to miss me and how much she loves me." Giuliana looked around and stopped on a picture of the family that hung on the wall. "Mommy was a special lady."

Gabriella felt the tears welling up in her eyes. She wondered if there would ever be a day that the thought of her mother would not result in tears streaming down her face.

"Yes, she was." Jason reached out and squeezed Giuliana's hand. They all sat there in silence, each no doubt recalling a special moment that they had shared with Clare.

Giuliana broke the silence. "Gabby, I'm finished eating. Can I go watch some TV?"

"Sure, just put your plate in the sink." Gabriella got up to help her rinse off her plate, and then Giuliana skipped into the living room, humming to herself. She walked back over to the table and sat down, without knowing what to say to her best friend. She had to admit that it was slightly awkward. They hadn't really had a normal day together since her mom's accident. There was an unspoken tension between them, an attraction, or embarrassment—she couldn't figure out which.

After several sheepishly exchanged glances, Jason finally took out an imaginary knife and cut the tension. "This doesn't have to be weird."

Gabriella laughed. "What?" But her face turned red, and she looked at the clock on the wall to avoid his mesmerizing eyes.

Jason gave her a look of derision. "C'mon, really," he said, pointing in between them. "Us. It doesn't have to be weird."

She laughed, still feeling embarrassed. "But we are—"

"Stop." Jason put up his hand. "We are best friends, and the best relationships come from friendship."

Gabriella felt her heart flutter at the mention of a possible relationship with Jason, but was their friendship worth risking? What if it crashed and burned? She didn't know what she would do without him in her life. "That is true," she started to say.

Jason didn't give her a chance to say anything else. "Good. I think we should hug it out."

"Hug it out?" Gabriella repeated. Even though the thought of being in his arms again did send goose bumps up and down her body, she didn't want to seem overeager. She had not quite decided within herself if she wanted to travel down that road with this boy whom she had known since grade school.

"Yes." Jason didn't give her time to think over anything. He flung his arms around her and pulled her tightly into his body.

She resisted briefly in the same way that she would resist an overbearing aunt (if she had one), but almost immediately she gave into the fresh oceanic scent that radiated around him. She allowed herself to be submersed in his arms, swirling the hairs on the back of his head around her finger and daydreaming of simpler times when being her boyfriend didn't come with so much baggage. She remembered the nectar taste that he had left on her lips, the perfectly timed movements as his lips had intertwined with hers, and she wanted him to kiss her again.

"What?" he whispered. His smile said that he knew what she was thinking, but he wanted to hear her say the words.

She didn't say anything with her mouth, but she looked into his eyes that were a brilliant shade of green and hoped that would be all the talking she had to do.

Jason chuckled slightly, and with his hand he cupped her cheek and brought her lips to him.

She could feel his arm grasping her around her waist, pulling her as close as possible. Their movements were synchronized, their kiss felt natural and not forced; she was drunk from the taste of his kiss, almost hypnotized, not wanting it to end. Gabriella pulled away from him suddenly and sat back down at the table.

Jason stood looking confused, trying to figure out if he had crossed a line. "Is everything okay?"

Gabriella looked up at him and smiled weakly. "Yes." She couldn't say anything else, because she had fallen in love with her best friend. That line that she dare never cross no longer existed, and she feared that she might have just complicated her life more than she could handle.

Gabriella thought of her mother and what she had always told her about love. She would say, "You will know, there will be no question of its validity. It will make you want to laugh and cry at the same time." And at that moment, there wasn't a better way to describe the way Gabriella was feeling.

Jason knew better. He sat down next to her and put his hands on top of hers. "You can tell me anything." He massaged the inside of her hands softly. "Are we okay?"

She smiled warmly. She felt foolish how his mere touch made her feel so much better, but she couldn't think like a teenager, no matter how much she wanted to. "I just think we should take it slow."

Jason nodded in agreement. "Yeah, slow, that's good." He leaned over and gently kissed her cheek. He smiled. "So what are you going to do?"

Gabriella confused. "About what?"

"Um, your sisters, and the custody hearing or meeting, or whatever it is?" Jason asked as if he thought it should have been obvious what he was talking about.

"Oh that." Though it had been weighing heavily on her mind, she really hadn't thought too much about it. She was mostly focused on the outcome, and she still hadn't figured out how she was going to get there.

"Have you talked to Mr. Morgan?" he asked.

"No," she admitted.

"Don't you think you should?" Jason's eyes seemed bigger staring down at her. She felt like she was getting in trouble for not finishing her homework.

"Um, yeah." She stumbled over her words, feeling disappointed in herself. "I'll do it today."

"You have to be on top of this stuff. You know your da—I mean, Austin, will be on top of it." Jason lingered for a moment, but then continued, "Did you at least tell Mr. Morgan that you will not be getting married?"

"Oh, that." She'd tried to push the embarrassment from her mind and forget that she had ever asked Jason to marry her. "I don't think I really ever understood the reasoning for that." She lingered in her thoughts for a moment. "I guess it made sense on the surface, being married probably would make me look mature on paper somewhat—you know, the girls in a stable home with a mother type and a father type, but I'm not ready for that, and I don't want to be my sisters' mother. I know that if Austin gets custody, that bitch Alice will try to replace our mother. Phase her out of Giuliana's memory."

"Well," Jason began.

"Don't defend her," Gabriella snapped.

"Sorry." Jason held up his hands in surrender. "So Giuliana seems to be doing okay. How is Gemma?" he said, quickly changing the subject.

Gabriella looked down at the table, feeling disappointed in herself once again. "I thought she was doing great, but..." She stopped.

Jason grabbed her hand, his expression genuinely concerned. "What is going on with her?"

Gabriella took in a deep breath. "Well, today, she was in a very bad mood and snapping at me all morning. I mean, it was the smallest things that set her off, and what set her off this morning I have no idea. She has been distant all week, well, since it happened. Even if she's down in the living room with me and Giuliana, she still isn't there." She paused, trying to construct her next thought. "So this morning, I was coloring with Giuliana, and she asked me if Mom had left her letters too. At first I felt incredibly guilty because I had forgotten all about hers, and I didn't know where they were. Giuliana told me that Gemma had the letters in her room, so naturally I went to Gemma's room to get them. Gemma wasn't in her room, and you know how she is so organized; everything has a place."

"Everything has a label," he finished for her.

Gabriella nodded and continued. "Yes, but today everything in her room was a mess. Books were everywhere, clothes strewn all over the place, and there was a pile of paper in the middle of her bed. It was the letters that Mom left us. She had literally immersed herself in them. I think the thought of Mom not being able to experience those moments with us overwhelmed her in a bad way. Now she won't talk to me, and I don't really know how to talk to her."

Jason's expression said that he was thinking over everything she had just told him, and then he spoke. "Gabby, have you read all of your letters?"

Gabriella was surprised by the question. She had thought about it many times—just going through and reading them all—but she had always managed to forget about it and move on to something else. She had put them away the day of the funeral and had been back only yesterday, when she needed answers. She feared that reading them would slow down her determination to move on with her life by hanging onto the past and always longing for her mother to be there with her.

"No," she replied, "I have not."

Jason looked surprised by her answer. "Really? I figured you would have."

"I know." Gabriella knew that she could usually never wait for a surprise. She had to know right then. Patience was not her strong suit.

A broad smile stretched across Jason's face. "Do you remember that one year when you were determined to find the Christmas presents before Christmas Day?"

She smiled back. She did remember, and it was a fond memory. They had drawn out a map of the house where they had lived at the time, and they put "Xs" where they thought Clare's hiding places may be. "Yes, I remember the treasure map. We never did find them though," she recalled.

Jason chuckled. "Your mom was pretty good at hiding gifts."

She smiled at him for the sentiment. For the first time, a good memory of her mother did not bring her to tears. "Baby steps," she whispered to herself.

"Gab, you cannot expect Gemma to be okay in a couple of weeks. It's going to take some time," he told her. "You too. You're going to need time," he added.

She sighed. "I know. I just worry about her, and I don't know how to talk to her without her wanting to slap me in the face." Gabriella remembered Gemma shoving her so hard that she had almost lost her balance earlier in the day. "Not to be overdramatic, but she was really hostile this morning. When she found me in her room, I really thought she was going to hit me."

Jason smiled at her. "How many times have you almost hit her?"

"This is different," Gabriella insisted. "She pushed me, and I almost lost my balance."

"Gabby, relax." Jason stroked the upper part of her leg. "She has lost her mother. I would think it would be *not* normal for her not to be angry."

Gabriella knew Jason was right, but she was still apprehensive about blowing Gemma's hostility off as a normal stage of grief. "You are probably right," she said, trying to end the topic of conversation and move on to anything else.

Jason sensed Gabriella's urgency and changed the subject. "My mom offered to watch Giuliana so we could go out one night this week, or whenever you're ready."

"Oh, okay." She thought Jason might be asking her out on their first real date, but again she did not want to seem overeager. "Yeah, that would be great."

They talked for another hour until Jason got a call from his dad asking him to come home.

"Sorry, Gab, but I have to go help my dad." He got up from the table and started to move toward the door.

Gabriella followed him. "No worries," she said with a soft smile and light shrug of her shoulders.

"Try not to worry about Gemma too much; she'll pull through," he assured her.

Gabriella nodded.

"So." He lingered before going out into the open, where they would not be in full sight of Giuliana.

She blushed. "So?"

He bent down and kissed her. She felt the electric impulses flowing through her body. She wanted him to stay. She did not want him to go help his father. Gabriella wanted to be alone with Jason in her bedroom. She wanted to confess her love for him. His tongue whipped around in her mouth. The kiss became more intense. He pulled her in so tight and began to caress her body. His hands traveled up right underneath her breasts. It felt so right. She wanted him to touch her. He pulled away and stared into her eyes.

"Why have we waited so long for this?" he whispered.

She smiled. "I don't know." She was wondering why he had pulled away.

"I have to go, Gabby, but how about Friday you bring Giuliana over to my mom's, and we can go out on our first real date?" He pulled her in again and kissed her.

She tried to gulp for air, but she would rather suffocate than stop his kisses. "That sounds good," she said as his lips traveled down her neck.

"Okay, okay," he said, making himself pull away from her. "I have to go, but I will see you soon, and I'll call you later tonight."

"All right," she said. She watched his car pull out of the drive. She heard Giuliana humming to herself as she watched television, and Gemma's stereo was rattling the entire house. Three weeks ago she would probably not have been home to hear these sounds, but now she loved those sounds. Those sounds gave her a sense of normalcy, a sense of comfort that she would never be able to find anywhere else in the world. She knew that being here for her sisters was her place in life right now. She knew that Jason would be there too when she needed him. Her thoughts stayed with him for a moment. She was in love with her best friend. The boy she'd witnessed eat a worm for three dollars, a boy who had a known obsession with the Ninja Turtles, a boy who knew everything about her already. Jason Throne. She wondered if she had always known that she was in love with him but just did not want to admit that the rumors were true. He had agreed to marry her, which was not something anyone in their right mind would do, but maybe Jason really did love her, or perhaps he was just feeling sympathy for her unspeakable loss. Gabriella's thoughts settled as the dust did outside. She and Jason were in love, and everything would work itself out.

12

Gemma's temper had only gotten worse with time as the days slowly passed until eventually it was time for Gemma and Giuliana to return to school. Gemma would come up with a new reason everyday as to why she could not return to school, each one as pathetic as the last. Gabriella had tried to reason with Gemma. Gemma had told Gabriella on more than one heated occasion that she was not her mother, and she did not have to listen to anything that she said. Gabriella knew Gemma was struggling with all of the recent changes, they all were, but every time Gabriella tried talking to Gemma, it just seemed to make things worse.

Gabriella wished that she would have spent more time on her family than on her not-so-important life. She had only been home on mandatory weekend nights that were designated for family game night, and most of those had ended in Gemma and Gabriella fighting over who was cheating and winning. She had missed out on so much time that she could have spent with her mom and sisters together, and now she had been thrown into this role that she was not prepared for. She had not been a great big sister to Gemma or Giuliana, and that was definitely showing now with Gemma's attitude getting worse with every day that passed.

Gabriella had made steps in the right direction by turning on her phone again, trying to explain to her friends why she couldn't attend their going-away parties, why she herself was not going away, and why she was in fact okay with her decision. Her decision to put her sisters' needs first was the easiest one she'd made since her mother's death, but it seemed to receive the most backlash. No one could understand why an eighteen-year-old girl would put her life and dreams on hold to be the sole provider and caregiver to her sisters, but no one really knew Austin Knope. And if they did, Gabriella was sure they would not blink an eye and see why she'd had no other choice and she was the only one who was fit to raise them properly.

Even though she had emerged from hiding, she'd lamely sent Jason a text message saying that she wasn't ready to date yet and refused to talk any further about it. She had been doing a good job of avoiding his calls and his unannounced visits with the help of Giuliana telling him that she was taking a shower or that she wasn't feeling well. Her feelings for Jason scared her, and she didn't have the energy or the time to deal with them at the moment. He was never too far from her mind, though, and his face had been invading her dreams over the last week.

With the hearing approaching, Gabriella felt that her sole focus needed to be on her sisters, and nothing else. She had actually started to accept phone calls. There were a few calls from Mr. Morgan, trying to pin her down, a few from the Thrones, assuring her they would be there for her, and some from nosy neighbors who wanted the inside scoop.

Gabriella looked up at the clock in the kitchen. She had two hours before Mr. Morgan was due to arrive. She decided that she would make another attempt to make Gemma talk with her, whether she liked it or not. Gabriella walked into the living room where she found Giuliana reorganizing her backpack again. "What are you doing?"

Giuliana barely glanced up. "Oh, I have to make sure I am prepared for Monday."

"Oh." Gabriella laughed. "What was wrong with the way you had it?"

Giuliana let an annoyed sigh. "Nothing, but I need to double-check my list." She looked up and rolled her eyes at Gabriella's lack of understanding. "Gabby, you can never be too prepared for the first grade."

Gabriella laughed again at her sister's enthusiasm. "You know, you have reorganized your backpack at least four times today."

Giuliana finished counting her pencils before responding, "You just don't understand."

Gabriella thought about making a retort, but she decided to let Giuliana have her fun. "I guess not." Gabriella then heard Gemma stomping down the stairs in case anyone thought there was any mistake that she might be in a good mood. The only time Gabriella saw Gemma was mealtime and that was never pleasant. Gabriella wasn't sure how to handle Gemma, but she had to try.

"Hey Gem," Gabriella called from the living room. "Come in here for a second, please." Gabriella realized that the consequences of this could be dire, but she couldn't concern herself with how uncomfortable the situation may be; she had to help her sister in whatever way that she could. She could hear Gemma approaching with each stomp harder than the last. As Gemma got closer, she heard her swearing under her breath. It almost sounded like a growl.

Gemma looked annoyed, offended, and potentially violent. There was no hint of a smile anywhere on her face, and there hadn't been for a few good days. "What do you want?" she asked through gritted teeth.

Gabriella took in a deep breath and said as nicely as she could, "Please sit down."

Gemma glared back at her sister, but surprisingly she obeyed and sat down on the couch.

"Baby steps," Gabriella whispered to herself.

"What?" Gemma snapped.

Gabriella decided to reveal her strategy to Gemma. She might be grateful for the advice. "Baby steps," she repeated.

Gemma looked overly agitated as if she were trying to decide whether to storm off or just punch Gabriella in the face. "What the hell does that mean?"

"It means," Gabriella said, irritated with Gemma's temper, "I know you are hurting, and we are hurting, so if we take baby steps, maybe everything won't seem like such a huge task. We can feel better about the smaller things that we do. For example, you sat down on the couch, baby step."

Gemma jumped up at once. "I don't need your stupid baby steps," she screamed. "I'm fine."

"Really." Gabriella stood up next to her so they were at the same eye level. "Well, let's see, you haven't been nice to anyone for about a week now. You snap at poor Giuliana if she breathes the wrong way, or you snap at me if I look at you in the wrong way. You won't talk to me, you won't talk to your friends, and you have no interest in seeking any professional help, and you have no interest in going back to school. So tell me, please. Please tell me what you need." Gabriella didn't mean to get so upset and raise her voice so much, but she didn't know what else to do. Gemma had no respect for her, and she had no problem making it an obvious fact known to all who walked into their home.

Gemma looked furious. Her face was red, and tears stung her eyes. "Gabriella, you wait," she threatened. "Wait until you read what she wrote." The tears came in full force now, and Gemma collapsed on the couch. She let out a cry loud enough to get Giuliana's attention.

"Gem." Gabriella tried to sit next to her, but Gemma curled up and jerked away. "Gemma, please don't shut us out," Gabriella pleaded. "We have to stick together. We are all we've got."

Gemma looked at her through the tears. "You think you are so strong? Well, wait until you read what she wrote for you when you get married or when you graduate from college; you won't be strong then."

"You think I am strong?" Gabriella pointed directly to her heart. "I am dying inside. I miss her too. We all do."

"You don't know how I feel," Gemma screamed. "Stop pretending to be her."

"*What*?" Gabriella was dumbfounded. "I couldn't be her if I wanted to. I am just trying to do the best that I can do, and honestly I don't know what the hell I am doing." Gabriella began to cry with Gemma.

"You are always telling me what to do. You want me to be a mini you, and it isn't going to happen." Gemma stood up and prepared to storm out.

"Gemma, if you walk away you will be sorry." Gabriella stood up with as much confidence as she could muster. "Gemma, I am telling you right now that you have to respect me. I am in charge, and if we do not work together, this is not going to be easy."

"Gabby, I don't respect you." Gemma looked around for something to throw at her sister.

"Both of you stop right now!" Giuliana yelled at the top of her lungs. They stopped shouting at each other at once.

"Do you think that Mommy would want us to fight like this?" Giuliana's voice was firm. "No, she would not. You both need to get along with each other." Giuliana, the youngest by far, was now the most mature in the household, it seemed.

Gabriella felt a rush of guilt take over, and she took a deep breath. "Giuliana, I am sorry. You are right." Gabriella gave Giuliana a tight squeeze, and then turned her attention to Gemma. "Gemma, I am sorry I was so harsh. There is no excuse for that. We are all hurting and mourning in different ways. I need to respect you just as much as I expect you to respect me. This is going to be an adjustment, and I need to realize things are not ever going to be like they once were. We need to find a new normal." Gabriella was praying silently to herself that Gemma would accept her apology.

Gemma's expression did not look favorable. She did not look like she cared what Gabriella had to say, or Giuliana for that matter. Gemma grunted and muttered under her breath. She threw herself on the couch and crossed her arms tightly across her chest. It looked like she was searching for something to say, but she said nothing and buried her face in her hands.

Gabriella moved over to her and took Gemma in her arms, rocking her back and forth and humming. Gabriella's tears began to flow freely, and Giuliana laid her head on their laps.

"I miss her so much," Gemma sobbed. She sounded in pain, as if someone was causing her physical harm. "It's not fair. She should be here."

"It's not," agreed Gabriella. "But anger is not the answer." She stroked the back of Gemma's head. She knew that Gemma was not angry with her, but angry with life and God. Gemma stopped rocking with Gabriella and sat straight up, causing Giuliana to move. She sat in silence for a moment, searching her thoughts. "I know that you are try-ing, Gabby. I know…" She paused again to figure out what she wanted to say. She looked up at the ceiling and took in a deep breath. "I don't mean to be so mean and hateful. I just feel so angry all the time. I feel like I was robbed of a mother, and all I have left are those stupid letters that just make me miss her more."

"But being angry is not going help anyone. Those letters were not meant to torture you. They're meant to be something to help you through when things get tough and you need her. We were lucky to have her as long as we did, and we just have to do what we can to keep her memory alive. Think of all the memories as happy times and blessings, and don't let them upset us because they are glimpses of our mother, and her beautiful life." Gabriella wasn't sure where she'd summoned the courage from, but she was grateful.

Gemma hugged her sister tightly. "Gabby, I am so sorry. I know that you're trying, and I have not made any of this easy on you."

"Don't take this wrong way," Gabriella began in a gentle tone, "but if you want to talk to someone like a therapist, it's nothing to be ashamed of, and it could help you."

Gemma nodded. "It's hard to move on. I know when I go back to school, everyone is going to be asking me how I am doing and what really happened, and what you are up to." The tears crept back into her swollen eyes. "I just don't think I'm ready for that."

Gabriella understood. She wasn't sure if she would want to go back to school under the circumstances. They did live in a very small town, and she was sure word had gotten around about their mother's untimely pass-ing. Gabriella was also positive that the upcoming legal battle was in the mouth of every housewife across Laking, Ohio. "Gem, we can't change when school starts." Part of Gabriella wanted to give in to Gemma's desire not to attend, but she knew that would not solve anything. "You have to go."

"I know," Gemma replied.

"See, this is what Mommy would have wanted," Giuliana said from the floor.

Gemma and Gabriella exchanged looks and chuckled at their younger sister's newfound maturity.

"Okay, guys." Gabriella stood up, shaking out the nerves. "Mr. Morgan will be here shortly, so we need to clean up a little bit."

They nodded, and Gemma took Giuliana upstairs to straighten up her room.

Gabriella was alone once again, alone with her thoughts. She glanced around and saw pictures of her mother looking back at her. She wanted to think it was her mom's way of telling her everything was going to be okay. She was going to make it. Gabriella's confidence level fluctuated from day to day. Some days she felt like she could conquer the world, and the next day she would feel like she were inches from losing control. Gabriella sighed and closed her eyes. She wondered about what Gemma had said, how she would feel when she read all of her mother's letters. A clear image of Clare danced in Gabriella's mind. She saw her twirling around with a broom, laughing and pretending to sing. Tears came back into her eyes. The image stayed with her, and she did not want to let it go. Gabriella hoped that her mother was watching over her. She sighed deeply and began preparing for Mr. Morgan's visit.

One hour later Mr. Morgan arrived, right on schedule. He wore the same brown suit with a mustard-stained shirt, a tie that his grandchildren had obviously picked out, and the same ratty briefcase in hand.

"Good afternoon, Gabriella." Mr. Morgan removed his hat as Gabriella ushered him in.

"Hello," she replied. She led him into the kitchen, where she had brewed a pot of coffee and prepared a few finger snacks. She had done her best to make sure she looked to be a mature young woman about to take on one of the most powerful men in Laking. "Can I offer you a cup of coffee?" Gabriella asked before she sat down.

"No, no, thank you." He held up his hand. "Gabriella, let's get right down to business."

"Okay." Gabriella's voice was shaky. She was a ball of nerves; there was so much riding on the hearing, Austin's actions, her actions, and what Mr. Morgan had to say.

"Gabriella, I know that you decided that you did not want to marry despite my advice," he said, sounding a bit annoyed, "but I think we can salvage the situation." Mr. Morgan pushed up his glasses and pulled folders from his briefcase.

"Sir, with all due respect, it is not the eighteen hundreds. I am not ready for marriage, and I think it was pretty irresponsible on your part to ask me to make such a rash decision. A judge would look at that like a rash, irresponsible decision. I do not need a husband, and I want you to remember that you work for me, so please treat me with a little respect as well." Gabriella's confidence had apparently carried over from this morning.

Mr. Morgan barely acknowledged her statement. "Austin Knope has acquired Mary Thompson as his attorney. Her reputation speaks for itself. She has lost only one case in her fifteen-year career. She is tough, but so am I. I need you to trust me and my experience and do not question my advice."

Gabriella felt the anger start to boil inside of her. "Mr. Morgan, I feel that I don't have anything to fear as long as I am honest. I am eighteen years old. I am not going to marry someone before I am ready. I don't need the stress of an arranged marriage when I am trying to take care of my sisters." Her self-confidence was at a new high. "I know I am young, but Austin is a liar, a bad father, and he had an affair with my mother. That can't possibly look good for him."

Mr. Morgan looked at her as if it were the first time he had seen her all day. He studied her, looking for a sign of weakness or possible cue cards behind him. "Gabriella, what you are saying has merit, but you have to realize that Austin is the father of the minor children in question. The only reason this case has a chance of succeeding is because Austin did not sign your birth certificates. But it is well known and never denied that he is indeed your father, and you carry his last name. He has a lot more money than you do, and in a case like this, money talks. It talks a lot. This is going to be an uphill battle the whole way."

Gabriella nodded. Mr. Morgan was not telling her anything she did not already know. She knew from the moment that Austin had said he wanted Giuliana and Gemma to live with him that none of this would be easy. Gabriella knew that she had a fight in her future, but she was willing to do what needed to be done.

"Gabriella, are you listening?" Mr. Morgan interrupted her thoughts.

"Yes," she barked.

Mr. Morgan ignored her tone and continued. "We have a meeting that will take place next Friday. This is so we can sit down with a mediator, no judge or courtroom. Just you and Austin, and the lawyers," Mr. Morgan explained. "We want to see if we can reach a settlement without the use of a judge." Mr. Morgan paused to let Gabriella grasp what he was telling her.

"So," Gabriella said, trying to wrap her head around it. "We have to meet with Austin before we can see a judge?"

"Yes," Mr. Morgan replied. "Can I trust you to keep your emotions in check?"

Gabriella knew he wanted to hear a definite yes, but if she was being honest, she could not promise that. She knew that if Austin said something to offend her mother, her sisters, or herself, she would probably snap. Gabriella's thoughts swirled up at once. "Can I bring someone to be with me for moral support?"

"Yes," Mr. Morgan told her encouragingly, "I recommend it. I think that is a great idea." He sifted through his paperwork. "Now I would like to go over what I expect of you at the meeting next Friday."

Gabriella nodded, took a deep breath, and gave Mr. Morgan her full attention.

"First off," he said, beginning what was going to be an incredibly long list, "you must make a great first impression because it will account for a lot of your character profile. There will be a representative from social services, a court reporter, and a mediator. All will make their own recommendations to the judge, if we make it to court. You must present yourself as a *responsible* adult." He emphasized the word "responsible." "I think it would be best if you had a job by then. I know you are a courier for the newspaper, but I suggest you move on to a full-time position." He wanted to make sure she was taking mental notes. "Under no circumstances," he said, raising his voice, "should you lash out at Austin." To Mr. Morgan, this was his most important statement. "I understand your feelings toward him, and quite honestly, I do not blame you, but trust me, those outbursts will not help you in legal proceedings; if anything, they will only weaken your case."

Gabriella gulped. "Mr. Morgan." She feared she already knew the answer, but she had to ask. "What are my chances?"

He removed his glasses and massaged his temples. "Gabby, this is an odd case, and I am going to be honest with you. The chances are slim." He let out an exasperated breath. "I am not telling you this to discourage you, but I want you to be aware of what we are up against. Austin is a powerful man in this town. I think that if you two can work out a custody arrangement without getting a judge involved, then you and your sisters will be much better off."

"There is no arrangement. They live with me; that is the only option. You can't—I can't—let him take them from me." Her voice broke, and she had to choke back tears. "He only cares right now because he thinks it will look good for his image. His next political campaign. He doesn't love us. I know that, and I am afraid once he has custody of them, he won't love my sisters like they deserve, and we have already lost so much." Gabriella stood up. "I am not going down without a fight," she declared.

Mr. Morgan smiled at her confidence. "Keep your spirits high, and if you remain positive, and like you said, honest, then you should not worry."

"Mr. Morgan, thank you for everything," she said politely.

As Mr. Morgan started gathering his papers, he stopped and looked at her. "Gabriella, can I be frank with you?" he asked.

Gabriella nodded. "Of course."

"No one wins in custody battles," he said. "Maybe try to compromise with Austin a little."

Something inside of her snapped. She was tired of the way people gawked over Austin Knope as if he were some sort of prodigy. She was tired of people telling her what she could and could not do. She felt like Mr. Morgan had no faith in her. "Mr. Morgan, can I be frank with you?" Her anger boiled over. "If you do not believe, or you do not want to win my case, you need to let me know so I am not wasting my money. I need a lawyer, not someone who is afraid of Austin Knope." She folded her arms sternly across her chest and stood with poise and confidence.

Mr. Morgan stared, almost like he was waiting for an apology, but sensing that was an unlikely result, he tried a different approach. "Gabriella, you are angry right now, and probably scared."

Gabriella cut him off. "Yes, Mr. Morgan, I am. I am scared, but I am not going to walk away. Austin has done that one too many times. And yes, I am angry that my lawyer is telling me that I haven't got a chance in hell to win." She had enough. "The world is against me, but I will prevail. So if you are not on board, then there is the door, and I will find someone else."

Mr. Morgan nodded. "Gabriella, if you will accept my apology, you are absolutely right. I will show more faith in you. Your spirit reminds me a great deal of your mother. You are more like her than you know. I would very much like the opportunity to represent you and help you win this case." Mr. Morgan bowed his head in her direction.

Gabriella sensed that Mr. Morgan was seeing her as an adult for the first time. "Mr. Morgan, to be clear," she said, "I will not be getting married. I may yell at Austin Knope, but I will try to remain calm. I will tell the truth, and I will do what I need to win this case for my family."

He nodded without protest. "I know you will." He stared at her. "Gabby, your mother raised a beautiful daughter, and I know from the bottom of my heart, she would be immensely proud of you."

Gabriella saw a single tear fall from Mr. Morgan's eye. She blushed at his heartfelt compliment before walking him to the door and bidding him good-bye.

It was the last weekend before her sisters started school, and she had one week until she had to face Austin Knope. She feared that he would win and there was nothing she could do about it. She feared he would take everything away from her, and she feared that she would be alone forever.

13

Gabriella took the first day of school as an opportunity to scour theLak-ing, area for a full-time job. Andrew Speck at the *Laking Daily Journal,* where she currently worked as an errand girl, could not offer her a full-time position, and her current position could not accommodate her newly minted schedule. Gabriella had a few interviews scheduled, and she was confident that something would pan out. She had been to the bank and a financial advisor that morning as well. She had made some investments with the money that her mother had left them to ensure Gemma and Giuliana's chance for higher education. Even though she had enough money for their immediate future, she had to think long-term about the years of groceries, taxes, utilities, and other day-to-day expenses.

Gabriella finally made it back home with a few hours to spare before her sisters would be home from school, and with all of her interviews scheduled for the coming days and the house already taken care of, she found herself to be bored. She thought hard about what she could do, but nothing came to mind. She would have been away at college, probably sitting in a lecture hall at the moment, but everything was different now. She was different.

Gabriella wandered up the stairs in to her room. It had not changed from this morning. She had gotten pretty good at making sure it was somewhat tidy. Her clothes were picked up, the bed was made, and everything was in its place. She sat down on her bed, looking around for something to occupy the time. Her eyes drifted over to her desk. Her desk was the place where she spent the most time, probably more time than her own bed. She could spend hours upon hours just writing, but she could never bring herself to finish anything. She never felt like her work was good enough. She used to think that a great story would just come to her and she would not be able to stop writing, but now that hope seemed dismal. She got up from the bed and walked the few steps over to her desk. Papers were sticking out from folders, sticky notes with fun words she'd come across were placed sporadically on the desk and walls, and an envelope with her name scribbled across it was visible from the drawer that was slightly ajar. She sat down on the antique chair, which had small splinters of wood missing and creaked with every movement. An odd sensation of comfort consumed her. She assumed it must be seeing her mother's handwriting; it had become her antidote for everything. Gabriella had done well not to open the letters before she was meant to, but she wondered if there might be something in there to help her prepare for Friday, the day she must face Austin. The reality was that she was in fact a teenager very angry with her father. She pulled out the envelope and started sifting through the letters.

Gabriella was looking for one that might say *"Day before court case"* or *"You can do anything,"* but instead she found one titled *"When you are feeling down."*

"Well," Gabriella said out loud, "thanks, Mom." She looked up toward the ceiling and then out the window. She was wondering if this is what people meant when they said they could feel someone with them. Gabriella felt Clare's presence. She could feel her love; she felt like Clare's hands were on top of hers, guiding her to open the envelope. A small tear fell from her eye. Her hands trembled as she pulled out the precious paper and unfolded it. She took in a deep breath as the words were revealed, only to be interrupted by the sound of her phone ringing.

She wanted to throw it across the room, but she remembered it could be someone calling about a potential job. It could also be someone at Giuliana or Gemma's school contacting her because they had gotten in trouble or sick, or maybe Gemma had snapped at someone for asking about their mom's death. She rummaged around in her purse for it. "Yes," she said to herself as she retrieved it from the depths of her bottomless pit.

Jason's name was flashing across the screen. She hesitated. What would she say when she answered? She had been avoiding him since last week. She could say that she'd been busy, which was true, but what would be her excuse for the text message she sent him? Since then she had basically fallen off the grid where Jason was concerned.

She was too late; the phone stopped ringing. Now she would have to be the one to make the call. She held the phone a little longer to see if he would leave a voicemail, but to her surprise the phone rang again, causing her to drop it on the floor. She scooped it up quickly so not to miss her chance again.

"Hey Jason, sorry—I didn't get to my phone in time," Gabriella said quickly.

"Oh, I just figured you were still ignoring me," he said, his voice somber.

"No, I am not ignoring you." Gabriella tried to play dumb. "I've just been busy," she said lamely. She sensed the urge to come up with more excuses, and she rambled on, "My sisters started school today, so I have been dealing with that. Mr. Morgan came over last Friday to go over stuff for this big meeting I have to have with Austin before we go to court. I've been looking for a job, full-time—apparently being an errand girl isn't responsible enough—and I've just been busy, trying make the best of all this for them."

Jason laughed in a mocking way. "Really, busy? Do you know how many times I've used that excuse?" he asked. "Of course you do, because I tell you about it every time," he answered for her.

"Jas," Gabriella began, not wanting to lie to her best friend, but also not wanting to hurt him.

"Gabby." He sighed. "Just talk to me. I haven't heard from you since you sent me that text. So I know something is up. I miss you. I miss my best friend."

A warm rush illuminated her cheeks to a rosy red. He missed her, and he still wanted to be her friend. She didn't know what to say, she didn't know how to respond; she was sure that she had probably ruined their friendship with that kiss. That kiss. Her thoughts went back and relived the moment as if it were happening right now. She started to wonder what he was wearing, what he was doing, and if he would ever take her in his arms again.

"Gabby, are you there?" Jason asked, sounding worried.

"Yeah, sorry," she replied, remembering she was on the phone. "I was thinking."

"About?" Jason asked.

Gabriella blanked; she couldn't think of anything to say without sounding lame. "Umm..." Her voice trailed off.

She heard him take in a deep breath before he spoke. "Gabby, I am not mad at you at all, if that's what you're thinking. I know you are going through a lot right now, and I just want to be there for you, and if you only want to be friends, then that's that, but don't shut me out."

"You don't think things will be weird between us?" She didn't want to lose what they had.

"Well, yeah," Jason said honestly. "I do think it will be weird if we have to fight our feelings for each other a little longer, but I don't think it is anything that we can't deal with."

She laughed, knowing that he was probably right. Part of her wanted to move their relationship to the next level, but she just didn't feel ready to explore the possibility. Even though in her heart she knew that she was in love with her best friend. It was complicated.

"Gabby," Jason began, sounding hopeful that the silence didn't mean that she had hung up the phone. "Can I stop by as I find my way home from under all these books—"

"Find my way home," she repeated. Something about that phrase made something in her mind go off. She wasn't sure what it was, but she could not stop repeating it to herself over and over. "Um. No, not right now, I have a few things to do, but would you mind coming to the meeting with me on Friday morning?" Gabriella knew she would need his support, and she did not want to leave anything up to chance.

"Of course," Jason answered without hesitation. "Are you sure you don't want me to come over?"

Gabriella wanted him to come over, but she did not trust herself to be completely alone with Jason. She wasn't ready to let her guard down all the way. "I have a few errands to run before I pick up Giuliana and Gemma, but how about later tonight?"

"Awesome, I'll be over a little later then, around five-thirty." He sounded excited. "I'll help you fix dinner, or better yet, I will fix you dinner tonight," he added. "Then you can fill me in on everything."

She smiled at his enthusiasm, but realizing he could not hear a smile, she said, "I can't wait."

"All right, so I will see you around five-thirty then, okay?" Jason asked her.

"Yep, sounds great. See you soon." Gabriella's heart fluttered with excitement as she hung up the phone. She could not wait to see him.

Gabriella smiled and looked out the window. The hot summer was beginning to fade. The flowers were stretched to soak in the last of the sunlight, and there were already a few leaves that had made the change and fallen from the trees. She thought back to the times when they would all rake the leaves together. At first it would be a heinous task that no one but Clare wanted to do, but they would give in eventually. And at the end, there wasn't a dry eye because they were laughing uncontrollably from jumping in and out of the leaf piles together. They would submerse themselves until not a tiny scrap of clothing could be seen from the outside.

Her thoughts came back to the present, and she glanced over and once again saw the beautiful scrawl that had come from the hand of her mother. Gabriella walked back over to the rickety old chair and sat down. She pondered to herself if she should read the letter, because she wasn't feeling as sad as she was earlier, but she thought of the advice and power she would need when it came to the meeting on Friday. She let the temptation take over, and she began to read:

Dear Gabby,

You are reading this letter because I am not there to give you advice, to boost your spirits, and knowing you, you are most likely being faced with a tough decision (please don't buy mod clothes; they were not cool in the sixties, and they are definitely not cool now). If I didn't just solve the biggest dilemma you will struggle with in your life, it must be pretty serious. You are most likely facing a problem that you cannot research the answer to in a book, or confide in a friend. It may be something that only a mother can help you with, and since I am no longer there with you in the flesh, I will do my best through words to help you through this tough time.

I could go on for days telling you how great of a daughter you are. How poised and graceful you are. How much I admire your big heart, and how sometimes I wished I had your sense. I know you will make mistakes, but that is the beauty of humanity and life. So I hope you do make mistakes, but do not let them define you. Let them make you stronger. Something you may look at now as a mistake you may look back later on in your life and say it was the smartest decision of your life. This also works vice-versa. Let your mistakes help you learn to your fullest potential. Gabriella, I knew from the moment you were born that you were destined for greatness. Anything that you put your mind to, you can achieve. I want you to do things for yourself, not for me.

I will be proud beyond measure no matter what you do as long as you are happy (this excludes drugs and murder ☺). Even though you are feeling down at this moment, and you feel I am the only one that can help you, I don't have the answers, sweetheart. But I know that you have the answers. They may not appear right away, but search your heart, and they will come to you. Without failure we would not have determination, and without determination we would not have hope. Gabriella, keep your head up and know that I am watching over you and your sisters. I love you dearly, and I miss you more than you know, but someday in the kingdom of heaven, we will meet again.

Love always and forever,
Your mother,
Clare Marie LaFrace

PS: Don't forget your greatest strength is writing—if you can't find the answer, maybe you should start writing and it will come out.

Gabriella found herself crying once again, but this time they were tears of joy and sadness mixed into one. Her heart smiled that her mother could still make her laugh and guide her in the right direction, but at the same time, it broke because Gabriella would never be able to thank her for the gifts that she left behind. Gemma was right—reading the letters would make it harder to move on, but her mother was still guiding her, so in a way she wasn't gone. She was still there with them.

Gemma and Giuliana returned home from school, and they were eager to share their adventures from their first day of school. Giuliana babbled on about the politics of first grade and how she already held an esteemed position. Gemma admitted that going back to school wasn't as bad as she thought it would be.

Gabriella was surprised at how much homework Giuliana had for only being in the first grade. Gabriella could not remember having homework until her sophomore year of high school.

"Giuliana, are you working or playing?" Gabriella called from the kitchen.

"When are you coming back into the living room?" Giuliana yelled back.

"Now!" Gabriella put down the cleaner and headed back into the living room.

"Oh well, I am working then," Giuliana called back innocently.

"Yeah, yeah," Gabriella said, entering the room to find Giuliana shoving some toys underneath the couch. "Gemma," Gabriella called up the stairs.

"Yeah?" she answered back.

"Can you come downstairs please?" Gabriella yelled back. She heard Gemma making her way down, but in no particular hurry.

"What's up?" Gemma asked.

"Can you keep—" Gemma didn't give her a chance to even ask.

"Why are you so dressed up? Why did you change your clothes?" Gemma demanded.

Gabriella's face turned pink. "I am not dressed up. I just changed because I spilled something on my shirt," she lied.

"Right." Gemma rolled her eyes.

"Whatever," Gabriella said, annoyed. "Can you keep an eye on Giuliana and make sure she does her homework while I straighten up the kitchen?"

"Sure, if you want to tell me what is really going on, and why you look like you are ready for some sort of date," Gemma teased.

"Gemma, I spilled something on my shirt, and I am out of clean clothes, so that is all that's going on." Gabriella knew that Gemma was not going to drop it, so she tried to make a quick exit back to the kitchen.

"Oh Gabby," Gemma called after her in a mocking tone. "Jason called while I was on the phone with Maggie, and he said he was running late." Gemma folded her arms in a satisfied fashion and waited for her sister to turn around and admit that she was right.

Gabriella's face turned red. She knew that she was probably way overdressed, and if Gemma got suspicious so quickly, then so would Jason. She began to feel embarrassed, and she didn't want to admit to her sister that she was indeed correct about the secret feelings that she had been harboring for Jason.

"Are you going to tell me what is going on?" Gemma asked again.

Gabriella took in a deep gulp of air and turned around to face her. "Nothing is going on. Jason is coming over to fix us dinner, that's it."

Gemma wasn't fooled for a second. "Really? Gabby, that is your"— she used air quotes to emphasize her meaning—"'look at me' shirt and 'wow, aren't my legs awesome' skirt." Gemma's smug smile spread across her face, signaling she felt she'd just won a battle of wits. "And today you are wearing both, and you expect me to believe that there is nothing going on with you and Jason?"

Gabriella gave her sister a warning look. "Jason and I are just friends."

"Right." Gemma rolled her eyes. "You think I was born yesterday?"

"Gemma!" Gabriella yelled. "I really do not want to have this conversation with you. Now drop it."

Gemma gave her an evil-looking smirk. "Yep, that's all I needed to know. I knew you two couldn't be that close and be only friends."

Gabriella shook her head. She started looking for something to throw at her sister.

Giuliana laughed. "I think you two will get married someday."

Gabriella was caught slightly off guard. "What? Why do you think that?"

Giuliana rolled her eyes. "Because you love him, duh."

"What, Where do you get that from, we are just friends?" Gabriella never thought that there was that much flirtation between Jason and her. She wasn't even aware that she had feelings for him until recently, but it seemed that her two sisters had known all along.

"Be-*cau*-se." Giuliana drew out every syllable to make sure Gabriella understood her. "You love him."

"Giuliana," Gabriella began only to be cut off again.

"Gabby, don't try. You love him, just like Gemma loves that boy band kid from England." Giuliana continued working on her worksheet without missing a beat.

Gemma's face turned bright red, and she looked at Gabriella to punish her in some way for what she had just said, but Gabriella found it hilarious, and she didn't think that Giuliana should be punished for being honest. Honesty was Giuliana's signature trait; she told it how it was, and she never apologized.

"Giuliana," Gemma whined, "you shouldn't go telling people that all the time. You need to watch what you say."

"Oh man." Giuliana sat up. "You guys are weird. At least I didn't say you were in love with that boy Brad in your class. The one you are always talking about to Angie on the phone."

Gemma looked like she was going to pounce on Giuliana and try to pull her vocal cords out so she could not reveal any more secrets. "Giuliana!" Gemma screamed.

"All right, that is enough." Gabriella stepped between them, trying to suppress her urge to laugh. "None of this leaves this room. When Jason comes over, let's not talk about who loves whom, and all the rumors we hear." She turned to look at Giuliana. "Rumors don't make friends. You might need to think a little bit before you say something like that out loud, because it may not be true."

Giuliana started to say something but decided against it, and she nodded.

Gabriella turned to Gemma. "Are you good?"

"Whatever, sure." Gemma was looking at Giuliana to warn her that payback would be coming.

"Okay." Gabriella eyed them both suspiciously. "Then we are all going to be on our best behavior?"

Gemma and Giuliana smiled at each other and nodded. Gabriella feared that they were secretly planning to do everything they could think of to embarrass her in front of Jason. They seemed to be under the impression that it would be hysterical, but Gabriella most certainly did not agree. She didn't want to make things more awkward between them than they already were. She told herself to think happy thoughts and relax, and she started to clean nervously until he arrived.

An hour later the doorbell was ringing with Jason waiting on the other side. She felt her stomach begin to flutter with a swarm of butterflies, but this time Gabriella had had time to prepare for Jason's arrival. She had fixed her hair so that there wasn't a flyaway, she had ensured her makeup was perfect, and she was wearing, just as Gemma had said, her "look at me" shirt and "don't I have amazing legs" skirt. She peeked down the stairs, waiting to hear Jason come inside. She heard Gemma talking and laughing and the sound of the door closing; that was her cue.

Gabriella wanted to make an entrance when she entered the living room. She wanted to make it a moment, like in the movies. She wanted to be sure to have his attention. She held her head up high and began a slow, sexy walk with her arm extending just enough to graze the handrail. She peeked down to get a glimpse of the man she was in love with, but Jason was nowhere to be seen. Her heart sank when she heard Gemma and Giuliana laughing hysterically in the kitchen. She sighed at the results of her over-the-top effort and her dismal entrance.

"Hey Jason," Gabriella said as she entered the kitchen. She closed her eyes and flipped her hair back in a slow-motion sort of way and gave Jason a seductive smile.

He barely glanced up "He—" Dumbfounded, he stopped in the middle of the word. He was looking at her as if it was the first time he had ever seen her.

Gemma laughed and rolled her eyes. "So, Gabby." She gave her sister another smug look. "You look really nice. What is the occasion?"

Gabriella glared at her. "I told you earlier," she said, forcing a smile, "I am out of my casual clothes. I need to do laundry."

"Right." Gemma rolled her eyes and went back to tearing up lettuce for the tacos.

"Wow." Jason nodded his head in approval. "You look incredible."

Gabriella blushed and looked at her feet. "Thanks."

"So, laundry problems?" Jason asked, giving Gabriella the same look Gemma had.

"Yes," Gabriella said quickly. "What can I do to help?" She tried changing the subject.

Jason winked at her, knowing full well what she was up to. "Start cutting up the tomatoes."

Gabriella walked toward him in a come-hither sort of way. She reached out to take the tomatoes from him. As their hands touched, it sent a warm wave through her body, and she smiled and made sure he watched her as she walked away.

Gemma openly rolled her eyes and gave a sigh of disgust. "Oh god."

Jason and Gabriella turned a bright shade of red, but they chose to ignore Gemma's outburst and went on like nothing was said.

"So, Jason," Gabriella began. "How is college?"

He nodded. "It's not too bad, I only go three days a week."

"Three days," Gemma whined. "That is not fair!"

"You will be there soon enough." Jason winked at her.

Gemma continued to whine, but Gabriella was too intoxicated to hear what Gemma was saying. Jason's oceanic scent filled the room; he himself was well dressed in a pair of pants that defined his shape and a collared shirt that seemed to be more filled out, as if he had been working out. His hair was stacked neatly; his shave was clean, highlighting his already distinct cheekbones, and with every curl of his mouth, small dimples appeared that made Gabriella go weak at the knees.

Gemma jabbed Gabriella in the ribs to let her know she was practically salivating over Jason. Gabriella shook her head, trying to concentrate. She dropped the knife she was using and walked over to replace it with a clean one. Jason was standing in front of the drawer that contained the knives.

"I'll be right back," Gemma told them. "Come on, Giuliana, let's go wash our hands." Gemma led her out of the kitchen against Giuliana's wishes.

Gabriella seized the opportunity and leaned up against Jason, whispering, "Excuse you."

He smiled at her seductively. "Are you sure you want me to move?" He took her in his arms, causing her to let out a small squeal. He kissed her like he had the first time. They were becoming experts with each other's rhythm. It wasn't forced. He started to run his hands up and down her back, pulling her in tight. She let herself go, forgetting where she was. She wanted Jason to take her, and then suddenly he stopped kissing her.

"This can't be real," he whispered. He trickled kisses down her neck.

Gabriella heard the chatter from her sisters getting closer. He smiled at her and gave her a lingering look, but she forced herself to pull away from the most welcoming arms she had ever been in. Gabriella reached into the drawer and pulled out the knife. She wanted to smack herself for telling Jason that she wanted to take things slow. Why did she do that? Why was she trying to run away?

"All right, dinner is ready," Jason announced.

Dinner was a great time as they laughed and told silly stories. Gabriella looked around the table and saw Giuliana and Gemma laughing uncontrollably at Jason's stories. They looked happy, kind of like a normal family. Everyone melded together. Jason always brought out the best in everyone he was around. It was one of the many things that Gabriella loved about him.

"Jason, this is way better than when Gabby cooks," Giuliana confessed.

"Hey now." Gabriella laughed. "I cook just fine."

Jason and Gemma were laughing so hard they were almost choking on their food. They had to reach for their drinks to wash down the parts that got hung up in their throats.

"Well, it's a little better than it used to be, but Jason should come over more often and teach you how to cook better." Giuliana beamed at Jason.

Gabriella rolled her eyes. "Whatever."

"I don't mind coming over at all." Jason winked at Gabriella and rubbed his leg against hers under the table.

"All right," Gemma said, catching the slight embarrassment on Gabriella's face. "Are you finished?"

Giuliana rubbed her belly. "Yes, I'm stuffed."

"All right, let's go wash up." Gemma took Giuliana and led her out of the kitchen.

"Thanks for dinner, Jason," Giuliana said over her shoulder.

"No problem. See you guys later," Jason called after them.

"Thanks, Gemma," Gabriella called to her. She saw Gemma raise her hand in acknowledgement. Gabriella got up and started clearing the plates.

Jason watched her. He sat back for a moment and just smiled as she started to rinse dishes in the sink. "Do you need help?" Jason asked her.

"No, you cooked, I got this," Gabriella replied.

Jason got up to help anyway. He walked up behind her, wrapped his strong arms around her waist, and kissed her.

Gabriella was surprised she was able to keep her balance as his kisses made her knees buckle. "Jason, about what you said on the phone," she began. "Not being mad at me. Am I sending you mixed signals?" She laughed to herself and felt stupid for asking the question.

"Mixed signals," Jason repeated sarcastically. "No, not at all."

She playfully jabbed him in the shoulder. "I know, I'm sorry. I just feel like all of this is happening so fast. And our friendship is so important to me. I don't want to lose that, and if we go down this road—"

"Gabby." Jason turned her around to face him and brought his finger to her lips, and then he kissed her. She closed her eyes and got lost in his lips. His lips were a sweet nectar that she was quickly becoming addicted to. She bit her bottom lip and pulled away slightly so she could see his eyes. He was so close to her she could feel his breath on her face. He stroked her cheek with one finger. "Gabby," he said, staring into her heart through her eyes. "There is no way that we can kiss like that and it not mean something."

She knew that he was right, but it didn't change her fears. "Jason, I know and I agree to a point, but we have been friends for so long. You aren't somewhat worried about losing that if things go south?"

"Gab, there is not a doubt in my mind that this is going to be something great, and if things go south, I'm sure after some time we can go back to where we were four weeks ago." He pulled her in for a tight embrace.

She nodded, but she didn't know what else to say. Gabriella pulled away from him and busied herself with the dishes. She had just one more question, something that had been eating away at her, and something she needed to know the answer to, even if she did not agree with it. "Jason." She put the plate into the dishwasher and took in a deep breath. "How long would you say you've had feelings for me?"

He looked caught off guard by the question, but he smiled and laughed. He started picking up the rinsed dishes to put into the dishwasher. He seemed to be thinking of an exact date. He looked up at the ceiling and then down at her and flashed his charming smile. "I have always thought you were beautiful, and as you got older, you got more gorgeous." He paused, looking her up and down. "Gabby, I can tell you honestly I have always felt something for you besides friendship, but I couldn't fight it anymore after senior prom. I mean, you looked like a princess, and I had never seen anyone so beautiful, and you were my best friend." He turned a tad pink in the cheeks, and he began looking for something to busy himself with to avoid eye contact.

"I think I have been in love with you my whole life," she admitted. She couldn't believe she had said it out loud, but there it was. It was out in the open, and there was no time machine to take it back.

He stopped what he was doing and looked into her eyes. "You're in love with me?" Jason repeated in disbelief.

Gabriella loved Jason Throne, and she was not afraid to admit it any longer. "Yes, I do." Gabriella felt a weight being lifted off her shoulders. "My mom always used to tell me that I would know in my heart when I was in love, and there would be no question. She used to say that the boy you fall in love with, the one you are supposed to be with forever, will make you want to cry and laugh at the same time. I never understood what she meant by that until you kissed me." Gabriella paused for a moment, remembering that kiss and her mother's words of wisdom. "After that, there was no question that I was in love with you. I could not deny it any longer. I think I'd been lying to myself about it for a while." She stopped speaking. She could not believe how easy it was to tell him anything. She could be like Giuliana and talk to him without a filter because no matter what, he would understand. "I just did not want to admit that the rampant rumors about us were true. People always said that girls and boys can't be friends like we were without wanting something more. I guess I wanted to prove them wrong," she admitted.

He chuckled. "I know what you mean." Jason led her away from the kitchen and into the living room. They sat down on the sofa; he took her hand and started caressing it with his own. "Gabby, I wanted to ask you how long you had feelings for me, because I was worried that I was taking advantage of you," he confessed.

"Jason, no," she said at once. She understood where he could think that, though. They had decided to get married for five minutes, and then they were making out like it was the most normal thing in the world. "Jason, I want this to happen, and I am not sorry that it did." She smiled to assuage his doubts.

He nodded. "Gabby, don't take this the wrong way," he told her. "But I want to take things slow. You've been through a lot, and I don't want to rush this. I have never had a girlfriend for more than a couple of months. I know you were with Alex off and on for two years, but—"

Gabriella brought her fingers to his lips to silence him. "Jason, slow is good." She reached up and brought his head to hers and kissed him. His lips were so inviting and spellbinding. She could not get enough of his kisses.

"Gab." Jason pulled away slightly and started tucking loose strands of her hair behind her ear. "I want to take you out on a real date."

Gabriella blushed. There were very few things she wanted more than for Jason to take her out on a date. "Well, this week might be kind of difficult with the meeting and all."

Jason nodded. "Do you want me to pick you up for that?"

She smiled at him, feeling so lucky to be wrapped in his arms. "Yeah, sure, that would be great."

"How about Saturday I take you out on a real date? I'm sure my mom would watch Giuliana if you needed her to," Jason told her.

Gabriella wasn't going to argue. "That would be great." She was ready to start a normal relationship with Jason Throne. She couldn't believe it was happening. She was in love, and she felt happy; for once, she felt like everything was going to be okay. Jason pulled her in close and kissed her once more.

14

The next few days went by faster than expected, and Gabriella was not as well rested as she hoped she would be for today. She decided after the fourth snooze she could not put the day off any longer. She was going to have to face Austin Knope. She wasn't afraid, but she wasn't exactly confident, and the fear of losing her sisters that she had managed to push to the back of her mind had slowly crept back up to make its presence known. She wondered if it would make a difference if Jason was holding her hand or not when she was told that she was not fit to raise her sisters. She shook her head ferociously. "Positive thoughts," she whispered to herself. She knew the fears would only make her more anxious, and not in a good way.

Gabriella took a deep breath, finally pushed herself out of bed, and began to get ready for the day ahead. She dragged her feet along the carpet, stopping to look at herself in the mirror. She practiced a few smiles, trying to find the right one that made her look the most responsible. She flipped through her closet, trying to find an outfit that would say "I am responsible. I can take care of my two sisters who happen to be minors."

Gabriella had made strides in becoming more responsible. She had interviews lined up every day for full-time employment. She had almost gotten a schedule down for her sisters for school, and she had not woken up from nightmares in four days. It was the first week that she thought that she might be finding a new "normal." She had started to smile again, and it wasn't as forced as it had been in the previous weeks, and the thought of her mother didn't reduce her to inconsolable tears. It hurt to think that her mother wasn't there, but she found comfort in the words that Clare had left for her. Gabriella stretched her arms, took in a few deep breaths, got dressed, and started her morning routine.

She walked down the hall and poked her head inside of Giuliana's room. "Hey Giuliana, time to get up." Gabriella heard muffled, disgruntled noises coming out from underneath Giuliana's blankets. She was always the hardest to wake in the morning, and she did not keep it a secret that it was her least favorite time of day. Giuliana always begged Gabriella for ten more minutes, convinced it would make all the difference. Gabriella learned quickly that ten minutes in real time was much different than Giuliana's version of ten minutes. The first few days of the school year, Gabriella had given in and let her have the ten minutes, but that soon turned into twenty minutes, and then they were late. Gabriella walked in her sister's bedroom and sat down on the edge of her bed. "Giuliana, time to get up."

Giuliana tossed and turned in her bed. "Gabby," she said in a muffled voice, "I think it's the weekend."

Gabriella laughed loudly at her new approach. "I don't think so. Giuliana, get up; we've got a big day ahead."

Giuliana didn't budge.

"Don't make me get the bucket of water," Gabriella threatened.

Giuliana popped up at once. She had learned early in the week that Gabriella was not bluffing. Gabriella waited until she heard Giuliana turn on the shower before going downstairs to get her breakfast and lunch ready.

"Good morning, Gemma," Gabriella said as she entered the kitchen.

Gemma was helping herself to a bowl of cereal before she had to catch the bus. "Are you nervous?" she asked.

"About what?" Gabriella replied in casual tone.

Gemma rolled her eyes. "Really, Gabby? The meeting?"

"Oh, yeah, right." Gabriella shrugged her shoulders. "I guess not."

"Really?" Gemma wasn't fooled by her newfound confidence.

Gabriella let out a bothered sigh. "Well, being nervous isn't going to help me any, so I am just going to do what I have to, and that's that." She tried to discourage Gemma from talking about it any further by busying herself making Giuliana's lunch.

"You're different," Gemma said as she started to gather her notebooks for school.

"What?" Gabriella stopped what she was doing.

"You're different, and I know that you aren't telling me everything." Gemma met her sister's eyes. "Normally, you would be ready to have a panic attack. You are so calm and collected."

Gabriella laughed. "So let me see if I understand—you're worried because I am calm and collected."

"Yes," Gemma shrieked. "It's not like you."

"Well." Gabriella went back to making Giuliana's lunch. "I guess I have a new perspective on everything, and it's just been a good week, so today should go fine. I'm not worried." She wasn't being completely honest, of course, but there was no reason to make Gemma stress out about it too.

Gemma zipped her backpack up. "I guess Jason will be going with you."

Gabriella blushed slightly. "As a matter of fact—"

"You guys weren't doing much talking the other night," Gemma finished for her.

"Gemma." Gabriella's tone was harsh. "Don't start. We are just friends."

"Whatever," Gemma replied. "I guess that's why you are going out with him on Saturday night." She didn't give Gabriella a chance to respond. She waved and left for the bus stop.

Gabriella was left feeling embarrassed and annoyed. She didn't know why or how Gemma always seemed to get the best of her. Gabriella wasn't ready to tell anyone about her relationship with Jason until she knew what it was, and they had both agreed to keep it under wraps.

Giuliana came scurrying down the stairs with her own version of acceptable hair. Gabriella walked over to help her fix it while Giuliana ate her cereal.

"Are you excited for school today?" Gabriella already knew the answer.

"No," Giuliana replied, unimpressed. "Today is music class day, and I don't like it because it isn't real music."

"What do you mean?" Gabriella asked, trying to suppress her urge to laugh.

"Well." Giuliana sounded annoyed. "They don't even let us play on the triangles."

"Oh." Gabriella chuckled. "Well, maybe they will today."

"You never know," Giuliana said in between big bites of cereal.

There was a knock at the door, and there was Lee Ann Gable, peering through the open glass to see if she could see anything that would jumpstart her gossip for the morning.

Gabriella and Giuliana rolled their eyes. "All right, time to go." Gabriella helped her get her things together.

Giuliana whined, "I think she's really early today."

"No, she's right on time. You are late. Come on now; it's time to go." Gabriella pulled Giuliana to the door.

"Good morning, Gabby." Lee Ann's voice was overly cheerful to the point where it sounded rehearsed. She wore a sweater tied around her neck and way too much makeup, and her hair looked like she'd stepped out of a magazine from the eighties, Gabriella assumed that she had picked a new out of date decade to imitate. "How are you doing today?" She tried to cram as many questions and small talk into her twenty-second window that she could. "My, my, you look great. What do you have planned for today? Any luck on the job front?"

Gabriella always did her best to evade her questions, and usually Giuliana was cooperative enough that there was never enough time for a sit-down interview with the nosiest lady in town. "Oh, you know, Lee Ann, a little of this and a little of that," Gabriella said as politely as possible.

"Well, if you ever need anything at all, Gabby—" Lee Ann started to say.

"I will let you know," Gabriella finished for her. "Love you, Giuliana. I will see you at four today." She bent down and gave her sister a hug and a kiss, and then Giuliana left with Lee Ann for school.

Gabriella closed the door behind them, and she realized that today was the first day of the rest of her life. Today would set the tone for the coming year, and today would reveal if Austin Knope had grown some type of heart, or if he was adamant on making her life miserable.

She started to walk back into the kitchen to clean up the breakfast mess, but the doorbell rang again, and her heart skipped a few beats knowing exactly who was waiting on the other side. She pulled open the door and leapt into Jason's arms. She did not care who saw, and he apparently did not either, because he kissed her as if it had been weeks since they last saw each other. She wanted to do that every day for the rest of her life. She could not help but feel utterly happy as her lips intertwined with his. Gabriella thought at that moment that nothing could ruin her day; all of her fears had subsided, and she allowed herself to become engulfed in the sense of normality again, no matter how brief it was.

Gabriella and Jason arrived at the courthouse thirty minutes early, and they were surprised to see that Mr. Morgan was waiting outside on the steps for them. Gabriella checked her watch to make sure she was as early as she thought. Mr. Morgan was in his same attire, except the mustard stain was smaller than usual and his tie did a better job at covering it up.

"Good morning." Mr. Morgan shook Jason's hand, and Gabriella followed suit. Mr. Morgan smiled politely. "Ready?" He motioned her inside the building.

She nodded and took in a deep breath. Gabriella knew despite her positive thinking she was in for a rough road ahead. She knew it would be an uphill battle the whole way, but she was determined to prove to whomever she needed that she was the best to care for her sisters and not Austin Knope, who had no problem walking away from them in the past.

As soon as they entered the courthouse, Gabriella spotted Austin and his wife, Alice, talking quietly. He was dressed in an expensive custom-tailored navy suit and a yellow tie, and Alice was dressed in politician's wife attire: a nice dress suit with the perfect pearl necklace resting against her tiny neck. Gabriella looked down at her own outfit, wondering if she had made the right choice. She worried that her black dress with a white cardigan looked amateur.

Jason noticed her second-guessing herself. "You look great," he reassured her.

She smiled weakly at him. Even with Jason there, the fears crept back in and were more prominent than ever. She felt out of her league. She thought that everyone around her, including her own lawyer, probably thought she was a joke.

Austin flashed a toothy grin as they came near. He shook Mr. Morgan's hand. "Nice to see you again, Jacob."

"Mrs. Knope." Mr. Morgan smiled courteously at Alice and stretched his hand toward her.

"Good morning, Gabby." Austin shook his head with a rueful smile. "I mean Gabriella." He tried to meet Gabriella's eyes, but she refused to look at him.

"Good morning, Austin," Jason said, trying to ease the tension.

Gabriella felt Jason nudge her slightly, but she really didn't care. There were no court reporters or social workers. Austin's lawyer wasn't even there, so in her mind she did not have to be nice yet. She thought back to when she had actually slapped Austin, and an odd sense of relief washed over her. She felt that she had made a dent in his debt to her family after everything he had put them through. She felt Jason nudge her again. She sighed and cleared her throat, and with all of the effort she could muster, she said in a civil tone, "Good morning." Gabriella began to worry. If a simple hello took so much effort, how was she going to be able to hold a mature discussion when the time came?

After Alice's lame attempt to make small talk about the weather, the Knopes' attorney finally arrived. Mary Johnson was rushing over as if she were five hours late instead of five minutes. "Hello, Mr. Morgan, great to see you as always." Mary Johnson was a sophisticated woman with all the makings of a cutthroat attorney, according to Mr. Morgan, but Gabriella thought that she looked normal and friendly.

"Are we ready to proceed?" Mr. Morgan asked, motioning everyone toward an empty corridor.

"Yes, we are." Mrs. Johnson led the way. She gave Gabriella a broad smile and nodded in her direction. Gabriella returned the gesture.

Jason slowed to Gabriella's pace to hang back while the power couple followed Mr. Morgan and Mrs. Johnson. "Are you okay?"

She peered into his eyes and saw genuine concern. He had been there for her in ways that she never could have imagined. She beamed up at him, feeling a little more at ease that she did have someone on her side. "Yes, I am fine."

He looked around to make sure no one was watching him, and he pressed his lips against hers. Gabriella felt her whole inside shake, and a surge of happiness burst through her.

"We can do anything together," he whispered.

She blushed and followed him down the long corridor. As they walked Gabriella felt like she was in a museum, with all of the older portraits of the former judges and city councils of Laking, Ohio, looking down at her. It had been their one shot at fame, and they had probably sold their souls to the devil to make it in the dirty game of politics, Gabriella thought. She started to feel apprehensive about the meeting that was about to take place. She had been telling herself all along that she did not have anything to worry about and a judge would see who should keep her sisters, and that would be her, but what if she was wrong? What if they did not pick her? How would she explain that to Giuliana and Gemma, who'd have to adjust to losing their mother and the place they called home all in the same month? Gabriella felt a tear slide down her cheek. She immediately wiped it away without thinking and told herself, "Be strong, you can do this."

They reached the conference room, where a huge table with too many chairs stood in front of them. Mr. Morgan and Mrs. Johnson took seats on opposite sides of the table. There was a woman with a laptop, most likely to record everything that was said, and there was a man that Gabriella had never seen before, but Mr. Morgan and Mrs. Johnson seem to know him, so he must be someone important. Gabriella started to get a feeling in the pit of her stomach that she may have overestimated how far her hatred for Austin would take her. Jason grabbed her hand to offer some comfort, but it did not bring much. Gabriella was fighting the urge to cry hysterically and call out for her mother.

"Good morning, ladies and gentlemen. Please take your seats, and we will get started," the unidentified man stated.

Gabriella and Jason sat next to each other, and she caught Austin staring at her with what she thought was a smug smile across his face. Gabriella felt a rush of anger. She wanted to lash out and punch Austin as hard as she possibly could.

"My name is Harry Lawrence, and I will be your mediator today," he explained. "What is going to happen is your legal representatives will present both sides and the expectations of the parties involved. Then, if you do not agree upon the terms presented, then we will try to mediate the matter into a solution. If no solution can be met today, we will set a date for the court to hear your case. Do we all understand the terms?" Harry Lawrence looked from Austin to Gabriella, and they both nodded. "Mrs. Johnson, we will start with you. Proceed when you are ready." Harry Lawrence sat down in his chair and took out his pen to begin taking notes.

Gabriella made sure to make eye contact with Mrs. Johnson. She felt that Mrs. Johnson might have more sympathy for her and perhaps even refuse to represent Austin any longer after she found out what kind of man he really was.

Mrs. Johnson straightened her paperwork, like she was deciding on a starting point. She cleared her throat and began. "First of all, we want to deal with this matter with the utmost sincerity and sympathy. Gabriella, I am personally terribly sorry for your loss, and I do apologize for the added pressure." Mrs. Johnson grimaced sympathetically at Gabriella.

Gabriella managed a weak smile, and she gave Mrs. Johnson her full attention.

She cleared her throat again. "We feel that it would be in the best interest of Gemma and Giuliana Knope if they were in the full custody of Austin Knope, their biological father, and their stepmother, Alice Knope. We realize that this situation is untraditional due to the parenting circumstances, but in most cases, custody would not even be a question if one parent were to pass away unexpectedly when minor children are involved."

Tears swelled in Gabriella's eyes at the mention of her mother's death in such a casual manner. She felt Jason squeeze her hand to remind her that he was there.

Mrs. Johnson continued. "Austin Knope was never given his parental rights that should have rightly been given from the beginning. He is the undisputed father of all three of Clare LaFrace's children. There is no doubt, nor has there been any speculation, that Austin is not their father. We feel that Mr. Knope could provide a much more stable home for the two minor children in question, and Mr. Knope would like to let Gabriella know that she would be more than welcome to live with them, or come and visit whenever she pleases." Mary Johnson adjusted more papers and looked directly into Gabriella's eyes with a hard stare. There was no sympathy in her eyes now. "We feel that the home, plus the stable environment that Austin could provide, will not compare to the unstable environment that will inevitably be present if the minors remain in the custody of Gabriella Knope." Mrs. Johnson's tone was unemotional.

Gabriella's anger had been taken over by hurt. The things Mrs. Johnson was saying only Austin could have put into her mind. She knew she wasn't good enough for him. She wasn't worthy to be his daughter, but the other two, he wanted to know. She struggled with that question for a long time. Why them and not her? But Gabriella knew that after the victory of putting her down for good, he would walk away from them as he had done in the past. Why did he hate her so much? What had she done to deserve these words from her father? Why didn't he love her like he loved his other children?

She saw that Mary Johnson's lips were still moving. She must still be speaking. Maybe Gabriella had missed out on the exact verbiage of the insults, but she had gotten the gist. Austin Knope's ammunition was that Gabriella was an irresponsible and angry young girl who would provide an unsafe environment for two children to grow up in.

Gabriella tuned back into Mrs. Johnson's speech. "Let us be honest with one another. Gabriella Knope is only eighteen years old—that is barely old enough to vote. There is no way that she can care for two young adolescent children. The fact that her mother left her a substantial amount of money does not create the parental guidance that these children will so desperately need."

Mr. Lawrence looked to Mrs. Johnson to confirm that she was indeed finished with her speech. She nodded, and Mr. Lawrence then gestured to Mr. Morgan to begin.

Mr. Morgan patted Gabriella on the shoulder. She took in a deep breath, hoping he would redeem her.

"I would firstly like to say," Mr. Morgan began, "that Gabriella Knope is a young woman beyond her years in maturity. She has had to take on so much at her young age, and give up so much, but she does so with pride and understanding and being selfless enough to put her sisters' needs before her own. She is a better mother figure than many young mothers I have come in contact with." Mr. Morgan smiled warmly and gestured toward Gabriella. "Now, in the matter of custody of Gemma and Giuliana, Gabriella is the only suitable person to take such control. These young girls have already had to deal with a terrible loss; any more change could possibly stunt their social development. Gabriella knows Gemma and Giuliana better than anyone, and they do not need to deal with another adjustment. We feel that Austin Knope is not a suitable candidate for full custody, despite his so-called parental rights." Mr. Morgan used the air quotes. "Mr. Knope fully and blatantly abandoned his children and had no contact with them in the beginning part of their lives. In any normal court setting, Austin's record would be against him. Children are not an option, but a responsibility, which Austin chose to ignore until it was convenient for him." Mr. Morgan paused for a moment to collect his thoughts.

Gabriella felt a sense of victory fill her up and an unfamiliar confidence beginning to wash over her. She knew the truth would be the best way. Gabriella was best for her sisters, and anyone with a right mind could see that.

"We propose," Mr. Morgan continued, "Austin and Alice Knope could be granted visitation rights every other weekend, and Gabriella will retain sole custody. She will remain fully responsible and be considered their legal guardian." Mr. Morgan sat down to confirm that he had finished.

Mrs. Johnson looked a little shaken up. It was obvious that she'd thought that Mr. Morgan was an old goat who would not have an argument in his back pocket.

"Well, it appears we have separate ideas. Now, Mr. Knope and Ms. Knope, you may have the floor. Say whatever you feel necessary, and we will try to strike a compromise," Mr. Lawrence explained.

Austin spoke first before Gabriella could say anything. "Thank you." He nodded toward Mr. Lawrence. "Gabriella, I want to do what is best for you and your sisters. Someday I think you will fully understand and you will thank me. I cannot let you give up on your life. You have so much potential, and now you are going to flush it all away."

Gabriella rolled her eyes, and then she remembered where she was. She had to remain calm and speak clearly and professionally. She could not let her feelings get the best of her. She could not let Austin Knope win.

"Austin," she said, her tone cold and rigid, "I will not put myself first because of the so-called bad timing in my life. I will do what I need to because I feel—no, I *am*—the best thing for them. Let's be honest, Austin, Gemma and Giuliana barely know you, so how can you think forcing them to live with you is a good way to help them to get over our mother's death?" A small tear fell from her eye.

"Gabriella, I know that you are angry with me, and you are not thinking clearly," he replied with the deepest sincerity in his voice. "You don't have to give up your life to be a good sister, or a good daughter to your mother."

Anytime he mentioned her mother, Gabriella felt fury stirring inside. She wanted to reach across the table and strangle him with all of her might. She decided that she needed to swallow her pride, and her anger, and she needed to try to be calm and collected.

"Please do not pretend like you know me or my sisters. I don't think you really knew my mother either. We will never agree, because we are different people. You run away when things get difficult, and I stay to do what is needed." she took in a breath to keep herself from crying. "Austin, you did teach me something. You taught me about the person I do not want to become. I do not want to run away from my family. I don't want to pretend that they do not exist. I want to be around them and love them. So unless you are willing to accept our offer, you are wasting everyone's time. We will let a judge tell you that you're unfit to be a parent." Gabriella glared at her father, daring him to say another word.

Austin shook his head and whispered something in Mrs. Johnson's ear.

"We will need to set a court date," Mrs. Johnson announced, closing up her folders. "There will be no agreement reached today."

"Mr. Morgan, do you concur?" Mr. Lawrence asked.

Mr. Morgan looked at Gabriella, and she nodded in agreement.

"Okay then, I will be in touch with your attorneys with a court date when one is scheduled." Mr. Lawrence stood up, shaking their hands and thanking them for their time.

"I think that went as well as could be expected," Mr. Morgan said in an upbeat tone.

Jason hugged Gabriella. "You did great."

She smiled up at him and thanked him for being there. They began to file out of the room. Austin was waiting to catch Gabriella's attention.

"Gabriella," Austin said. "Can I speak with you privately?"

Gabriella did not want to oblige, but Jason and Mr. Morgan encouraged her to do so. "What do you want?" she asked impatiently.

He wasn't looking at her, but at his feet, and fidgeting with his keys nervously. "Gabby, I don't want to go to court with you. You are my daughter, and I don't want to drag it out like that. I was hoping today we could come to some sort of understanding."

Gabriella refused to buy into his sad story. "Austin, you don't want to go to court because you know that you have no chance of winning, so why don't you do the decent thing and just drop this?"

"Gabby." He managed to look up at her. "I am going to tell you something. You won't believe me, but I think you have a right to know."

She was ready to go until she saw tears in the corner of his eyes. "What?"

He sighed deeply, trying to keep his emotions in check. "The night your mother got in that accident. I drove out to the Valley to see her."

His voice broke up through muffled sobs. "We'd been speaking more, and I'm sure that you've noticed I've been around the past few years." He buried his face in his hand as if he were ashamed to look at her.

Gabriella was bewildered. "Austin, please just tell me," she said, her tone almost pleasant.

"I..." He tried to say it again. "I was going to leave Alice, and I was going to be with your mother. We were going to get married. I've always loved her, and I have never regretted anything more in my life than the moment I turned my back on her." The tears in his eyes were flowing freely now.

She wasn't sure if she had heard him correctly, but it didn't matter. He was right; she wasn't going to believe him. All he'd admitted to was leading her mother on once again and then going straight back to his wife. "Austin," she began, "thank you for telling me, but you are right. I don't believe you." Gabriella Knope walked away from her father, as he had done so many times to her.

15

The next day Gabriella woke from a fitful night of sleep. She tossed and turned and for reasons she did not expect. She thought that she would be restless from her slam-dunk victory over Austin and excited for her first real date with Jason, but life yet again had thrown her for another loop. She kept replaying her conversation with Austin over and over again in her mind. Gabriella did not want to believe him, and despite her worthy attempts, it had consumed all of her thoughts. She wanted it to be another one of his tricks, but something inside told her that it was not, but what difference did it make if they really were going to get back together? They did not because her mom had died, and he went right back to Alice without skipping a beat. She remembered Alice being there that day at the Thrones' home right after her mother had passed away, so was he really going to follow through with his plan to reunite with her mother? Gabriella was too skeptical to believe anything Austin had to say. She tried to push the thoughts as far away from her mind as she possibly could.

Gabriella heard Gemma and Giuliana bustling around in their rooms—more noise coming from Giuliana knocking things over, but Gabriella was more than sure that she didn't have access to anything that could burn the house down, so she decided to take some time for herself. She made her way over to her desk, sat down in the antique chair, picked up a pen, and opened up a notebook to a blank sheet of paper. A blank piece of paper used to be her best source of therapy, but now it was almost alien, and she didn't know where to begin. She used to write every day, but life had gotten in the way. Her mother had always told her that the words lived inside of her, and the world needed to hear her stories. She sat back in the chipped chair and let out a deep sigh of regret. She saw her dreams of touching others with the written word floating away. She was missing out on the great learning opportunities at Brown, but someday she would follow her dreams. It was just not in the foreseeable future. She was now and would be the legal guardian to her sisters, and that didn't leave much time for writing. "I miss you," she said to the empty room. She put the pen down on the wordless paper and left the room.

Gabriella tried to act as if nothing were wrong, but Gemma knew better, and even Giuliana could tell that Gabriella was having a down day. Giuliana offered her unsolicited hugs, and Gemma badgered Gabriella to tell her what was going on, and it didn't matter if she were up for sharing or not; Gemma insisted on her so-called right to know. Gabriella's nerves were wearing thin and Gemma was causing her to develop a headache, and she began to understand the look that their mother would get sometimes. She would press her fingers up to her forehead and smile, but she would be looking around the room for any possible exits when the incessant whining, talking, and fighting wouldn't stop. Unfortunately the house didn't contain any places that were off-limits, so there was no escape to be found.

"All right, guys." She stood up from the couch. "I am going to take some aspirin. You guys are going to the Thrones' this evening. You both have friends down the block you can hang out while you're there, and I'm going to hang out with a few of my friends that I haven't seen in a while." Gabriella didn't want to give Gemma a chance to respond, but she didn't move quickly enough.

"Oh right, your date with Jason," Gemma said in a mocking voice.

"No." Gabriella turned around. "My date with my friends."

"Gabby," Gemma continued as if she didn't hear her, "I don't know why you try to deny, because everyone and their sister knows that you are into Jason. And you have been for a long time. So get over this secret kick you are on and 'fess up." Gemma winked at her sister.

It took a lot of effort, but Gabriella chose to ignore Gemma's tone and snarky wink. "Just get an overnight bag packed. I am going to shower. I'll be finished in a bit." Gabriella almost ran up the stairs to spare herself from anything else Gemma had to say.

Tonight was supposed to be a magical night, one that she wouldn't forget, but now it was tainted. Jason had barely entered her thoughts. She was consumed with what Austin had told her. She told herself over and over that it didn't matter if he was telling the truth, but why couldn't she stop thinking about it? She started to get angry because he was ruining her first date with Jason. Everything was off. *That's it!* she screamed silently to herself. No more. She wasn't going to give him the satisfaction. She refused. She pushed the thoughts from her mind and focused on her evening ahead. She wasn't going to let Austin Knope ruin any more moments of her life.

Downstairs Giuliana and Gemma were watching some kid show about preteens on a ship. Gabriella always teased Gemma, knowing that she secretly liked all of the "wholesome" shows that Giuliana loved. Gemma heard Gabriella coming and immediately picked up a magazine and pretended to be reading it.

"It's probably pretty hard to read a magazine upside down." Gabriella snickered.

Gemma turned red and then got mad. "Shut up!"

"All right, calm down. Are you guys ready to go?" Gabriella asked.

"I'm ready, Gabby," Giuliana answered. "But next week could I have a sleepover, or go to a sleepover?" Giuliana stuck out her bottom lip and looked up from underneath her eyelashes, and her blue eyes sparkled.

Gabriella pretended to be thinking it over. "I'm sure you could go to one as long as you do your chores and behave this week." Gabriella gave her a serious look. "Where is this sleepover going to take place?"

"Oh, I don't know, I just wanted to be able to go if I got invited," she replied causally.

"Gabby," Gemma whined. "I want go out with friends too."

"Okay," Gabriella said. "Who, where, when, what, and I need a number." Gabriella's response was so automatic she startled herself.

Gemma was taken aback as well. "Well, Mrs. Knope," Gemma said, "I have not really thought about it too much, but maybe a movie with Angie."

"Okay, well, I need the details, and I will need to, or Angie's mom will need to, take you and pick you up." Gabriella's protective nature had suddenly taken a step up to motherly.

Gemma looked confused by the authority in Gabriella's voice. "Okay, that's fair," she replied.

Gabriella nodded, feeling she had just won what could have been a battle of wills and wits with her younger sister. She made a mental note: start out strong and don't bend. She looked at the clock and gathered up Giuliana's overnight bag for the Thrones' house, and Gemma grabbed hers. As they were getting ready to walk out the door, the phone rang. Gabriella gave serious thought to ignoring it, but it could be the Thrones' cancelling or Jason cancelling. She dropped their things and picked up the phone.

"Hello?" she answered, wishing she had caller ID.

"Gabriella, it's Jacob Morgan." He sounded out of breath. "I apologize for calling so late."

Gabriella glanced at the clock. "It's only six-thirty."

"Yes, but it's family hour, you know." He laughed weakly. "I have important news."

Maybe Austin had withdrawn his case, and Gabriella was going to get full custody without a fight. Mr. Morgan was silent on the other end, and she was becoming impatient. "Well, what is it?"

"Yes, yes." Mr. Morgan sounded like he was shuffling through some papers. "Well, first of all, the date of the formal hearing has been assigned for November eighth at ten a.m.—make sure you write that down."

"Okay, thank you." Gabriella was wishing that she would have let the answering machine take the message; she was already running late.

"Gabriella, there is more," he said slowly. "I don't know how to tell you this, and I'm not going to sugarcoat it, but something has happened."

Gabriella tried to remain calm, but her mind raced. She tried to think of something that she had done wrong, but nothing came to mind. She wondered if it was about Jason—maybe being in a relationship would not be acceptable in a judge's eyes. "Please tell me!" she demanded.

"Mrs. Johnson has filed paperwork to gain immediate custody of your sisters. Austin could have custody of your sisters within two weeks," Mr. Morgan explained.

"What?" she screamed into the phone. Gemma and Giuliana stopped what they were doing immediately and turned to look.

"Gabriella, I understand your anger, and you have every right to be angry," Mr. Morgan said.

Gabriella was barely listening. She was so furious that she could smash Austin's head through a window. She could not make sense of what he was telling her. His words seemed like a jumbled mess. The room was spinning, her head was swarmed with thoughts, and she was ready to go on the attack. "Mr. Morgan," she interrupted. "Does this mean that Austin asked her to file for immediate custody?"

"Yes," Mr. Morgan said truthfully. "They had to have talked about it, but—"

She cut him off again. "Am I going to lose them?"

She heard him breathing heavily on the other end of the line. "Well, it's important that you come into my office next week so we can do some damage control and file our own paperwork to stop him from gaining immediate custody, but I don't know if it will work or not. But I promise you, I am going to do everything I can to help you. Gabriella, it is important that you do not do anything rash, please, for the sake of our case."

Gabriella knew what he was insinuating, but for the first time since her mother's death, she knowingly lied. "Yes. I won't." Gabriella did not give Mr. Morgan a chance to say anything else and hung up the phone. She smiled at Gemma and Giuliana and assured them that everything was fine, and they left the house.

She drove most of the way to the Thrones' home in silence. She had almost forgotten about her date with Jason, until Gemma made a snarky comment about it. The last thing on her mind was the date, and there was a good chance that it wasn't going to take place. The anger pulsated through her, causing her hands to tremble. She could feel the tears stinging her eyes. Everything that she had promised her sisters was about to be empty words, and the father that she'd never had was about to ruin her life, and she couldn't figure out why he had such a sudden interest. Was it guilt? Was it for appearances? Why couldn't he just leave them alone? Gabriella was going to find out the answers to all of these questions that night, no matter what.

Gabriella pulled into the drive, where she could see Cindy Throne peeking out the door, obviously very excited to spend some quality time with the girls. Cindy was ready to embrace each of them in an overbearing hug before they barely took a step over the threshold. They had not been back to the Thrones' home since the day they'd found out about their mother's death. A house, which not long ago held pleasant memories, was now a real-life reminder of her real-life nightmare that had unfolded there.

"Hi girls. You look like you've grown." Cindy beamed at Giuliana.

"I think I have." Giuliana stood on her tiptoes to seem taller.

They all looked up as they heard loud footsteps barreling down the stairs. Jason appeared within seconds, but he stopped in his tracks and stared at Gabriella. "Wow," he said, not realizing anyone else was in the room. "You look gorgeous." He started to walk toward her but stopped when he realized that they were not alone.

Gabriella blushed slightly and caught a glimpse of Gemma's smirk. "Thank you," Gabriella replied. She was trying to think of an excuse to explain why she could not go out right now. She tried to think of something she may have forgotten, but then Jason would just offer to go with her to get it, so that would not work. Her mind was blank; she had never lied to Jason, and she was not sure if she could pull it off, but she knew that she had to do what she needed to do alone. "Jason, can I meet up with you in an hour or so? I have to go by Mr. Morgan's office to sign some paperwork," Gabriella said.

"On a Saturday?" He sounded confused.

"Yeah, he called before we came over, and I need to go over and sign some stuff," she lied.

"Oh okay." He looked suspicious. "I'll go with you."

"Oh no," Gabriella said at once. "I mean, that is sweet, Jason, but I can just meet up with you in an hour or so. There's no reason for both of us to be late."

Jason realized that everyone was listening to their conversation and in an effort to keep their relationship under wraps, he decided not to argue. "Okay, then I will see you in an hour."

Gabriella did not waste another second. She hugged Giuliana and Gemma good-bye and told them she would pick them up in the morning. She rushed out the door, and Jason was left dumbfounded.

Gabriella drove furiously, allowing all of her anger to make its way to the surface. She knew there was nothing to sign at Mr. Morgan's office. She was going to her father, Austin Knope's, house to have a long-overdue conversation, where she could tell him exactly what she thought and where he could go. She had no doubts that she was about to make a huge mistake, but this time he had finally sent her over the edge. She didn't understand how he could be so cruel and so heartless. He was trying to rip everything away from her, and he didn't even seem to care. She wasn't going to stand by and let him just take her sisters away from her; she didn't care if it made more sense from a legal standpoint. It wasn't going to happen.

Gabriella pushed her doubts aside and decided it was now or never. She got out of her car, slamming the door to make her presence known. She stomped her way to the front door of the old-time colonial mansion, the home of a man who claimed to have her best interest at heart. Gabriella didn't believe that for one second. He was always on the lookout for how he could spin things to make himself look better in the public eye. She pounded on the door nonstop until she heard some faint chatter and commotion coming from the other side.

Alice Knope, who was obviously not expecting any visitors, opened the door slightly. "Gabriella?" Alice was shocked to Gabriella standing on her porch. "What on earth are you doing here?"

Gabriella had no desire to speak to the woman who was responsible for most of the unfriendly rumors that circulated the town about her mother, and she thought for a moment that she might have hated her more than she hated Austin. "I need to speak to my father." Gabriella almost threw up at the use of the word. It was the first time that she had ever called him that, but she needed Alice to know that she was serious.

Alice looked at Gabriella, unsure if she had heard her correctly. "Well, come inside," she said, standing to the side to allow her to pass.

"No," Gabriella snapped. "I don't want to go in there." It would be too hard to go and see where his real family lived, the family he had no trouble acknowledging.

Alice, obviously offended, gave her a nasty look and mumbled something under her breath. "Austin," she yelled over her shoulder, "you have a visitor." Alice tucked her blond hair behind her ear and crossed her arms. "Is everything okay?"

Gabriella was tapping her foot nervously and impatiently. "I want to talk to Austin, not you," she snarled.

"You know what, Gabriella?" Alice, probably fed up with the years of attitude that Gabriella had given her, appeared to be about to lay into her with the good scolding that she needed, but right then Austin appeared in the hallway behind his wife.

"Gabriella?" Austin was frankly shocked at her appearance. "I don't think you have ever been to our house." He didn't mean to say it aloud for them to hear; it was more of a thought than anything, but Gabriella's appearance was so unexpected. "What are you doing here?"

"I need to speak with you," she said through gritted teeth.

Austin was still unsure of his daughter's intentions, but he was foolishly hoping that things were about to change between them. "Well, come on in, and we can talk all night."

Gabriella shook her head and put her hand up in protest. "No, I don't want to come in, and I want to talk to you, not your wife." Gabriella stepped back from the door to make it clear that she was not coming inside.

Alice gave her husband an outraged look. Austin nodded in her direction. "Can you give us a few moments?" Alice did not hide her disapproval; she grunted and muttered something under her breath and slammed the door behind her. "Sorry about that," Austin said, trying to appear sympathetic and understanding.

Gabriella walked down the steps into the yard. She had the sudden urge to run away. She wasn't mature enough to face him. The sight of him broke her heart. Everything he had done to her and her mother and her sisters. Gabriella couldn't stand it. She felt like she was a helpless child with no way of stopping an evil monster from ruining her life. But she couldn't let him walk all over her any longer. "I need you to tell me the truth for once."

Austin looked baffled. "I always tell the truth."

"No, you don't," she snapped. "Did you mean it when you said you would do anything to make up for what you've done to me, my sisters, and my mother?" She could feel the water welling in the corners of her eyes. She didn't want to give him the satisfaction of crying; she didn't want to give him that power over her.

"Yes." He placed his hands on his chest. "With all of my heart I meant it."

"Then drop the custody case! Walk away! " Her voice was stern and absolute.

Austin shook his head. "Gabby, I can't do that." He walked down a couple of steps. "I know that you don't understand and you think I'm doing this to hurt you, but I am not. I'm doing this to protect you." His voice was dripping with regret and guilt.

"How can you stand there and lie to me?" she asked. Her face was hot from anger and strained from the fight to keep from crying.

"Gabby, I am not lying to you." He knew that it wouldn't do much good to defend himself, but he had to try. "I care for you. I always have."

"Bullshit!" she screamed. "Bullshit for every deadbeat dad that has said that to their little girls!" She couldn't hold back any longer. "You were never there! Why now?" she demanded.

"I've always wanted to be there," he said, his voice rising. "I'm sorry."

Gabriella shook her head repeatedly. She couldn't believe anything that he said. It didn't matter what he said. She couldn't give up more than she already had. Gabriella clasped both hands together. "Austin, I am begging you. Gemma and Giuliana are all I have left in this world, and you want to take that away from me. I need them—don't you understand that?" She had given into the tears.

Austin wanted to put his arm around his daughter, who now had her hands on her knees, gasping for air, but he knew his touch would only infuriate her further, and he really had no one to blame for that other than himself. He didn't know what to say to make her understand. "Gabriella, you have to believe me when I tell you that I am sorry for all of my mistakes. And I know that there are a lot. I think about them every night! Every night," he yelled. "I loved your mother, and I am not going to walk away ever again! I am not trying to take anything from you!"

Gabriella's urge to charge him and swing her fists with all of her might was almost too much to suppress. When he talked about her mother, it awoke a rage that did not dwell too far below the surface. In her mind, he had no right to anything after everything he'd put her through, but that didn't change the fact that if they went to court, Austin would end up with custody of her sisters, and she would eventually be blocked from their lives. She felt defeated. "Please," she said through her own sobs, "don't." She buried her face in her hands, feeling ashamed that she had to beg him. "Just let us be." The words were muffled but heard. It was the first time that she had asked her father for anything, and at the same time, she couldn't deny the little girl inside of her that wanted to run into her daddy's arms to make everything better.

Austin sat down on the porch steps and took some time to gather his own thoughts. His own face was wet with tears. He looked through the cracks in his hands and saw his daughter suffering because of his actions. He didn't know how to make the situation right, but he thought that honesty would be the best start. "Gabriella, you are right. I was not a good dad to you or your sisters. I wasn't there for you in the way that you needed. And there is nothing that I can say to make you believe me, but there is not a day that goes by that I don't regret walking away from my family with you and Clare. I took the easy way out. I was doing what I thought I had to do, and now I have to live with the consequences." He stood up, visibly crying now. "I am never going to do that again. I will not give up my chance to know my daughters, and I will never stop fighting for my chance to know you. I love you."

"What?" Her voice was almost a whisper, but it was loud enough for him to hear. "You love me?" She couldn't believe that could be true. "How do you expect me to believe that when you had your fucking lawyer file paperwork to seize immediate custody of the girls!" She was screaming now. "My mom was everything to me. I am barely hanging on, and you want to rip what shred of normalcy that I have left in my life right from me? How can you say that you love me? You don't even know me! You never wanted to know me! Can you imagine how that makes me feel? It isn't like you live across the country; no, you live in the same fucking town, and you wanted nothing to do with us! How could you? And you say that you love me? You have—"

"Gabriella." His voice was forceful. "What are you talking about, paperwork to seize immediate custody?"

Gabriella snorted haughtily. "Don't play dumb, and don't change the subject. I'm not so naïve to believe that you didn't tell your lawyer to file that."

He looked enraged. "Gabriella, I swear to you, I never agreed to that."

"Oh, and how am I supposed to believe that?" she demanded.

"Because everything you said before is true," he said desperately. "And I can't imagine how that made you feel, but I do love you, and I would never intentionally hurt you."

Gabriella laughed and shook her head. "Austin," she pleaded, "if you love me, then please, please, don't take my sisters away from me."

Austin stared at his daughter. No words were spoken, but he understood her hurt, and he was appalled at what his lawyer had done behind his back. He didn't want the girls to come and live with him like that; he didn't want to drag it out to an ugly court battle. He was only trying to give Gabriella the time that she needed. There was nothing that he could say to make her believe him, but maybe there was something. A moment of clarity, the answer he had been waiting for. "Wait right here. I have something for you." He didn't give her a chance to answer and walked back inside quickly.

Gabriella's head was pounding from the screaming, her face was hot and sticky from the tears, and her mind was a jumbled mess. She took in deep breaths to try to calm down and collect herself. She didn't know why, but she believed Austin when he told her that he didn't know anything about the custody papers. She had never seen him so upset before that she could remember. He seemed genuine, but she feared that as soon as she let him in, it would start over like a

197

reset button. She couldn't let her sisters go through the same rejection that she had.

Austin had never given Gabriella anything, at least nothing that she had accepted from him, but she admitted to herself that her curiosity was aroused. Then she began to wonder if maybe it was a trick—perhaps he was going to call the local authorities and have her arrested for trespassing. She started to take steps toward her own car, but before she could press both feet down, she heard Austin on the other side of the door, yelling at Alice to mind her own business.

He walked outside, carrying an old box. It was more of a decorative box with a keyhole. "Here," Austin said, trying to hand it to her.

"What is this?" Gabriella was trying to sound unimpressed, but she was curious to what it contained.

He forced the box into her hands. "I want you to have it." He sat down on the stairs and motioned for her to sit down next to him.

Gabriella was apprehensive, but she sat on the porch next to her father. She examined the box that he had given her; it was old, weathered, and dusty. They sat in silence, shoulder to shoulder. It was the closest that they had ever come to being a normal father and daughter. The sun was setting in the west over the horizon. The light was illuminating the ambers that had begun to change before the rest of the trees. The air was starting to get a bit colder, and Gabriella silently wished this wasn't the first time that she was watching the sun set with her father. She felt a tear slide down her cheek, but this time it wasn't one of anger, but her own regret.

"What's in here?" Her voice was softer than it had ever been before with him.

He gave her a weak smile and let out a sigh of relief. "Just take it home. When you are ready, go through it. It has all the answers to your questions." He ran his hand over the top of the box. "Your mom bought this box for me when we were fourteen, along with one for her. We agreed that when we were fifty, we would show them to each other. I'm sure she still has hers somewhere." He choked up. "God, if I could... well, I can't." He was talking to himself. It was obvious that he was full of regret and his heart was hurting as much as hers was.

Gabriella ran her hand over the top of the worn box in the same fashion that Austin had. She felt grateful to him for the first time in her life. "Thank you," she said.

He beamed at her. The stars were starting to litter the sky. The moon was rising over the Valley as the sun was saying good night. Never had he had the chance to sit with Gabriella, never had she been so cordial to him, and never had he been so hopeful for the future. He turned to Gabriella and took her hands in his. "I loved your mother more than I ever thought possible. No matter how hard I tried not to. I always loved her. I will never be able to make it up to her for the things that I did, and the choices I made, but I can start by making it up to you. When you see everything, you will understand why I can't walk away."

She wasn't angry this time. She almost did understand. She wasn't ready to let him back into her life, but there was something in his hazel eyes with the glints of amber that made her believe every word that he had said. She wondered, was this what she had missed out on her whole life by not having a dad? Late summer nights fighting, but then watching the sunset together, knowing somehow that everything was going to be okay? She didn't know what was going to happen, but she knew that she had a choice. She could trust Austin or not. They sat in silence for a while. Neither spoke; they just stared up into the sky, both probably wondering if Clare had found a new home among the stars and wondering if she were looking down at them right now. Gabriella hoped that was true, and she wished upon a star that night for that very thing.

"Well, I better be going." Gabriella got up, feeling awkward by not storming off, as most of her encounters with Austin ended.

Austin nodded. "Gabby, I will make sure that my lawyer withdraws those papers first thing Monday morning. We will do this the right way." He looked at her as she walked away. "I love you," he said.

She gave him a rare smile, and for the second time in her life, she said, "Thank you."

Gabriella got in the car. For the first time, it wasn't the sight of headlights that she had to remember her father by. She finally had something tangible to hold onto, and with that thought, she pulled out of the driveway and headed home.

16

Over the next several weeks, Gabriella had accomplished quite a bit. After a great deal of begging she finally convinced Andrew Speck of the *Laking Herald* to give her a full-time job as a copywriter for the local ads. She had managed the routine of full-time work and full-time care-giver into a better flow, and she had somehow managed to find the time to go out with Jason on their first real date. They had decided—again—to take things slow, but they were no longer denying their relationship, to which Gemma was quick to point out that she had known all along.

However, Gabriella's mind was always somewhere else because of the pending custody hearing, which was only a month away. She had assured Gemma and Giuliana that she had everything under control, even though that was basically a lie. She knew the chances of keeping her sisters with her were slim to none unless she could come to some kind of an arrangement with Austin.

The night Gabriella had gone to Austin's home had changed her opinion slightly, but not enough to trust that he would never leave them again, and she couldn't let her sisters experience that kind of pain. Gemma had already felt it too much, and Gabriella wasn't going to be the reason she had to endure the pain of abandonment for her entire life. The fear of Austin walking away again overshadowed the small ray of light she had seen inside of him that night, so she had to set aside her dreams and wants for the time being.

She thought back to the box he had given her—she had not been able to bring herself to open it. She was afraid of what she might find;

she didn't know if she could handle all of the intimate reminders of her mother. She wasn't quite ready to explore the truth of her parents' relationship, not yet.

On this particular evening, Gabriella was taking Giuliana to a birthday slumber party. Giuliana had not stopped talking about it all day. She had unpacked and repacked her bag at least ten times. Gemma also had big plans for the weekend, and tonight was her first real date. The boy she was going out with was sixteen and a licensed driver. He was on the honor roll, and Gabriella had already spoken to the boy's parents to make sure he was suitable enough to take her baby sister out. Gabriella felt a sense of responsibility when it came to dating, and she did not want her sister getting into anything she could not handle. She knew Gemma would only get more stubborn as time passed, so Gabriella was taking advantage of what influence she did have until that time came.

Gabriella was ready to take Giuliana over to her friend Shelby's house, and then she would have just enough time to see Gemma off on her date. She readied Giuliana's things by the door. "Giuliana, let's go, let's go, let's go," Gabriella called up the stairs.

"I'm coming," Giuliana yelled back. "Hold your horses." Giuliana came trouncing down the stairs with two more bags.

"What are you doing?" Gabriella pointed to the extra bags.

"Going to a sleepover," she replied in a mocking tone.

"Really, with all of that?" Gabriella laughed.

Giuliana let out an annoyed sigh. "Yes, someone has to bring the entertainment." She smiled brightly up at Gabriella.

Gabriella shook her head. "Okay, well, I'm willing to bet a million dollars that there is entertainment already there," she told her sister.

Giuliana looked to be thinking over the possibility of a million dollars, and then she confidently extended her hand to shake on it.

Gabriella laughed loudly and threw her hands into the air. "Sometimes you are too much." She went back to the foot of the stairs. "Gemma, I'll be back in twenty minutes."

"Okay," Gemma called from her room. "See you then."

Gabriella walked back to the front door where Giuliana was waiting impatiently. "Let's go."

It took her a little longer than twenty minutes to get Giuliana over to the slumber party. Giuliana had a minor meltdown when Gabriella was getting ready to leave her, but she comforted her younger sister and said all the right things. Giuliana thought it over and then joined the party. On the ride back, Gabriella thought about how quickly her motherly instincts had come into play. She assumed that since she'd had such a great mother, it was only natural. Gabriella was learning so much about herself, and she realized how quickly she could catch on to things when time wasn't a luxury.

She walked through the door into the room that held the over-sized portrait of her family. She saw her mother smiling down, frozen in laughter. She wondered what she would have wanted her to do. Would she have wanted Austin to have full custody of her sisters and for Gabriella to continue on in her life like nothing had ever happened? Was she really going to give him another chance? Gabriella's mind had been a muddled mess for the last few weeks. She wished for one last chance to speak to her mother, to hear her soothing voice, for her to give her guidance and direction. She closed her eyes tightly, trying to make something happen, but nothing did. She could not hear her mother's voice like she had promised in the good-bye letter. She wished that she would not have taken the time that she did have with her mother for granted. She wished that she would have cherished the time more. Gabriella realized that she was crying, not loudly or uncontrollably, but just softly to herself, consumed in the memory of her mother.

She wiped her eyes, trying to compose herself. She had to go upstairs and help Gemma get ready for her first date. Gabriella remembered her first date and her mother standing behind her, offering her own words of advice. Gabriella let the memory wash over her as time stood still.

"Gabby." Clare clasped her hands over her chest. "You look so beautiful."

"Thanks, Mom." Gabriella was smoothing her yellow summer dress in the mirror. "You don't think it's too much, do you?"

"I think it's perfect." Clare radiated the way any proud mother would. She couldn't believe that her daughter was fifteen years old already.

"Goodness, it seems like only yesterday that you were asking me to kiss your boo-boos." A small tear trickled down her cheek.

"Mom." Gabriella tried to console her. "Don't cry."

"I can if I want," she insisted. "You are my little girl, who isn't so little anymore." Clare stood behind Gabriella in the mirror. They were both almost the same height, and Clare herself was very beautiful and young-looking. They looked more like sisters than mother and daughter. "You are just growing up so fast." Clare rested her chin on Gabriella's shoulder. "I am so proud of you, and this Alex guy seems like a great kid. I think you guys will have a great time." Clare made Gabriella face her. "All right, remember—no drinking, no sex, no drugs, and don't go anywhere unless I know where you are." Clare gave her a stern motherly look.

"Mom, I know." Gabriella was annoyed that her mother had to remind her for the thousandth time. "I am not stupid."

"I know you're not, but I'm your mother, so it's my job to tell you those things," Clare replied. "Oh wait." She ran out of Gabriella's room and back in as quickly as she had left. She put a silver chain with a stunning blue diamond oval pendant around her neck.

"Mom." Gabriella gasped in awe. "Where did you get this? It's beautiful."

"This necklace is very special to me, and it was given to me by my very first love, and I want you to wear it tonight for luck," she told her.

Gabriella looked down at the stunning necklace, and she hugged her mother tightly. There was a knock at the door, and Clare hugged Gabby one last time and watched as she walked out of the room to go on her first date.

Gabriella opened her eyes, and she was crying again, wishing she would have hugged her a little longer and a little tighter. She felt guilty that she got to share her first date with her mother, but Gemma would not get to have that special moment. Gabriella shook out all of her nerves and tears and practically ran up the stairs.

Gemma looked stunning in a blue dress with a white cardigan. Her hair was curled and clipped back, and she had even put on a small amount of makeup that made her look like a young woman.

Gabriella felt very proud of her sister. She realized how quickly she had grown up, no longer that annoying eight-year-old that would tattle on her constantly. "You excited?" Gabriella sat down on her bed.

"Nervous," Gemma admitted.

"Well, don't be. You look gorgeous," Gabriella reassured her. She stood up behind Gemma in the mirror as Clare had done for her.

"I wish Mom were here." Gemma sighed.

"Me too," Gabriella admitted.

"I read my first date letter this morning," Gemma told her sister. "She said no sex, no drugs, no drinking, and someone has to know where I am at all times."

Gabriella laughed. "That's what she told me too."

Gemma hung her head low and let a few tears flow out.

"I have an idea; come with me." Gabriella pulled her sister by the hand, forcing her to follow. They walked to the end of the hall, to the room no one had entered for months now. The room that their mother had spent her nights in, a place where they would go for late-night chats, a place of refuge and comfort from everyday life.

"Gabby." Gemma planted her feet firmly, refusing to take another step. "I don't want to go in. I'm not ready."

"Mom has a necklace in there that she gave to me to wear on my first date, and I think you should wear it tonight, and I need you to help me find it." She hoped the promise of the necklace would be enough to convince her, because Gabriella did not want to go in the room alone. Thankfully Gemma agreed, and they pushed open the door together. A floral scent that had been barricaded for a few months now clambered through the opening, and they were overcome with a slew of memories they had made in their mother's room. They closed their eyes to visualize her beauty, her voice, and her soothing nature.

Inside the room stood a four-poster bed with a blue-and-white comforter set with some kind of swirly decoration. If they sat there long enough, they could make out all sorts of shapes as if they were looking up at puffy clouds in the sky. There were two nightstands, a vanity with a chair that Clare had sat in every day, a tall chest of drawers, and pictures of the girls in every corner of the room. The room looked like it had always looked except for some extra dust. It could be mistaken that their mother was away on a short business trip, but they both knew that was not the case.

"It's probably in there," Gemma said, pointing to a jewelry box that had gathered a layer of dust.

Gabriella had spent many days admiring the box that contained such beautiful jewelry. She always thought that her mother moved with grace and poise, and elegance. Clare had never been one to flaunt her jewelry, but she would pull it out for special occasions and sometimes for Gabriella and Gemma to play dress-up with. The images danced in Gabriella's mind to a painful reminder of what Giuliana would miss out on, but she told herself she had to stop thinking that way, or else she would never stop crying.

Gabriella hesitated before sitting down on the satin-upholstered chair that her mother had been the last to sit in. There was still an imprint of her mother's presence having sat there every day for as long as Gabriella could remember. She ran her fingers over the fabric, trying to soak in any remnant that she could, and she felt the instant comfort that she had been longing for. Just the simple smell, the simple fact that her mother had been the last to have touched the chair, was all that she needed.

Gabriella had almost forgotten why she had come into the room, but then Gemma's impatient stare reminded her. "Right," Gabriella said, returning her focus to the necklace.

Gemma was looking around, trying not to touch anything. She looked a little uncomfortable being inside the room, almost like she was in a museum and touching something would set off an alarm, but then something caught her eye. She walked over to one of the nightstands next to her mother's bed.

"Gabby," Gemma said, picking up a book, "did you know that Mom kept a journal?" Gemma was examining the journal carefully, as if it would break with too heavy of a grasp.

"No." Gabriella lost interest in the necklace once again.

Gemma walked back over to Gabriella, flipping the book over and over to make sure she knew what she was holding was real. "Do you think we should read it?"

"I don't know." Gabriella knew how private her journal was, and even if she wasn't around any longer, she wasn't sure how she felt about people going through her most intimate thoughts.

Gemma looked disappointed. "I think we should. I think it would help us."

Gabriella knew that she would eventually give in to the temptation. "Okay, but not tonight."

"Why not tonight?" Gemma protested.

"Because tonight is about your first date, and whatever is in that book is not going to be dating advice, so let's do it tomorrow or Sunday in here with Giuliana, like we used to watch movies with her." Gabriella went back to looking for the necklace. "Here it is." Gabriella pulled out the gorgeous blue diamond pendant necklace that her mother had let her wear on her first date. Gabriella got up so Gemma could sit down at the vanity. She stood behind her so she could put the necklace on Gemma like Clare had done for her. "Mom told me that this necklace was a gift from her first love and it was very special to her, and I want you to wear it for good luck." Gabriella felt tears slide down her cheek again.

Gemma stared at her reflection in the mirror, touching the small but noticeable pendant. "Do you think her first love was Austin?"

Gabriella had never really given that much thought because she did not want to admit that her mother had actually loved him, but she knew deep down that Gemma was probably right. Austin probably did give her mother the necklace.

"You look so beautiful, and you are going to have a great time." Gabriella was beaming with pride. "This Brad seems like a really great guy, and you seem to really like him." Gabriella hugged Gemma tightly. The doorbell rang, and Gemma gave Gabriella a nervous look. She hugged Gabriella very quickly and ran down the stairs.

"Have fun," Gabriella called after her. Gabriella heard the door shut behind them, and she smiled to herself, knowing that she had managed to get Gemma off on her first date successfully.

Gabriella stood there for a moment, lost in her own thoughts, and then realized that she was still in her mother's room. She looked around and saw the brown tethered book sitting on the dresser where Gemma had left it. Gabriella knew that she would not be able to resist the temptation of taking a peek inside. She grabbed the book and walked so quickly in her excitement that she tripped over her own feet and fell down. She was embarrassed but thankful no one was around to see the tumble. As she was pushing herself up, something underneath her mother's bed caught her eye. Gabriella crawled over to the foot of the bed to get a closer look. She pulled out what looked like an old decorative box with a keyhole. It was identical to the one Austin had given her to go through. She ran her hand over the box, realizing that this box contained her mother's most precious memories of her father.

Gabriella was thankful that her mother was a logical person; the key wasn't too hard to find. It was in a drawer of the elegant jewelry box that stood on her mother's vanity. She heard the rust click away as she unlocked the box. Gabriella opened the lid and found herself staring at mementos and notes from her mother's relationship with Austin. Gabriella put the box carefully on Clare's bed, and she raced back to her room to grab the box that Austin had given her. She raced back to her mother's room. She took in a deep breath and opened the box that Austin had given her. She was nervous about what she may find. She was aware that she was most likely going to have a new understanding of her parents' relationship. She took a long moment to consider if she really wanted to dig into their past, but there was no resisting it.

Gabriella started with Clare's box first. There were old movie ticket stubs, some old notes from high school, dried rose petals, a bus ticket to Los Angeles, California, and a few old pictures. There really wasn't anything of merit that would mean anything to Gabriella. They were trinkets that only meant something to Clare. Gabriella sat back on the bed, slightly disappointed. She picked up her mother's journal and turned to the last entry. She read the date: *August First*. Her mother had written the day before she died. Gabriella thumbed through the other pages and discovered that her mother had written almost every day. An excitement filled her heart, and she could not wait any longer. She started to read her mother's final entry.

Another day, another dollar, another chance to laugh. It was actually quite a good day if I am being honest. It started with Giuliana making me laugh the way that only she can. Giuliana informed me she would like to be a spy for the CIA and all the Bourne Identity *movies were her inspiration. When I asked her how she had watched them, she began to explain her spy-like techniques to retrieve them from Gabriella's room. I don't know how she comes up with this stuff. Everyday it's something new, it's a new adventure...She makes my heart smile.*

I think today was a turning point for me and Austin. He has been so true to his word lately. I know I have traveled down this road so many times. I know that the pages of my journals are littered with the "I love him" or "I hate him" or "I can't believe he did that" in good ways and bad, but at the end of the day, I can't help it. No matter what I do, it comes back to the simple fact that I love him and I want to spend my life with him. He promised he would come and see me tomorrow in the Valley, and if he keeps his word, I will know that this will be different. We have reached a place where we both understand our needs and wants. I know he has a family with Alice, and I would never want to destroy that, and I don't think I am. I think she knows why he married her; it was more an arranged marriage than anything. He has children with me as well, and as hard as I have tried, I have never stopped loving him. If it hadn't been for his parents opposing us when we were sixteen, we would be married now. When I think of how much time we have lost, it hurts. I knew from the moment I met him when I was ten years old that I would be his wife. He knows me better than anyone else, and I know that he would not have left Gabby and me when we were sixteen if that had not been the only way to survive. I really have no doubts that he is going to show up tomorrow. I know that he will be there and we will be able to seal everything with a kiss. That's the fairytale version, of course. Or he might not show. Who knows?

I think about Gabby and Gemma and how hard of a time they will have with it if we get back together. Gabby despises him, and I guess that is partly my fault. I let her. I don't push her, and maybe I should, but I think she just needs time. And I know that she loves me, and if she sees how happy he makes me, then I think she will come around. I love him so much. I hope all three of my daughters find the love that I have found, but I hope they don't have to go through the heartache I went through, but in all honesty, true love like ours is worth the wait.

Gabriella was crying again and not because of the sight of her mother's handwriting, but because of herself. She had spent her life shutting Austin out, she had spent her life hating him, and she would have never admitted that her mother could have actually loved him. She remembered the day of the funeral. Austin had been so upset and he had tried to talk to her, but she was so cruel to him. She didn't care; she thought it was all an act. She had been so blinded by her hatred that she had missed the blatant signs that were everywhere; she just didn't want to see.

Gabriella tried to think of the days that surrounded her mother's passing more thoroughly. A letter from her mother titled *Austin Knope* flashed in her mind. She had assumed that it was a mistake and the letter was meant for Austin, not her. She'd had the intention to read it twice, but every time something had distracted her, and she would forget completely about the letter. But now she knew the letter was meant for her. Her mother would have known how hard it would be for her to accept her death, and she would not accept Austin Knope as part of her life, no matter the circumstances, even if she thought that was something her mother desperately wanted. Gabriella buried her face in her mother's pillows, suffocating in the fading scent of lilac and roses, crying and wishing she could go back in time and change some of her actions.

She didn't want to be alone anymore, she couldn't handle the adult persona she had created for herself, she wanted someone to hold her and tell her that everything was going to be all right. She had to open the box to her mother's past through Austin's eyes; she had to read the letters. She had to know the answers. She needed to know the truth no matter what it was, and she needed someone to be there when she found out.

Gabriella picked up her phone and called the only person who would understand. Her breathing was heavy as the generic ringing tone sounded in her ear.

"Hey babe, I was just getting ready to call you." Jason sounded delighted on the other end.

"Hey." But Gabriella had only mouthed the word; no sound came out.

"Hello?"

She cleared her throat loudly and told herself to buck up. "Hi, Jason. I need you," she said at once.

"Are you okay?" Jason sounded worried.

"Yeah, I went into my mother's room—" she started to explain, but he cut her off.

"I'll be there in fifteen minutes." He hung up the phone.

Jason brought comfort to her because he always seemed to be one step ahead, and he always seemed to know what she was thinking. He never hesitated. He was always there for when she needed him the most. She wondered if her mom had felt the same way about Austin as she did for Jason, and if that were the case, it made a little more sense why Clare couldn't let him go.

Jason arrived within fifteen minutes as promised. She ran downstairs as fast as she could and swung open the door, flinging herself into his arms and kissing him so passionately he almost fell over. She grabbed him by the hand and brought him into her mother's bedroom.

Jason was happily surprised with Gabriella's greeting, but she still hadn't spoken a word to explain what was wrong. "Do you want me to start guessing, or are you going to tell me what's going on?" He looked around the room, and his eyes fell on the contents of the bed. "What is all this stuff?" he said, moving over to touch it.

"Don't," Gabriella commanded. "I'll tell you everything, but sit down over there. This may take a few minutes."

He looked apprehensive but did as she had asked.

"Okay." She took in a deep breath. "I can do this," she said aloud. She saw that Jason was looking more confused than ever and even a little bit worried. "All right." She took in another breath, and for some reason she felt like she was giving a school presentation.

Jason started to look impatient. He motioned her to speed things up.

She nodded and sat down at the foot of the bed. "I'm not okay." It was the second time she had said that out loud, and she instantly felt a weight had been lifted from her shoulders. "I have not been okay since my mom died. I told myself I was okay, but that wasn't true, not in the least. Jason, I lost my mom, and she isn't coming back." Her voice cracked. Jason looked like he wanted to say something, but she put her hand up to stop him. "If I stop I won't be able to finish."

He nodded and gestured for her to continue.

"You of all people know how I feel about Austin." She waited for him to nod in agreement. "Well, the day after the meeting, Mr. Morgan called me and told me that he had submitted paperwork to take immediate custody of Gemma and Giuliana." She paused again so he could process the information. As Gabriella had anticipated, Jason's mouth fell open. "Yes, yes, I know; it was low, even for him. So the night that was supposed to be our first date was the night that I found this out, and that is the real reason I blew it off. I went to Austin's house to talk to him."

Jason interrupted instantly. "Gabriella, what did you do?"

She laughed off his concerns. "Well, listen and I will tell you." He sat back and gave his attention to her once more. "I went over to his house, and I talked to him. The most I have ever really talked to him. I told him how I felt in a somewhat rational tone, but he claimed he did not know about the papers. He said that his lawyer had talked about it, but he didn't want to go that route, and I kind of believe him because he had them withdrawn the next day. He gave me that box." She pointed over to the bed. "He told me to look through it, and then I would understand why he couldn't give up his rights to Gemma and Giuliana. Well, naturally, I did not look in the box because I couldn't bring myself to. I think I was scared of what I would find out." She paused to collect her thoughts, making sure she had included everything. "Oh yes, and I forgot to tell you. At the meeting, he told me the night of my mom's accident he was in the Valley with her, and they were going to get back together for real this time. He was going to leave Alice for my mother and they had plans to get married, but I did not believe him. So the night I was at his house, he was telling me the same things and how much he loved her. And I didn't believe him, but I found my mom's journal. And it was all true. She loved him, and she was going to be with him again. And she was so happy. So happy." Gabriella stopped speaking when the tears started to resurface.

"Okay, let me get this straight," Jason said. "Austin and your mom were planning on getting back together. Austin's lawyer did something snaky behind his back. You confronted him, and he gave you a box. Is that everything?" he asked, summing up what had taken her five minutes to explain in three sentences.

"No." Gabriella broke off. It was something she hadn't been able to say out loud. It was something that she didn't want to admit.

"What?" Jason got up to approach her.

Gabriella felt tears coming into her eyes. "I think my mom wants Austin to care for Giuliana and Gemma, not me. But I could be wrong," she began. "She left a letter for me and titled it *Austin Knope*. At first I assumed that Mr. Morgan had mixed up the letters, but now I know that it's for me." She stopped fighting the tears and let them come.

"Gabby." Jason kissed her hand. "We will figure this out together." He kissed her softly on the lips.

They both got comfortable on the bed. Gabriella grabbed one of her mother's pillows and drowned herself with the familiar scent that still lingered. She handed Jason the letter with Austin Knope's name scribbled across the front.

He gave her a confused look. "Do you want me to read it?"

She nodded and began to weep quietly. "Yes, read it to me please."

"Okay." He rubbed her back tenderly and carefully opened the letter. "Are you ready?"

She could not speak, but managed a head motion. She was terrified of what was written in the letter. She was afraid it would confirm her suspicions that it was her fault that she had missed out on a relationship with her father.

"All right," Jason began. "Here we go." He unfolded the paper carefully so not to tear it and began to read.

My Dearest Gabriella,

I hope you are doing well. If you are reading this letter, I have probably been gone for some time now, and I hope that you know I will always be with you no matter how much time passes. I felt it was important to write to you about your father because I do not want you to hate him. I understand your reasoning, and it is partly my fault. With the burden of my death upon your shoulders, I am sure that you feel that everything is your responsibility. I have no doubt that you will try to keep the girls living with you if they are at that age, and I have no doubt that you will do everything in your power to keep them safe. I cannot tell you what is right and wrong, but Gabby, please do not feel alone in the world. Your father loves you very much, and I know that you don't think that is true. But he has done a lot for us. He's always kept his distance from you as of late, out of respect for your feelings. I know it is hard to understand, and it has taken me a long time to get to this point. We were sixteen when we got pregnant with you, and we lived in this small town. Your father was the quarterback, and the son of Congressman Knope; his family did not want to admit that something like that could happen to them. They did not want to face the reality. If Austin were to stay with me, his family was going shut him out and disown him. We would have had a very hard life, so he sacrificed us to provide us with a better life. He tells me every day that he would rather have nothing at all than his oldest daughter hating him, but he lives with that. He wants more than anything for you two to build a relationship. Gabriella, please be cordial with him for me. I love him, and he was my soul mate. We almost got the timing right, but we were never quite there. I honestly hope that you never have to see this letter, and that we are spending Christmases together as a happy family. It is what I want more than anything in the world. I have to tell you something, because actions speak louder than words: Austin funded your full scholarship to Brown. He did not want you to know because he knew that you would not accept it. Gabby, sometimes the best things in life are the hardest things we ever have to do. I love you no matter what you decide, but remember, he loves you just as much as I do. Give him a chance to make up for his past. I have.

Love you forever and always your mother, Clare LaFrace.

Jason looked at Gabriella, who was crying as if she were in a fragile state. Jason wrapped her up in his arms. "Gabby, I love you," he said. "It's okay to be angry at him, and I know your mom understood that. I think she was saying don't push him away, and give him a chance, and maybe have some type of relationship." He kissed her on the top of her head and held her the same way he had when she had found out about her mother's accident.

Gabriella felt sick to her stomach. She felt disgusted by her own actions. She had jumped to so many conclusions about Austin, and she never wanted to hear anything different. Every time he had tried to explain himself to her, she shut him out. She would lash out at him like he was some kind of criminal. She looked down on the bed at the box Austin had given her. She had yet to sift through the contents, but now she was ready. She kept spouting to everyone who would listen that she was an adult, but now it was time for her act like an adult. "Actions speak louder than words," she whispered to herself.

Gabriella whimpered as she saw what the box contained: it was not only the contents of his relationship with Clare, but some trinkets from her own past as well. On top were three letters. Two were in Austin's handwriting, and the third was in Clare's handwriting. It was the good-bye letter she had written him, Gabriella was certain. She pulled it out with every intention of reading it. Underneath the letter there were pictures of Clare and Austin during their happy times, newborn baby bracelets that contained Gabriella, Gemma, and Giuliana's information, and he also had a bus ticket to Los Angeles, California.

"Gabby," Jason said, reading a letter that was in Austin's handwriting. "Austin wrote this to your mom when she got pregnant with you."

Another tear trickled down her face. She knew she had to read it for herself; she had to know everything. Jason handed her the letter with messy handwriting that was unfamiliar to her, and she began to read.

Clare,
First I want you to know that I love you, and I would never inten-
tionally hurt you. I have never felt worse in my life when my words

caused your tears to flow. I am so sorry, I was a coward, and when my mother told me to ask you to get an abortion, I listened to her. Please believe me when I tell you that I never wanted you get an abortion and the only reason I said it was because my mother was with me, and she made me. I know that is no excuse for the hurtful things I said, but I did not mean them. You know what you mean to me, and you know how I feel about you. You make my heart beat faster and slower at the same time, and when I am not with you, I don't feel complete. You make me want to laugh and cry at the same time. I love you with every fiber in my being, and I know that you know that.

My parents have made me a deal, and I have taken it. I think it will be the best for our son or daughter because my happiness no longer matters. It is all about our child. They have agreed to provide financial support for her or him for their entire life, and for you, as long as I agree to never see you again. I promise when my parents are not controlling my life, we will be together. When I reach the age of twenty-one, my inheritance will be available in full to me as long as I meet certain expectations. I will never stop fighting to make my way back to you, I promise. I know you might be angry that I am giving up on our love, but please understand, this is the only way. We are only sixteen, and this will make it much easier on us, I promise. I will always love you and our child, and I will be there when our child is born whether my parents like it or not.

Clare, you are my soul mate, and the most beautiful woman I have ever met. This is not puppy love, but it is real and true. I will always love you, and I will always be here for you. Please forgive me for what I must do to keep you safe and taken care of.

Love you forever and always, Austin Knope

Gabriella felt that everything in her life that she thought she knew was not true. She felt confused and angry. She didn't know what to think about Austin. He was a man who had left her and her mother, only to provide a life without struggle. She didn't know whether to be grateful or upset, because no amount of money could replace someone's father. She never had gotten that chance to know him. Why

215

didn't her mom tell her about Austin's contributions? She had so many questions. Austin had promised that his box would answer all of her questions, but it only created more. There was one more letter. Perhaps one more letter would make her understand everything.

"I have to read this one too," she told Jason, holding up her mother's good-bye letter. Austin had left it in the box for Gabriella to read.

My Dearest Austin,

I cannot tell you how many times I have written this letter. I have written it angry, I have written it happy, and I have written it sad, but no matter what, I always seem to be in love with you. There is nothing more in the world that I want other than to be your wife and you my husband. I understand that it is not in the cards for us this go-around, but I hope someday that we get our chance together. You and I looked on together today as we watched our oldest daughter graduate from high school and begin the next chapter of her life. So I decided that I would write this letter to you honestly.

We have three beautiful children who are the light of my life. They are my connection to you forever, and I am so grateful for that. I know giving them a childhood with the kind of upbringing that I never had was what you thought was best, and I agree to a point, but I can tell you no amount of money can replace our love for each other.

I know how you feel about me. I have never really doubted it, even when I have been angry with you, but as I write my good-bye letter to you, I am oddly at peace. I sincerely hope that you never see this letter, and I hope that I have somehow drummed up the courage to tell you how I feel. I know that you have always known in a way. I think we are destined to be together, and I know that if we had been a few years older when we had Gabby, we would be happily married. Life got in our way, and that is okay because I had you in my life, and you gave me three gifts beyond anything I could have ever imagined, and Austin, I truly do love you.

Now, if I am gone, you will need some advice on how to raise our three lovely daughters. Gabriella will do everything in her power to resist you. She is very angry with you, and only you can fix that. I don't know how, but I am sure something will come to you. You must not pressure her. You must let her come to you. You must not walk away from her. You must understand her feelings. If you are patient, then I promise she will come around. Do not give up on her. I know that she loves you, and she secretly longs to have a relationship with you.

Gemma is strong-willed but not quite as stubborn as Gabby. If you comfort her and don't talk down to her, I don't think it will take her long to warm up to you. You have not been in their lives as much as a normal father, so it will take some time and patience on your part. Gemma is very studious, and she is very involved in school. If you notice that start to slip, then step in and guide her in the right direction.

Austin, you must remember that they are teenage girls, very volatile, so don't push them. Try to let them come to you. I know they will see the great man that I fell in love with. I know it will be hard for them at first, but you mustn't give up on our children. They will be depending on you.

Giuliana is in love with you, and nothing gives me more pleasure than when she lights up at the mere mention of your name. She is learning to tie her shoes, and we use the bunny ear song. Also her favorite stories are Cinderella and Winnie the Pooh, and I know it might sound a little vain, but if God forbid I am gone at her young age, keep me alive in her heart. Tell her stories, show her pictures. And please tell them all that I love them and I am never far away.

Austin, you will be fine without me, and I have every confidence that our daughters will excel in the world, with or without me. They have an inner strength about them, a defiance; no matter what life throws at them, they will prevail.

I suppose this is really it. I want to thank you for giving me the chance to experience true love in my life. I will take that with me wherever I may be going after I am gone.

Keep me close to your heart always. Austin, you have never strayed far from mine. I love you and I always will, and I always have.

Love always and forever, Clare Marie LaFrace

Gabriella's life had changed once again in a matter of hours. There would be no turning back now. She knew the truth. She knew that Austin loved her, and he wasn't going anywhere. She cried in Jason's arms for a while. There were no words to be spoken, only exchanged looks of understanding. Gabriella had a lot to think about, and she didn't know where to begin.

17

The next morning Gabriella awoke cradled in Jason's arms. Her face was hot and sticky; her eyes were burning from the lack of restful sleep. Gabriella had wrestled with her thoughts until Gemma came home from her date last night. Gabriella had filled Gemma in on what she had found in the journal, the letters from Austin to their mother, and their mother's good-bye letter. Gemma was silent for a long while, while she processed the information. Neither knew what to say or do—they were dealing with things far beyond their maturity level—but then they began to talk and delve deeper into Clare's personal thoughts. They learned a great deal about Clare that night, so much that the next step was clear, but neither sister wanted to admit that they might have been wrong. They spent the night crying over their anger and confusion, but mostly just the loss of their mother. It was still a fresh wound that couldn't seem to heal. Her words made it seem like she would come barging through the door at any moment to scold them for looking through such an intimate book. They really had no way to clear their doubts without talking to Austin, so they called him late last night and asked him to lunch.

Gabriella didn't know where the conversation would go or what the outcome would be, but she kept telling herself to have an open mind. She wanted him to have the answers she was looking for, and she wanted him to be the man that her mother had written about. She wanted to let herself meet him in that light. She wanted to know the man that loved her mother unconditionally and only broke her heart because of circumstances out his control. She wanted it to be true. She wanted a chance to have a father. The idea was scary—opening herself up to that kind of disappointment if Clare's words were just a nice story, a wonderful idea that reality had ruined, but Gabriella pushed the negative thoughts away, and knew that it was time to really listen. It was best for her sisters, and that's all that really mattered.

Gabriella picked up Giuliana from her slumber party. Evidently there wasn't much slumbering; she was so tired she fell asleep in the car on the way home. Jason was waiting to help get her inside without waking her. She looked so peaceful it seemed cruel to make her live with her choice not to sleep. Gabriella tucked her in her bed and kissed her forehead as Clare had always done until Gabriella had gotten too "cool" to be tucked in by her mother. At that moment she wished that she hadn't ever thought that she was too grown up to feel her mother's touch; it was the one feeling that she wished that she could have back over anything in the world, and it didn't matter if she were granted three wishes. That was something that would be forever unachievable.

A tear slid down Gabriella's cheek. "Don't let her sleep too long," Gabriella whispered. "She won't sleep tonight."

Jason looked at her for a long moment and then bent down to kiss her. "You are going to make a great mother someday. They are lucky to have you."

Gabriella wasn't sure why that meant so much to her at that moment, but her heart was engulfed in pride and love. She blushed and threw her arms around him. They'd embraced for only seconds until Gemma walked around the corner, making her disgust known.

Before the bickering could begin, they were silenced by a knock at the door. It couldn't be eleven o'clock already, she thought, but a glance at the clock on the wall confirmed that it was indeed. Her brain kicked into overdrive, the same second-guessing took over her thoughts, and the fidgeting and heavy breathing set in. She felt a ball in the pit of her stomach turning and twisting. She had told herself that by the time Austin had actually arrived to their home that she would have a game plan and her line of questioning would be ready. But of course, that was not the case. She was nothing but nervous, like she had a big class presentation or something. There was another knock at the door.

"Are we going to let him in?" Gemma asked.

Gabriella opened her mouth to speak, but no words came out.

Jason put his hands on Gabriella's shoulders. "You can do this. It's going to be okay." He kissed her on the cheek. "Trust your instincts." He wrapped her in his arms for a quick but meaningful hug. "I'll stay up here in the office and strain my ears to eavesdrop in case Giuliana wakes up." He winked at her and left her sight.

Gabriella smiled after him, lost in her thoughts again until another knock at the door brought her back to reality. She gave Gemma a look of concern and confusion. Gemma didn't say anything; she grabbed her sister's hand, and they walked down the stairs together. There they were, in front of a door that Gabriella had shut many, many years ago, and now she was finally going to open it and let him in. She reached her hand out to grab the handle only to jerk it back at the cold touch of the silver metal. A shudder ran through her; doubt swept over her, but it didn't overtake her. Gemma gave her an encouraging look, realizing that it was a bigger step than they both had anticipated.

Gabriella nodded, and pushing through her own thoughts, she opened the door. There he was the man who had loved their mother with everything he had. The man who gave up his own happiness for the comfort of her family. The man who she'd treated like dirt almost her whole life. She smiled. He smiled and looked back into her eyes. They were his, green hazel, with the flecks of amber glistening as the water rushed over them. She wanted to throw herself into his arms, but that had to wait. She had to know everything.

"Please come in." Gabriella stepped aside so he could enter.

"Thank you." Austin walked inside. He stood in the foyer, looking at his daughters. He wasn't sure if he should hug them, and history had taught him that the answer to that was no. He could hardly deny the urge, but he didn't want to set Gabriella off, so he opened with conversation. "Where is Giuliana?" He looked around, thinking she might be hiding under a table or behind the coat rack.

"Oh, she's upstairs sleeping," Gemma answered. "She was at a slumber party last night, and I think the poor thing stayed up all night long."

Austin nodded. "I'm really glad that you called."

Gabriella realized that she was staring. "Oh yeah, let's go into the kitchen and talk."

Austin sat at one end of the table, and Gemma sat down in the chair diagonal from Austin. Gemma motioned for Gabriella to take the chair across from her, but she hesitated. She didn't know why she was so worried about being close to him. She wanted to talk to him. He wasn't invading her space or showing up uninvited this time. This time she wanted him to be there, but yet something was keeping her from getting too close. She felt shy and unsure of how to proceed.

Gemma must have seen the panic on Gabriella's face because she walked over behind her and helped her sit in the appropriate chair. Gabriella didn't fight it; she was still silent, just staring at her father, almost like she was in shock. Gemma elbowed her hard in the ribs to bring her back to reality.

"Would you like some coffee, Dad?" Gemma asked.

"Dad," Austin repeated without meaning to. Gemma had never been as cold as Gabriella, but she also had never thrown out the word "Dad" on a regular basis. Austin felt warmth gush all over his face, and he took a moment to compose himself. "Sure." He started to get a good feeling about where the conversation might go, somewhere productive and happy.

Gabriella took a few not-so-discreet deep breaths to calm her nerves. She was counting backward in her mind. She knew that there was no turning back; she had to talk to her father; she had to know everything. She closed her eyes, opened them quickly, and finally spoke. "Austin, we read the letters."

Austin smiled. "You did." He sounded relieved.

Gabriella nodded. "And Mom had a box like you said that she would."

A genuine look of excitement and curiosity spread across his face. "What was inside?"

"Her life with you," Gabriella replied. She was silent, studying his reaction. She saw small tears forming in the corners of his eyes. It might have been the kindest thing she had ever said to Austin.

Austin couldn't stop himself; he reached his arms in both directions and put his hands on top of his daughters' hands. "I miss her more than you will ever know, but I am grateful that I have you girls in my life. You are so much like her. Both of you in different ways, and that's how I know that she will go on forever."

Gemma and Gabriella exchanged looks of understanding and choked back the tears. Gabriella pulled her hand away, but Gemma put her free hand on top of Austin's.

Gabriella took in another breath. "I"—she shook her head—"I mean, we," she said, pointing back and forth between her sister and herself, "have some questions for you."

Austin didn't let go of Gemma's hand. "Okay." He nodded. "I figured you would."

Gabriella cleared her throat and asked the question she had planned on asking last. "Why did you marry Alice?"

Gemma gave her sister a warning look reminding her that Austin was not there to be attacked. He was there to have an actual conversation.

He laughed accidently. "I'm sorry, you just don't hold back." He seemed to be remembering something and then shook his head. "That's a fair question."

"Okay," Gabriella said impatiently. "Are you going to answer it?"

Austin nodded. "I married Alice because of my parents. It was the only way to keep my inheritance, and then I swore once I got control of the money, I would leave Alice and come back to your mother, but then my parents made other stipulations. I had to have a child with Alice; otherwise the money would be gone. And I couldn't let that happen, because I had you two girls to think of. It was before your mother's career took off, and I had to still provide, and they wouldn't let me touch a cent unless I did what they asked. Then my sons were born, and I couldn't walk away again. I was in a corner, and I didn't know what to do. I didn't know how to dig myself out of the hole that I had gotten into. I got so caught up in keeping up appearances that I couldn't walk away. And I love Alice, but not the same way I loved your mother." He paused, and his voice became muffled by quiet sobs. "I really did love her very much."

Gabriella tried to wrap her mind around what Austin had just told her, but anger overrode her intentions. "You did everything for money. How could you possibly think that money would replace having a father? Obviously we could have made it work; I mean, you don't have to be rich to be happy."

"Dammit, Gabby," he snapped, startling both of them. "I live with that every day. I live with that mistake. I was young, and I was accustomed to a certain lifestyle, and I didn't want you guys to want for anything. I wanted you to have everything." He buried his face in his hands for a moment and sighed, wrestling with his own regret. "By the time I figured out how wrong I really was, it was too late. You hated me, and your mother was very angry at me, and Gemma hardly knew who I was, and I have no one to blame but myself for that."

"Austin," Gabriella began, but he cut her off.

"I know it's no excuse. But it's my explanation, and if you give me the chance to make up for it, I can. I promise." His eyes and voice were sincere.

"Austin." Gabriella couldn't hide her anguish any longer. "I know that if I go to court, I'm going to lose. I know that, I'm not stupid, but how can I be sure that you won't walk away? You can't let them feel that pain of abandonment. You can't leave them. You can't treat them as if they are second-rate; you can't let them feel that way."

"Gabby." He took her hand. "I never once thought of you as second-rate, and there is nothing I can do to make up for that, but if you will let me, maybe we can start fresh." He tightened his grip on her hand, squeezing it gently. "I am never going to walk away again. I have been trying to walk back into your lives for a while now, and I understand that you won't heal overnight. But I am never going to stop trying to build a relationship with you." He looked deep into her eyes. "I lost your mother, and I don't know you or Gemma that well. Perhaps my punishment for being a bad father is losing the love of my life, and it's because of her that I can't give up, and I can't let you give up your life. She wouldn't want that."

He reached down and pulled out his wallet and opened it to a picture of Clare and him from one of those five-dollar photo booths. They were making goofy faces at the camera. Clare looked incandescently happy, happier than Gabriella had ever seen her mother—no worries, no stress, just in love. There was nothing to be said. The three of them looked on as if they were imagining what Clare had said that night, what she had been thinking, and how she really felt, but the picture explained it all, the memory frozen in time.

Austin spoke again. "I have loved your mother with all of my heart since I was ten years old. I waited too long to stand up to my family. I was too scared to do what was right, and I have to live with that regret for the rest of my life. I will have a hole in my heart that can never be filled." He was crying openly now. "I love you."

Jason's voice came into Gabriella's head: "Trust your instincts." Gabriella nodded, feeling sure of herself for the first time since her mother passed. "I believe you." Gabriella put her free hand on top of his. She wasn't fighting her tears anymore. "Austin, I am angry with you, but I think that I should give you a chance, and I think that we all should give you a chance."

Austin gasped and sobbed loudly, pulling his hands free and cupping her face. "Thank you so much for this. I love you so much. I promise from this day forward, I am going to make it up to you. To all of you." He started brushing her hair away from her face, and she leaned into his hand. "Gabby, I love you so much, and I am so sorry for all the hurt that I have caused you."

Gabriella pulled away, scared that they were moving too fast. All new relationships need boundaries. She read Austin's look; he was worried that he had done something wrong. "Austin." She softened her tone to reassure him. "Giuliana, she doesn't know you very well."

"I know." Austin nodded in shame.

"So I think we should start spending more time with each other, and you should get to know all of us." She smiled warmly at Austin. "Austin, I cannot let her get hurt. So I have to make the transition easy on her. I am not going to sell this house. And if Giuliana cannot adjust to living with you, she will be able to live with me here."

"I understand, Gabriella." Austin took a second, and then a light went off. "Wait, what are you telling me?"

Gabriella interrupted him. "If all goes according to plan, and Giuliana is okay with it, I am going to go to Brown in the winter, and Gemma and Giuliana will live with you. We have to make sure that Giuliana understands, though, and that she doesn't think I am abandoning her."

Austin's floodgates had opened; he put his head down on the table. Gabriella and Gemma smiled at each other. Gabriella had her father in her life. She had longed for the moment in which she could call him Dad, and the joy on his face made her heart swell with joy.

Austin jumped up and pulled Gabriella into a tight hug. "Thank you so much. I love you."

"I love you too, Dad," she whispered back.

Epilogue

Six Months Later

My Dearest Gabriella,

Your first semester of college is behind you. I am so proud. I know that your father is very proud too. I know that you are wishing I was there to pick you up from your dorm room, but I am there with you in spirit. I knew that you had this greatness in you since you were about five years old. You brought home the first poem you had ever written; you were so excited, and so proud. I was so proud that my daughter had written such beautiful words about a bunny and a butterfly. I want you to know that you are a great writer. The words live within you. You only need to figure out how to let them out, and that will come with your life experience. College will change your life. You will learn about yourself, and you will probably (if you haven't already) realized that you are in love with Jason Throne (just saying). Gabriella, going after your dreams is the greatest thing you can achieve in life. Never settle for anything less than what you want. You can reach beyond the stars. I have said this many, many times before, but I am so proud of the beautiful person that you have become, and I know that in the near future you will be on the bestseller list. I love you with all of my heart.

Love always and forever,
Your mother,
Clare Marie LaFrace

Gabriella sat at her desk with tears of happiness streaming down her face. The words of her mother always sent a wave of comfort, happiness, and sadness through her. She peered around the room that had become a tiny box, and she couldn't figure out how she had fit so much stuff into that small space. She chuckled to herself. She had spent the last four months at Brown University, submersing herself in the written word. She had made a lot of new friends and kept her childhood sweetheart, Jason, on speed dial. She couldn't wait to see him in two days, when she would be in his arms. She would be seeing her sisters for the first time in two months.

Last summer had been the worst of Gabriella's life, and she thought that the warm weather would give her the same queasy feeling she'd felt on that August day, but how wrong she was. This summer she would spend with the people she loved the most. She would spend it listening to Giuliana spin tales of the Wild West of first grade. She would listen to Gemma tell her of her devotion to her boyfriend, Brad, who she was completely in love with. She would get to be in the arms of the man that she loved with all of her heart, Jason, and she would work on her relationship with her dad.

She paused for a moment and looked down at the letter her mother had written. She saw the comforting sight of Clare's handwriting and remembered how much she had doubted her mother's love for her father. Gabriella had finally accepted that Clare and Austin had loved each other more than she would ever understand, but she knew that if given a few more days that they would have been together forever. Gabriella smiled to herself at the thought of actually giving her father a chance. She was finally going to experience having a dad, and the little girl inside of her was overjoyed.

Gabriella picked up her pen to write the foreword to her first completed novel, which she'd titled *Finding My Way Home.*

I lost my mother when I was eighteen; coincidentally, this was the same year I found myself. I found that I was not alone in the world. I found my words. I was fortunate enough to have a mother who cared about her children more than her own life. I will take her with me everywhere I go. She taught us that unconditional love is not earned nor deserved, it is simply given, and sometimes it is the second chances that mean the most.

She put down her pen and smiled to herself. Gabriella had finished her first novel. She looked at the photographs that had yet to be packed and thought of how proud her mother must be of her. She knew that she had done the right thing by letting Austin back into her life. She knew that it would be a while before their relationship was perfect, but she'd learned that a dysfunctional relationship was better than no relationship at all.

When she returned to her small town in Ohio, she wouldn't be welcomed back in any special way. She would have her sisters dying to know what went on, and she would have her boyfriend wanting to kiss her every second, but she would also have a father who would want her to come over for dinner. She never had that before, and it didn't make life seem as sad as it was a few months ago.

Gabriella's phone rang. "Hello?"

"Hi, Gab." Austin's voice popped up from the other end. "Are you on your way to the airport?"

"Getting ready to leave now," she replied.

"All right, call us when you land. Love you," he said.

"Love you too. Oh, the cab's here. I'm on my way home."

Allie Walker is a twenty-eight-year-old Missouri native who has always loved to write. This small-town girl with big ideas first began writing to cope with life's diversity, but an amazing story of family, unconditional love, and fate took over and eventually came to life as her first novel, *On My Way Home.*

As a general rule, Walker refuses to be a victim of circumstance and won't give up on any personal goals. She's grateful for the supportive people in her life and lives with her husband and their Siberian husky in St. Louis, Missouri. She has completed her second book, which she plans to publish in the near future